Scotsmen Prefer Blondes

A MUSES OF MAYFAIR NOVEL

Sara Ramsey

ISBN: 978-1-938312-01-4

For Sean Connery

And for Loro, in all its incarnations

CHAPTER ONE

MacCabe Castle, the Scottish Highlands - 23 September 1812

"Are you sure you want to do this, Prue?" Amelia asked.

Miss Prudence Etchingham turned away from the window. Her frown was answer enough. "No. But you must admit the tea Lady Carnach served when we arrived was better than anything my mother's housekeeper can produce. I would happily marry the devil for those lemon cakes."

Amelia crossed her arms. They'd had the argument in fits and starts all the way to Scotland, but there were only a few moments left before Prudence met her would-be fiancé. "Lemon cakes are all well and good…"

"More than well and good, I should think, if you've lived off my mother's housekeeper's soda bread," Prudence interrupted.

"You can't sell yourself for a cake," Amelia insisted. "Your worth is greater than that of anyone I know."

Prudence leaned against the edge of the bed, so high that she couldn't sit on the mattress without boosting herself up onto it. "You are the only one who thinks so. The marriage mart gave up on me ages ago."

They were in one of the castle's innumerable guest chambers, already dressed for dinner and waiting for the gong to summon them downstairs. Amelia did acknowledge that the castle was vastly preferable to the Etchinghams' lodgings in London. The castle was large enough that Amelia and Prudence had their own chambers — a luxury their spinster statuses rarely allowed.

If Prudence followed through with the plan her mother had made for her, though, she would have the entire castle, not a minor guest room. Most single women at seven-and-twenty would be delighted to entertain a proposal from an earl. But Prudence was pale under the light brown hair piled on her head. Her yellow gown only enhanced her pallor — it made her look sickly, not satisfied.

"You don't need the approval of the marriage mart," Amelia retorted. "If you could just wait a bit longer, perhaps one of your historical treatises could raise some funds for you."

Prudence smiled, but her brown eyes were sad. "History doesn't sell as well as fiction. And it's better to marry than be trapped in spinsterhood with my mother."

Amelia picked at a fraying thread on the edge of her glove. "I think we might escape in another year or two. Once I'm thirty, my mother will surely let me set up a cottage in the country. No one would remark upon it if you joined me. Then I could write my novels and you could study history as much as we like, without fear of discovery."

"With what do you suppose we will pay for a cottage?"

"If neither of us marry, our dowries should maintain us. And anyway, if my books continue to attract notice…"

Prudence cut her off again. "Your dowry, perhaps. Mine won't even buy a new pair of gloves. Mother says I should be grateful to have found any man at my advanced age and without a pound to my name. The fact that Carnach is an earl has her salivating even more."

Amelia stopped picking at her glove with a guilty sigh and pulled it onto her hand. "Don't you think that might be a reason not to marry Lord Carnach? You haven't met him. Our mothers liked Lady Carnach when they shared a Season with her, but they know nothing of her son. She said he wants to go into politics — what if he is such a prig that no other woman would have him? Or what if his tastes are *perverse*?"

Her voice dropped on the word, but Prudence giggled. "I've seen all the same illustrations you have, Mellie. I can tolerate a bit of perversion for those lemon cakes."

With a delicate blush sweeping across her cheeks, Prudence looked younger than she had in an age. Amelia sighed. "Don't decide yet, Prue. At least wait until you meet him. He could be an utter ogre."

"Of course I won't have him if he's an ogre. And I have no desire to be a political hostess, even for a hundred cakes. But I can't turn everyone down like you have. This is likely my only chance."

Amelia's heart twisted. Other than her cousin Madeleine, who had recently married the Duke of Rothwell, Prudence was her best friend. And she was the sweetest girl in London, with a secret streak of humor that Amelia adored.

But sweetness and good humor were wasted on a woman who had no dowry. In London, no one paid Prudence any notice.

Would the Earl of Carnach notice Prudence? The real Prudence, the one Amelia knew? Or would he see her as a desperate woman who would be grateful for his title and his fortune, one who would do whatever he needed of her?

"Still, know that I'll do anything you need to avoid this. If I have to write another book like *The Unconquered Heiress*, I will. It's still selling like mad."

Prudence frowned. "You shouldn't take such a risk again."

Amelia had written the satire in the spring, partly as penance for an argument with her cousin Madeleine, partly as revenge on the most repugnant of her would-be suitors. She preferred writing Gothic romances to social commentary, but the book had sold better than anything she'd written before.

"Perhaps it's a risk worth taking if it saves you from Carnach," Amelia said.

The dinner gong sounded — likely carried up the stairs by a footman and rung especially for them, since the guest wing was separated from the family wing by the vast expanse of the ancient great hall. Prudence pushed herself away from the bed and held out her hand to help Amelia stand.

"No, you can't write another," Prudence said firmly. "If anyone knew you authored the first one, you would have been ruined. And if you're ruined, my mother won't allow me to see you. So you have to stay safe, even if another book would buy you lemon cakes for life."

Amelia grinned at that. "Very well, no satire. What about a Gothic novel in which a dastardly seducer lures a beautiful woman to his mountain castle, then forces her to throw parties for Whigs until the end of her days?"

Prudence swatted her arm. "Let me at least meet the man before you cast him as a villain."

Amelia relented. They walked to the stairs that led down to the great hall. The castle was no longer shaped like a castle proper — as with many old estates, the original building had been added to, subtracted from, and renovated over the centuries. The great hall was intact, lined with tapestries, and the dais still held its ancient table for the lord and his family. Behind the dais, a passage had been converted into a portrait gallery, leading to the castle's only remaining tower.

Amelia shivered as they passed through the hall to the stairs that led up to the family wing, which was more modern than all the rest. "If you do stay, make sure Carnach buys you well-soled slippers. You'll catch your death here otherwise."

Prudence didn't laugh as easily as she normally did. "No more talk of death, Mellie. I need to concentrate."

Amelia sighed. It only took a few moments to climb the stairs and walk down the hallway to the drawing room. When they reached it, Prudence paused just outside the door.

"Lemon cakes," she muttered to herself.

Amelia laughed despite herself. "A battle cry that will live on for centuries, Prue."

Prudence's laugh was shaky, almost a sob. She squared her shoulders, cloaking herself in dignity like she wore the most expensive gown in England, not a plain muslin dress that was several seasons out of date. Then she stepped forward, ready to offer herself up as a sacrifice to replenish her mother's fortunes.

Amelia followed, feigning serenity as her anger grew. Prudence didn't want this, even if she needed it. And if Prudence wouldn't demand something more for herself than this, Amelia would do whatever it took to find an alternative.

The MacCabes' butler, Graves, greeted them at the door. "Lady Amelia Staunton and Miss Etchingham," he announced, even though the gathering was small. She knew the women — her mother, Lady Salford, sat with Prudence's mother, Lady Harcastle, and their hostess, Lady Carnach. Amelia's brother Alex, the Earl of Salford, was there too, having grudgingly escorting them to Scotland.

The only man she didn't know broke away from the group to stride toward them. Lady Carnach trailed in his wake, presumably to conduct introductions.

Amelia heard Prudence suck in a breath, felt her freeze beside her. If this was her would-be husband, he didn't look like an ogre. He didn't look like a politician, either — he looked like one of the old Celtic warriors come to life. He was tall, well over six feet, with a muscled frame that showed to complete advantage in his tailored eveningwear. His dark hair was longer than fashionable, and he had carelessly pushed it back in a sinful sweep that would make Byron foam with jealousy. His brows were thick over his eyes, and with just a quirk they would turn sardonic.

But for now, he was polite. He took Prudence's right hand as Lady Carnach murmured the introductions.

"Miss Etchingham, I am honored that you have come to Scotland," he said.

His voice rumbled, rough and sensual, under the cool welcome. Amelia's eyes narrowed. It had taken less than a second to register Carnach's appeal. With his title and his looks, why would he need to take a woman he'd never met as his bride?

Perhaps Prudence had the same doubts. She didn't let go of Amelia's hand, even after Carnach took her other hand into his. Instead, her grip tightened as though Amelia could save her.

If the earl noticed his would-be bride attaching herself to her friend like a barnacle — and with the sidelong glance he gave Amelia, he did notice — he didn't remark on it. "I trust you've found the castle to your liking?" he asked.

The sound Prudence made was not one of delight. It sounded like a mouse realizing it was clutched in a hawk's talons.

Just before it died of fright.

Damn. It wasn't a ladylike thought, but Amelia didn't feel like a lady. She felt like a general suddenly confronted with a suicide mission. She didn't think Prudence should marry the man.

But she didn't want Prudence to be embarrassed, either. Amelia squeezed Prudence's hand, hard and urgent.

Prudence finally remembered what she was supposed to do. She dropped into a curtsey. "You have a lovely home, Lord Carnach."

The curtsey was awkward, with Carnach holding one hand and Amelia the other, but Prudence successfully executed it. When she came up again, Carnach brushed his lips across her knuckles. "Thank you, Miss Etchingham. I hope you find much happiness here."

His tone was gentler than before.

Prudence made another strangled sound.

Amelia smiled, pretending this was like any other house party she'd attended. "You are so fortunate to live here, my lord. We could not stop marveling at the scenery, could we, Miss Etchingham?"

It was an uninteresting observation, the sort of statement that made men preen and think themselves clever by comparison. But Prudence stopped choking. If they both stayed vapid and boring, as the ton had trained them to, perhaps Prudence could overcome her panic. The tactic had successfully hidden Amelia's writing and Prudence's academic leanings for so long — surely it would work now.

Carnach's gaze shifted to Amelia. His eyes were grey, but grey was such a lusterless word for what they really were — the moody grey of clouds about to break, turning into quicksilver as he looked at her. His mouth turned up, just enough to show amusement without baring his teeth.

"The poets appreciate the scenery, I'm sure," he said. "Will you regale me with a discussion of the weather next?"

Amelia would have laughed. Carnach knew the way the

conversation was supposed to progress, and apparently had as little use for it as she did. But she couldn't be at ease with him — not when his plans for Prudence still bothered her.

She eyed him coolly, holding her ground when he raised an eyebrow. "Would you prefer to discuss the chance of sun tomorrow? Or the chance of rain? I am prepared for either topic, my lord."

"If it's weather you care about, my lady, you'll find the conversation here much to your liking," he said, suppressing a grin. "But what of you, Miss Etchingham? Shall we discuss the weather as well? I don't have any gossip to share that would interest you, I'm afraid."

Prudence was looking beyond him to where Alex and their mothers sat. She didn't answer, and the pause turned awkward. Amelia finally recalled her with another squeeze of the hand.

"I'm sorry, my lord," Prudence said, a flush spreading across her cheeks. "I was woolgathering."

Carnach smiled at her, but the quicksilver in his eyes had turned back into storm clouds. "We have wool as well, of course, if you'd like to discuss that instead."

Prudence didn't laugh at the jest. "Whatever you wish, Lord Carnach."

His smile faded. Amelia had never heard that note of resignation in Prudence's voice before. To Carnach's credit, he didn't seem to relish it either.

His brothers came into the drawing room then, and the relief on Carnach's face was obvious. When he turned to greet them, Amelia leaned in to whisper in Prudence's ear. "Don't let him think you'll be his chattel."

"That's what I'll be though, isn't it?" Prudence snapped. "No sense pretending otherwise. And no sense regretting what I might have had instead."

There wasn't time to try to convince her — Lady Carnach was already introducing them to the other MacCabes. The second son, Alastair, was the local vicar, and his angelic blond hair matched his role. Duncan and Douglas were twins, almost identical, with the same dark hair as Malcolm. But where Malcolm's eyes seemed capable of brooding, she saw nothing but amusement on his brothers' faces.

They were everything that was pleasant. Even a few minutes in their company made Amelia feel that she would enjoy her time in Scotland, regardless of the outcome.

And if any of them noticed Prudence's distraction, when she should have tried harder to be amiable with her potential new family, they were too polite to mention it.

When it was time to go in to dinner, one of the twins claimed Amelia's arm. "How do you find our weather, Lady Amelia?" Douglas asked.

She snorted, then tried to smooth it over with a cough when she realized he hadn't meant it as a joke. "Do you think we will have rain or sun tomorrow?" she replied.

Douglas started regaling her with an old wives' tale of how to predict such things. He turned her toward the door, and she looked up to find Carnach grinning at her.

The earl didn't say anything about her choice of conversation, though. He turned back to Prudence and spoke to her with the soft voice of a horse tamer. If Prudence responded, her voice was too soft for Amelia to hear.

Amelia followed on Douglas's arm, listening with half an ear to his stories. She'd been angry when she had walked into the drawing room, but she left it confused. She still found it suspicious that Carnach had fixed his attentions on Prudence — she loved her friend, but even Amelia knew Carnach could have looked far higher for a bride.

But why wasn't Prudence responding to his charm? Perhaps this was like one of the Gothic novels Amelia wrote, and Prudence had recognized some dark omen, some latent evil, that Carnach hid from everyone else.

If this were one of Amelia's stories, Prudence would try to escape. But Fate would have other plans.

Amelia shivered. This wasn't a novel. Prudence could certainly do worse than Carnach. He wasn't the villain Amelia had guessed him to be, even if he was entirely too smooth for her liking. She wouldn't scheme to end the match, as she had originally planned — perhaps it was for the best if Prudence married him.

But if Prudence wanted to escape him, Amelia would be more than happy to help her.

CHAPTER TWO

In his study with his brothers three hours later, after a remarkably wretched dinner, Malcolm slammed his empty whisky glass down on his desk. "Do not say another word, Duncan. I've made my decision."

Duncan and Douglas exchanged glances. Douglas gestured with both hands, an elaborate, sweeping movement ending with a suggestive curl, and Duncan laughed into his glass. The twins had developed their own language at a young age, and they still used it when they didn't want to share their thoughts with others.

Malcolm scowled at them. "I know what that one means. Buying myself a whore won't help matters."

Alastair rolled his eyes in sympathy. "Don't mind the twins, Malcolm. They're still more boy than man." Then he cleared his throat. "Of course, wisdom does occasionally come from the mouths of babes."

Malcolm and his brothers had adjourned to his study after dinner. The Earl of Salford had declined, instead choosing to work on his correspondence, which is what Malcolm would have done if his brothers hadn't forced him into retreating to the study and having a drink with them. "Retreat" felt like the right word for it. In the war to secure his clan's future, the search for a bride was his prime objective. Tonight's opening salvo had not gone as intended.

At least he had his brothers to commiserate with — although their commiseration usually made him feel better only because it redirected his annoyance to them rather than his other woes. At thirty-four, Malcolm was the oldest and had been responsible for all of them since their father's death the previous year. Alastair was three years younger than Malcolm, and was the village's vicar — not that he always behaved so piously. But the twins had just turned twenty-five, and with no wives, no incomes, and no houses of their own, they were a unified thorn in Malcolm's side.

"I should buy you both commissions and be done with you," he said, removing the stopper from the heavy crystal decanter to pour himself another drink. "Perhaps one of the India regiments so you can't come home on leave."

Douglas grinned. "You've threatened that since we were in leading strings. Send Duncan. He sports a uniform better than I do."

"Only because I bathe regularly," Duncan retorted. Then he turned back to Malcolm, ready to press his point again. "You cannot seriously intend to marry that chit, brother. It would be like legshackling yourself to a sheep."

"Or a dishrag," Douglas supplied.

"She's not a dishrag," Alastair said. "Miss Etchingham is just…a tad quiet for you, isn't she?"

Malcolm glared at his turncoat brother. Alastair usually sided with him, not the twins. "Why should I not marry a quiet woman? It would be a welcome relief from hearing the lot of you criticize me at every turn."

"Douglas and I are usually silent in our criticisms," Duncan said. He emphasized it with another gesture to Douglas that had them both laughing again.

Malcolm had had enough. "Miss Etchingham is a very nice young lady."

"'Young' is charitable," Douglas muttered.

"A very nice young lady," Malcolm repeated, raising his voice. "She was no doubt tired from her journey. As for conversation, I can't blame her for not wanting to talk to any of you."

"Did she talk to you?" Alastair asked.

They all knew the answer to that. Malcolm had escorted her in to dinner, made sure she had the choicest morsels on her plate, led her into discussions of the weather, the society pages, and everything else he could think of — but to no avail. Her answers were monosyllabic. Her countenance was almost bored. She kept glancing down the table as though hoping for a rescue. He coaxed one or two giggles out of her, but nothing that could be deemed joy.

He never failed to engage a lady in conversation. Even her mother, Lady Harcastle, who looked to be every bit the sour bitch his friend Ferguson had warned him about, had warmed to him.

Malcolm rolled his tumbler between his fingers. "You know why I have to marry. If I am to achieve enough influence in the House of Lords to save our clan's livelihood, I need a hostess who can give the right sort of parties. Ferguson has vouched for her. He claims she can speak quite nicely. She has never caused a scandal. And she needs a husband."

Alastair sipped his whisky. "Ferguson has only known her a few months. And why do you trust Ferguson's judgment on society issues?"

Ferguson was Malcolm's closest friend, but had left Scotland after unexpectedly becoming the Duke of Rothwell several months earlier. He was now married to Lady Amelia's cousin Madeleine, which was how he knew both Amelia and Miss Etchingham. When Malcolm had decided to find a suitable wife quickly so that the wedding plans didn't take valuable time away from his political aspirations, Ferguson was perfectly placed to recommend a possible bride.

"Ferguson understands society," Malcolm said. "He just doesn't care for it."

"But if you want a hostess, shouldn't you look for someone who can, say, host? And talk to people?" Alastair asked.

Douglas looked up from his silent side conversation with Duncan. "What about the blonde girl? She was quite talkative, if you didn't notice in your efforts to sustain speech on your side of the table."

The blonde girl. Such simple words for such a beautiful woman. When he had first seen her in the drawing room, it was all he could do to keep his attention focused on the woman he was supposed to marry. Amelia Staunton was lovely — taller than his would-be bride, with humor and intelligence shimmering in her sapphire eyes. She was also loyal, if her attempt to prop up her friend was any indication.

But she was not for him. "Ferguson said he doesn't know anything about her past, other than that many men have tried to win her and failed. He said Prudence is the safer bet. If one of you wants to tie yourself to Lady Amelia, you're welcome to. At least she would take you out of my hair."

"She would be better than India," Duncan mused.

Alastair eyed him as the twins returned to their conversation. "Lady Amelia does not seem unsuitable. She was all that was charming and witty at dinner."

Malcolm hadn't heard any of it. The formal dining table was simply too big, particularly when his mother seated him and Prudence slightly away from the rest of the guests to give them a chance to talk. But Amelia's low, seductive laugh had cut through him during the awkward silences with Prudence. He would have happily traded places with any of his brothers if it had put him within range of her words.

"If Miss Etchingham does not wish to continue our acquaintance," he started to say. Then he caught himself. "Miss Etchingham, given enough time, is far more suited for my needs. I want someone who is utterly beyond reproach, who will not bring any embarrassment or scandal, who will serve as my hostess and give me heirs. Her lineage is impeccable, and her financial position poor enough that she will be grateful for what I can give her. I am confident that we can manage each other quite tolerably. Lady Amelia can go to the devil."

Alastair stared at him, his jaw uncharacteristically slack. "So you do want a dishrag — a dishrag who is grateful for you."

Malcolm threw back the dregs of his second whisky. He thought about pouring a third, but it would only increase the censure in his saintly brother's eyes. "What else would you have me do, Alastair? I am destined to marry for duty, not love. It's the way of the world. And Miss Etchingham is good enough."

"There are surely other women better suited to this duty than Miss Etchingham."

"Perhaps. But I cannot spend months or years chasing after silly misses on the marriage mart. I must take up my seat in the Lords in November, and I'll have this marriage business done before then."

"I don't think such haste…" Alastair said.

Malcolm cut him off. "I want to be noticed for my speeches, not my search for a bride. Why not marry the first woman who fits my requirements? Really, you should thank me for it — the faster I gather influence, the sooner I may put a stop to the landlords who are evicting their Scottish tenants to make way for sheep."

Alastair shook his head. "Do you only see marriage as a duty? If I have learned anything from the church, it is that duty does not have to be joyless."

"I don't think that," Malcolm protested.

"When was the last time you went to Edinburgh for pleasure?" Alastair asked.

"Or gotten properly foxed?" Douglas interjected. "And this drink doesn't count — I mean well and truly soused, in the pub instead of alone in your study?"

"Or taken a mistress?" Duncan asked. "A female mistress, not an estate ledger."

They all knew the answers. He'd devoted himself to entertainments like those when he was younger, not seeking marriage because there would be time enough for duty when he inherited. But he hadn't done anything but estate business since his father's wake.

Malcolm scowled at them. "You can do as you please. But I won't have our clan forced to emigrate to America while I pursue some mindless pleasures."

He was overstating it. The look Alastair threw him said they all knew it. No one could evict the MacCabes except Malcolm himself. But his tenants were starting to trickle away on their own, driven by economic policies that ruined the small crofters' livelihoods.

And if none of the other Scottish landlords would stand for their tenants, Malcolm would try to stand for all of them.

Alastair rose, leaving his unfinished whisky on the table beside him. Duncan beat Douglas to the abandoned glass, draining it with a careless laugh. Alastair sighed, then looked back at Malcolm. "I will marry you to whomever you choose. But at least take care to make it a choice, and not just a business transaction."

He left after that pronouncement, taking his cursed wisdom with him. Malcolm didn't want to hear it. He didn't want to hear it from the twins, either. He left them to the decanter and slipped out onto the terrace. In the dark, in the chill of early autumn, he could be alone with his thoughts.

And if his duty felt distinctly joyless in that moment, he ignored it.

CHAPTER THREE

The gentlemen never joined the women in the drawing room after dinner. Alex had stuck his head in to say that the other men were adjourning to Malcolm's study, and that for his part he was off to bed.

"I must apologize for my sons," Lady Carnach said for the third time in an hour as she and the other mothers looked over their cards. "We do not entertain guests often enough for them to remember their manners."

One would have to be a complete boor to fail to join the ladies after dinner, but Amelia didn't interrupt the older women from the corner where she and Prudence sat embroidering. Dinner, after all, had not gone well. Who could blame the men for avoiding more of the same?

"It's no matter, Louisa," Lady Harcastle said, smiling tightly. "Prudence will still be here in the morning."

Prudence scowled and jabbed her needle into her linen.

"I do hope so," Malcolm's mother replied, although Amelia detected doubt in the soft cadence of her voice.

"You know how it is with young people," Lady Harcastle continued. "They sometimes need a few days to remember their duty, but they do in the end. We all went through the same experience during our debuts, if I recall."

Amelia's ears perked up at that, but she didn't say anything. She'd sat on the edge of her mother's conversations with Lady Harcastle for over twenty years, and knew that showing interest in the older ladies' gossip was the quickest way to end it.

"You may have doubted, but I didn't," her mother said, tossing a card to the table. She, Lady Harcastle, and Lady Carnach were playing whist, with a dummy hand to make up for the lack of a fourth player, and the ratafia flowed freely now that the men would not be joining them. Prudence and Amelia sat nearer to the fire, which made Amelia feel somewhat overwarm even though the extra light was welcome.

She forced herself to believe that the flush on her face was caused by the fire. It couldn't be related to the strange fluttering she'd felt since dinner, when she looked up occasionally and caught Lord Carnach watching her over his wineglass. It was travel fatigue, or indigestion, or perhaps typhus.

Yes, typhus. Better to believe she was dying than that she'd inadvertently solicited the interest of the man her friend needed to marry.

Lady Harcastle frowned at her hand. "Just because you made a love match doesn't mean you can still lord it over us, Augusta. And with an earl to boot — how unfair."

Her usual venom seeped into her voice. There had been a time, years earlier, when Lady Harcastle was quite charming. But she'd grown more difficult in recent years, and Amelia didn't understand why her mother still tolerated the connection.

Augusta took a long draught of ratafia, then sighed. "The fun of lording it over you was lost when Edward died."

Amelia's father had been dead a decade, but her mother's voice was still pained. Amelia looked down at her stitches. They were uneven, but she couldn't pick them out again; the linen was more hole than cloth. She stabbed at the fabric and wished she could steal some ratafia without her mother noticing. Really, it was no wonder Prudence wanted to escape Lady Harcastle — the woman was the worst.

"I am sorry, dear," Lady Harcastle said. Guilt replaced the venom, as though she had been sleepwalking through their earlier conversation and had just awoken to the reality of what she'd said.

Amelia's mother waved her glass. "It's been years. And for all that I loved him, I would rather have lost him than my sons. I don't know how you've survived it, Mary."

The silence grew, became absolute. Amelia looked up and saw her mother flush. Augusta was often blunt, but perhaps it was the ratafia that had added an edge to her voice. Augusta reached out a hand toward Lady Harcastle, but the other woman evaded her touch.

"I haven't survived," Lady Harcastle said, in a voice turned raspy with buried emotion. "If only Prudence…"

She broke off, looking over at her daughter. Prudence stood abruptly and thrust her embroidery into her workbag with all the fire she hadn't displayed for Carnach at dinner. "If you will excuse me, Mother, I have the headache."

Lady Harcastle nodded, covering her eyes with her cards. Amelia followed her friend from the drawing room, not waiting for permission. Amelia was only a few steps behind, but by the time she touched Prudence's shoulder, she knew the woman was already in tears.

She didn't say anything, just pulled out her handkerchief and wrapped her arms around Prudence. She was half a head taller, and she felt Prudence's tears on her shoulder as she glanced down the hall. There was no one about to find them, although she suspected the mothers would hear Prudence if she became much louder.

She patted Prudence on the back, waiting for her to calm down.

When her sobs subsided into sniffles, Amelia squeezed her gently. "Is this about your brothers, or something else?"

Prudence stepped back, wiping her cheeks with Amelia's handkerchief. "Both — or neither. I don't know, Mellie. It's been almost three years since they all…"

She still couldn't say the words. Prudence's father never should have let both sons buy commissions, not when the estate was entailed, but he wasn't stern enough to turn them down. When they died together, fighting under Wellington at Talavera, the news had caused Lord Harcastle to have an attack from which he'd never recovered.

Three years later, Prudence was no longer in mourning, but only at her mother's insistence. She was the only one left. And with the estate passing to a distant cousin, marriage had moved from a priority to a necessity.

Amelia held her hand and tried to reassure her. "If you want to marry Lord Carnach, I will support you."

She didn't like it, but she would. Prudence shook her head. "I don't want to marry Lord Carnach — at least, not really. Can you picture me as a political hostess?"

"No," Amelia said. "But are you sure? You were eager this afternoon."

Prudence sniffled again. "I was eager to escape London and settle this marriage business. But I had nothing to say to him. And I know he looks better than I had any right to expect. But I didn't feel the slightest desire to kiss him. All I could think of at dinner was how I would have to someday — and how I would rather run away to Egypt than do that."

"You'd rather run away to Egypt than do anything," Amelia pointed out.

"True. But the more I thought of living here, of giving up…

everything in London, the more I panicked. It was awful."

"It was awful," Amelia agreed.

Prudence smiled just a little. "That is not very supportive."

"You said it first. But perhaps if your mother wasn't there reminding you of how all her hopes rest on you, you could relax long enough to talk to him."

"What can I do about that? Ask her to leave? If it were as simple as that, I wouldn't be considering Carnach's proposal."

"No. But you need to spend some time alone with Carnach — or, at least, without your mother."

"There's no hope for it," Prudence said. She tried to return Amelia's handkerchief, but Amelia looked at the damp fabric and let her keep it. "Carnach and I would not suit each other. I thought I was ready and that the time had come to abandon my silly fantasies. But perhaps not."

Prudence sucked in a breath, choking back another sob. Amelia patted her shoulder, waiting. When Prudence spoke again, there was an edge of resentment to her voice. "It's so unfair, isn't it? That my mother would rather sell me to Carnach than let me find my own way?"

Amelia would have used a stronger word than unfair. "It's not your fault that you're all she has. And surely there's someone better suited for you than Carnach."

"I used to think that," Prudence said. "But if there is a man who is meant for me, I cannot keep waiting for him to realize it."

"Still, you shouldn't agree to be Carnach's hostess just because you need the funds. The man seems to be looking for a broodmare, not a companion."

Prudence giggled a little through her tears. "He did not impress you, did he?"

Carnach had impressed her — too much.

"The earl is better suited to be a villain than a hero," Amelia declared.

"Does he still have lemon cakes, though?"

Amelia smiled. Prudence's humor was back.

But then Prudence sighed. "Villain or hero, I cannot toss aside his offer. Not that he's formally made one yet — but as much as I may hate the circumstances, Mother is right. I'm not likely to do better."

"You shouldn't accept Carnach's suit just because of her," Amelia insisted. "We'll find another way, I promise."

"We likely won't. But I thank you for the charade."

Amelia didn't like the defeat in Prudence's eyes. It would be a relief if Prudence didn't give herself over to Carnach's ambitions, but it didn't solve her problems. "Do you want me to spend the night in your room?"

Prudence shook her head. "I need to think. You know I can't with you thrashing about and stealing the covers."

"I do not steal the covers," Amelia protested.

Prudence pecked her on the cheek. "Whatever you wish to believe. You're the one who creates fictions, not me."

She danced out of the way before Amelia could poke her in the ribs. As she walked away, Amelia sighed. Prudence's step was lighter than it had been when she left the drawing room, but her dilemma was far from solved.

That left Amelia alone in the hall. She wouldn't return to the drawing room. The mothers were laughing hysterically about something, and the sound of it wafted through the open door — the ratafia was doing its trick. Going back there would be like walking into a den of drunken hyenas. They were sure to gnaw on the bones of Amelia's shortcomings as a late-night snack.

It was too early to retire, though. She would rather cut her hand off with her needle than take up her embroidery again. She could go to her room, but her writing desk wasn't unpacked.

She wandered down the hall, away from the staircase, slipping past the drawing room door toward the rooms beyond it. Somewhere there was a library, and while Lady Carnach had not given them a full tour yet, she had claimed it was lovely.

Amelia found it on the third attempt, after stumbling across a well equipped but disused music room and another, smaller salon. None of the candles were lit, but the moon was nearly full. The light streaming in through the uncovered windows was bright enough to illuminate the room. Lady Carnach promised loveliness, but this was something else altogether. It was a magical space, this room, the kind of library she dreamed of having.

The size of it dazed her. The room was long, narrow, and two stories tall, with multiple doors to the hall and an equal number of French doors giving out onto a stone terrace overlooking the back gardens. Thick Aubusson carpets in the blues and greys of the MacCabe coat of arms warmed the chilly floors, complementing the comfortable chairs arranged in clusters by the windows. A small balcony circled the room, accessing the second level from a spiraling wooden staircase in one corner.

She walked down the first wall, running her hand over the books neatly arranged on the shelf. She loved the feel of book spines — some cracked with age and use, others smooth and sleek, like the book was a work of art. The light was too dim to make out the titles, but there were hundreds, likely thousands, of books in the room. It would take a lifetime to read them all.

By the time she reached the window, she was already in love. She never felt this passion for people — never let herself feel this passion, after she had realized the threat it posed to her independence. But books — books were safe. She could let herself long for this room.

Amelia lit a candle on one of the tables, shielding the flame as she looked around the room again. The books were well ordered, and it took only a few minutes to find a section of recent novels shelved between memoirs and poetry on the far wall. All the latest volumes were there. Either this library was a showpiece to impress guests, or at least one person in the castle was an avid reader.

She skimmed her fingers over the titles. Her light glanced off the gilt lettering. There were novels by Ann Radcliffe, Horace Walpole, and a wide variety of anonymous or pseudonymous authors. And there, near the end, was a slim red-bound book: *The Unconquered Heiress.*

Amelia lifted the volume from the shelf and turned it over in her hand. It had journeyed all the way from London to the Highlands and found its way into this library. She felt a brief flare of pride. And then, as always, annoyance.

Where her name should have been engraved, there was the lie that protected her: "A Novel by A.S. Rosefield."

She frowned at the letters. If the ton knew of her writing, she would likely be cast out. She didn't want to be ruined. But how would it feel to see her real name on the cover instead?

Would it give meaning to all the lonely hours she spent weaving stories in her room?

Someone rapped on the French door to her right, startling her. The glare of her candle obscured the person who demanded her attention. She moved closer, unconsciously gripping her book like a club, and saw Lord Carnach watching her through the glass.

Her throat closed up, but she set her candle on a table and opened the door with a remarkably steady hand.

"What a pleasant surprise, my lord," she said.

It was a vapid statement. He responded in kind. "I do hope my library is to your liking, Lady Amelia."

"Quite. But I should not like to be found alone with you…"

She trailed off, expecting him to leave. When he didn't, she turned her nose up to the precise angle that usually drove off would-be suitors.

He assessed her for a long moment with those strangely perceptive grey eyes, then pulled the French door shut behind him. "We're not so formal in the Highlands. If you can keep from kissing me, I'm sure your reputation is secure."

Amelia glared at him. "I wouldn't dream of kissing you."

He grinned. "If you haven't yet, it's only because we've just met."

She made a show of sliding her book onto the shelf. When she turned back to him, he still watched her, as though she was the most amusing thing he'd seen in an age.

"If you will not take your leave, then I shall. Good evening, my lord," she said, giving him the briefest curtsey.

Carnach caught her arm before she could walk away. "Stay," he commanded softly.

She brushed his hand away. "I'm not the woman you lured here to marry. You should seek her out, not me."

"I should." He shook his head hard, as though to clear it. "I should. And yet you have already said more words to me than Miss Etchingham said through all of dinner."

"Perhaps the company wasn't to her liking."

"Is any company to her liking?" he asked.

Amelia didn't have an answer for that. She also didn't have an answer for why she was still in the library, bantering with Lord Carnach, when she had spent so many years avoiding any hint of impropriety.

Perhaps the answer was to be found in the air of command about him — something about his imposing height, or the firm line of his jaw, or the way his dark hair swept back from his face as though he had just come in from a long ride.

Or maybe it was the way he regarded her so intently, his grey eyes looking almost silver in the moonlight — as though he intended to cast a spell to keep her there. She was accustomed to men worshipping her, despite her discomfort at their attentions. But this was the first time she thought she might be willing to worship him instead.

The fluttering in her belly intensified. And she knew it was for him — not from typhus, no matter how much she wished otherwise.

He regarded her for a moment, and in the silence her breath sounded just as fast and shallow as any heroine confronting a would-be ravisher. She was mad for even thinking in terms of ravishment. But if she was mad, her body didn't care.

"Would you like a drink?" he asked.

He sounded casual, as though he invited unwed ladies to drink with him every day, and possibly twice on Tuesdays. But his eyes were intense, watchful, weighing her with every gaze.

The need she felt was still weak enough that her mind could overrule it. She closed her eyes, thought of Prudence, and tried to kill her desire. "I really mustn't."

"I mustn't either. And yet…"

She opened her eyes. Carnach had walked over to stand beneath an ancient painting of a man in all his Highland finery, some distant ancestor who now watched over the decanters arrayed on the shelf below him. Carnach's hand hovered over the bottles as he watched her. Something on his face said he was considering some possibility, making some decision she didn't understand.

"And yet," he said softly, "I find I must. One drink, Lady Amelia. Will you stay?"

CHAPTER FOUR

In the half lit library, with moonlight and candlelight pooling between them, Amelia felt all her dormant desires stirring. She had channeled all her rebellion into her writing, behaving perfectly in public so that no one would suspect her secret career.

But writing wasn't her only desire. She wanted the adventures that she'd written for her heroines — the danger, the excitement, the dark deeds and heady passion.

"Must not," she said again.

He poured sherry into one glass, whisky into another. "Stay," he said. "You can't do better than me."

"Aren't you an arrogant one?"

Carnach laughed. "I meant you cannot do better at the moment, unless our mothers and brothers are more to your liking. I know you could reach far higher than me in the ton."

She took the glass from his outstretched hand. When his fingers brushed hers, she wished she wasn't wearing gloves.

She tried to focus on the conversation, not his slow smile as he sipped his whisky. "I don't know, my lord. An earl is hardly a stable boy."

"And yet even an earl would have no chance at your hand, would he?"

Amelia took a step back. "You're not offering, are you?"

"Your horror wounds me," he said.

"You do not appear to be wounded," she said, smiling despite herself.

"Deeply, deeply wounded," he said, thumping his fist against his heart.

Her smile turned into a laugh. "Never tell me you have a flair for drama."

"We all have our secrets, Lady Amelia."

She took a drink of her sherry. "Not me, my lord. I am an open book."

Carnach laughed. "I'm sure that's a falsehood. I don't know your secrets, but Ferguson tells me you're an absolute cypher."

When had her cousin's husband discussed her with Carnach? "Ferguson should know better than to meddle."

"You must not know Ferguson well — he was a born schemer," Carnach said. "But his scheme this time has left me in the dark. Why would he suggest a quiet woman like Miss Etchingham when you leave all other women in the shade?"

Amelia ignored the compliment. "Miss Etchingham is really quite lovely."

"I wouldn't know. She hardly said two words at dinner. You, though — while she was silent, all I could hear was your laugh."

And all I could see was your eyes. She didn't say it. She knew these games. And whatever Carnach's intentions were, she didn't need them, even if the part of her that dreamed of traditional passion wanted him.

"Thank you for the drink, my lord, but I really must be off to bed."

He set aside his glass, still nearly full. "My question remains," he said, as though she had said she would stay rather than go. "Why Miss

Etchingham? Why not you?"

"You would find me a poor companion," she said, in her coldest voice.

"Ah, the Unconquered shows herself," he said softly.

It was a reference to the unfortunate nickname she'd acquired in London — the one she had used to title the scathing satire she had just put away. By basing the heroine on herself, she had hoped to keep everyone from guessing that she had authored it.

"Ferguson has been a busybody, hasn't he?" she said.

"Is he wrong?"

He wasn't wrong. She did have a reputation for being unyielding on the marriage mart. But she had little love for the man who'd seduced her cousin Madeleine. "Ferguson doesn't know me, not really."

"I wonder," he said, leaning against the bookcase. "What would it take to know you?"

"Why do you care?" she asked. "Why would you want to know me?"

He shrugged. "Call it madness. Or call it intuition. But if I were the first earl," and here he jerked a thumb at the portrait above him, "I suspect I would have already carried you off to my bed."

She gasped. Other men flirted, feinted, obfuscated. This man declared and demanded, in a clipped and aristocratic voice with just a hint of brogue. If the library held the magic of a thousand books, Carnach was the sorcerer who could bring it all to life.

And perhaps he could bring her to life too. She already felt something she didn't have a word for welling up within her, dangerously close to the surface. When he uncoiled from his relaxed pose and reached out to take away her sherry, the graze of his fingers against hers felt like it could cut her open and make all her need, all her passion, all her wildness, bleed out between them.

"You shouldn't say such things," she said.

He stepped closer, beyond her usual boundary, into the space where her frigid walls usually froze suitors. But with him, there was no chill — only heat, and an odd certainty.

"One kiss," he said, cupping her neck with a firm, demanding hand. "One kiss to find out whether this is madness or intuition."

This is why girls fall into ruin, Amelia thought dazedly, seeing in a moment of perfect clarity that she was just as vulnerable to seduction as she had always feared.

But even the heat of his touch and the desire in his voice couldn't burn away every scrap of her brain. The last remaining shred of it may have forgotten what would happen if she was compromised, but it hadn't forgotten Prudence.

She planted her hands firmly on his shoulders and shoved. He dropped his hand from her neck, but he didn't apologize. He waited instead, like he thought he could still win her over.

She forced herself to breathe. "We mustn't do this, my lord."

"Malcolm," he said.

"I can't call you that."

"You could if we were married."

Panic rose in her throat, sharp and sudden. "I thought you weren't offering for me."

"I'm not a complete cad, Amelia. I wouldn't try to kiss you unless I was prepared for the consequences."

She took another step back, out of reach. "Nothing happened. Nothing will ever happen. And there will be no consequences. You should marry Miss Etchingham, if she'll have you. And if she won't, you'll find a hundred women in London more suitable than me."

Malcolm no longer looked like a sorcerer. Crossing his muscled arms over his chest, he looked more like a warrior of old, eager to pillage her. "I've decided. It was intuition."

"And I've decided it was madness," she retorted. "You can't possibly want to marry me after a single conversation."

"You're right." He stepped forward. "I still think a kiss is required."

Even though she was appalled, his grin made her laugh. "That wasn't what I meant, my lord."

"Malcolm," he reminded her again.

She took a deep breath, hoping she looked composed. "Very well, Malcolm." There was more of a sigh to his name than she intended, and the soft roll of her tongue on the *l*'s felt like the kiss she'd denied them.

If even his name could seduce her, she needed to run as far away from the man as possible.

"I must go," she said. It was abrupt and awkward, nothing like her usual command of language, but it was all she could manage.

"Until tomorrow, then," he said. He didn't touch her again, but he looked just as unyielding as the man in the portrait above him.

Tomorrow.

She turned and fled.

If her defenses had crumbled so quickly, how could she survive another round?

*   *   *

He agreed with Amelia. This couldn't be intuition. It was pure madness. There was no other explanation.

Malcolm watched her flee. It wasn't an orderly retreat — it was more like a rout. When she had looked at him, he thought she wanted him as much as he wanted her. Instead, his attempt to kiss her had scared her off.

He picked up his whisky glass and strode to the French door, turning the lock against the night. Through the window, the moon gave everything in his mother's formal garden an eerie silver edge. But the flowers were nothing compared to the wonder in Amelia's eyes before she remembered that she shouldn't want him.

He rolled his tumbler in his hand. She wasn't the type of woman he sought for his bride. There were secrets hiding in those eyes, and he didn't think they were the shallow secrets of a society miss.

Still, what was better? A woman with secrets and a backbone to support them, or a woman with no secrets who could barely feign interest in him?

Amelia was interested in him. He was sure of it, even if she wasn't. If she wasn't so loyal to her friend, he suspected Amelia would still be in the library with him — and they wouldn't be talking.

Malcolm cursed under his breath. He didn't intend to marry for passion. And he couldn't marry a woman with secrets, not if they were the kind that could threaten his clan. If she was truly unsuitable, he couldn't take her, regardless of what his intuition said.

He strode to a writing desk, yanked open the center drawer, and pulled out paper, ink, and a sharpened quill. His friend Ferguson had gotten him into this mess, recommending Miss Etchingham over Amelia. He surely had his reasons, even if Malcolm couldn't fathom any of them.

He scrawled a note to ask whether there was any reason not to pursue Amelia instead. Ferguson and his household had traveled to Scotland with Amelia's party, splitting off to go to Ferguson's manor. If Malcolm sent a footman with the note in the morning, he would have a response by evening.

While the ink dried, he sipped his whisky. Maybe he should go to London to look for a bride. Surely he could find a woman who would be as obedient as Miss Etchingham and as delightful as Amelia.

But when he tried to imagine that woman, he couldn't see her. All he saw was Amelia's smile.

He folded the paper, sealed it with wax, and took it down to the great hall to toss on a tray for Graves to dispatch in the morning. Then he looked up at the ancient swords hanging above the dais, protected by generations of Carnach earls. They were softened by the tapestries that added color to the stones, embroidered by generations of Carnach countesses.

Every one of his ancestors had done their duty to the estate. He needed to follow in their footsteps, not be led astray by passion. If Amelia could take up his duties with him, he would offer for her. If she couldn't...

If she couldn't, he wouldn't take her, regardless of what his intuition said.

CHAPTER FIVE

The next morning, Amelia was still in her dressing gown hours after the sun rose. She hadn't slept well after returning to her room. Even though she'd caught herself in time and refused Malcolm's kiss, it should never have come that close.

She knew better than to kiss anyone. She sometimes desired the adventures her heroines had — but in real life, it took only an instant to be ruined. She'd come close to being forced into marriage by the awful Lord Kessel a year earlier, when he had cornered her at a ball and tried to kiss her. Luckily, Alex had been watching, and he'd found her before the damage was done. After Alex broke the baron's nose, adding injury to the insult Amelia had caused by slapping him, Kessel had given up his pursuit of her.

But if Alex had to rescue her again, he might start to think she was better off married. She should have left the library as soon as Malcolm appeared. She certainly shouldn't have enjoyed their conversation as much as she did — was laughter and a bit of moonlight really enough to make her lose her common sense?

She'd remembered before anything disastrous happened. But even though she didn't want him — didn't *want* to want him — she still didn't want to face Prudence. Neither he nor Prudence seemed interested in each other, but Prudence wouldn't appreciate Amelia's meddling.

And if Prudence knew how close Malcolm had come to kissing Amelia in the library — what would that do to Prudence's only chance to escape her mother?

Amelia picked up her quill. She was curled in bed with her writing desk, even though she'd done more daydreaming than writing since unpacking it that morning. All she could do now was stay away from Malcolm, and hope Lady Harcastle gave up on the idea of Prudence's marriage so they could all return to England.

Ink bloomed on her fingers from her careless grip on the pen. She cursed softly to herself. She needed to work, not stare off into space and let the ink run down her hands. She placed the quill's nib on the paper and started to write.

Veronique walked slowly down the stone hallway toward the doom that awaited her. Her torch flickered in the draft, as though a great beast with cold, menacing breath slumbered at the end of the passage, threatening to extinguish her light with every exhale. Would her captor demand her embrace tonight?

Amelia groaned and scratched through the lines with a heavy, decisive hand. Her writing had been ruined by seeing Malcolm in the library the night before. If she stayed in Scotland, she would write a novel so lurid that even her greedy publisher might not risk the scandal of publishing it.

Someone tapped on the door. Prudence stuck her head into the room before Amelia said anything. "Aren't you starved, Mellie? I missed you at breakfast."

Amelia waved her in. She didn't want to look Prudence in the eye, but it was better than banging her head against her writing desk. "A maid brought me a roll and some chocolate an hour ago — or was it two?"

Prudence closed the door and sat on the edge of the bed. "I would tell you to take better care of your health, but I barely ate either. And you should see our mothers — they had enough ratafia last night to stock all of Vauxhall for a fortnight."

"You can't be serious," Amelia said, putting aside her writing desk and wiping the ink from her fingers with a cloth.

"Perfectly serious. Your mother must have switched to wine at some point — her lips are still purple. And my mother was so quiet from her headache that she didn't say a single word about my failure to land an earl."

Prudence was more cheerful than she was the night before. Amelia shifted in bed, pulling her coverlet up around her like a piece of armor. "I am glad you've decided against an alliance with that man. He's not the type I would see you with."

"Hmm," Prudence said.

Amelia eyed her suspiciously. "You haven't changed your mind?"

Prudence pleated the edge of the coverlet with her fingers. "Not precisely. But perhaps you are right. If I saw him alone, without my mother, would we suit?"

"No," Amelia said, more sharply than she intended.

"How can you know that? It was your idea, not mine."

She sounded bewildered — which was fair, since it was Amelia's idea she had grasped on to. Amelia sucked in a breath. If Prudence still wanted the marriage, she would support her — but only if Prudence was sure.

"Don't you want someone...safer than Carnach? Someone who will adore you, not just marry you to tick a requirement off his list? You should find a man who is interested in history, who loves books and quiet evenings at home, not public policy and Parliament."

"You make me sound so dull," Prudence protested.

Amelia laughed. "I want the same, you know. Without the husband lording his authority over me, perhaps — but quiet evenings at home would be lovely."

"Maybe I don't want the same," Prudence said slowly, smoothing the coverlet out before pleating it again. "I thought I wanted a scholar, but perhaps I should find a man who won't let me sink into all those ancient languages and dead cities."

"You can have that without the man."

Prudence shrugged. "You've had your chances at passion and refused them. I haven't. And I wonder if I've not done enough to find it these past few years."

"Passion isn't as necessary as freedom," Amelia said. "And passion with the wrong man…it may feel wonderful, but it ruins everything in the end."

She was thinking of Malcolm — Carnach, as she needed to remember to call him — but Prudence smiled sympathetically. "If you had found the right man to offer for you, rather than a string of wrong ones, might you feel differently? I know Lord Kessel's pursuit of you was awful, but there must be someone worth having. If not, why are there so many poems and plays about love?"

Amelia didn't want to revisit her old suitors — particularly not Kessel. She stood and jerked the bellpull. The library felt medieval, but the castle had been modernized. She could pretend she was still in London, not in a castle with the one man who had almost broken through her defenses. "I should dress and show myself downstairs, don't you think?"

"I know you're changing the subject," Prudence said with a wry smile. "But if you plan to dress, would you please put on something suitable for a picnic? It's why I came to your room."

Amelia walked over to the window, afraid that her face would give her away if she asked the question while looking at her friend. "Who is picnicking with us?"

"Lord Carnach and your brother. The mothers claimed they wanted us to enjoy ourselves, but I think it's the ratafia headaches keeping them at home."

Amelia looked out over the craggy hills toward the valley where a little village nestled beside a lake. It really was beautiful terrain — so wild compared to her family's estate in Lancashire, and yet so gorgeous in its untamed state. "Are we safe without a true chaperone?"

Prudence snorted. "Your brother will guard your virtue, and you can guard mine. Carnach's virtue is in his own hands."

Amelia flinched. "He may not have much virtue to concern himself with."

"Why are you set against him?" Prudence asked, coming to stand beside her at the window. "He isn't that bad. He was most civil to me this morning, and readily agreed to a picnic."

She needed to tell her everything. How could she let Prudence marry a man who was so easy with his affections?

Prudence would know that Amelia wasn't trying to steal Carnach away from her — Amelia had vowed off marriage years earlier, and her resolve was as strong as ever. But what was fairer to Prudence? If she told Prue what had happened, perhaps there wouldn't be a wedding. They could go back to England, and Prue could find someone better suited for her.

But Prudence thought she was out of options. Even if Amelia told her that Malcolm had almost kissed her in the library, Prue might put duty over fidelity and marry him anyway.

Would their friendship survive if Prudence always wondered whether her husband would lust after Amelia again? Surely Malcolm would settle into marriage, perhaps even fall in love with Prue the way she deserved — but if he didn't, would telling Prudence ruin everything? Was it better to stay silent, and just stay away from Malcolm?

If Amelia thought about it any more, she'd be a candidate for Bedlam. So she turned to Prudence with a bright smile. "You're right. Carnach is civil. But please promise me you will seek more than civility."

"Would civility and a title be enough? Civility and a comfortable living? Civility and a good family?" Prudence's voice turned sharp. "For one who advocates so strongly against a love match, you don't seem willing to accept that there are other reasons for marriage."

"Fine," Amelia snapped. "Marry the man. Even though you deserve better. Even though you would hate to be a political hostess. Ignore all that and marry him so he can keep you in gloves and books and lemon cakes."

Prudence glared at her, but her expression smoothed before Amelia could apologize. "You always were a stubborn one, Mellie. And I know you only want me to be happy. But someday…"

She trailed off. Amelia was too curious to let her stop. "What?"

"Someday I hope someone changes your mind. You aren't always right, you know."

"I know that," Amelia said.

Prudence laughed. "That sour look on your face says otherwise. But let's not argue. It's too beautiful outside to fight, and I don't want anything to mar our picnic. If Carnach and I still don't suit after spending time away from my mother, I won't marry him. Is that enough of a promise?"

The maid entered then, so Amelia didn't have to answer. But

Prudence left her with a look that said she noticed the lack of affirmation.

Amelia sighed. Prudence was so forgiving. Too forgiving. If she knew what Malcolm had done…would she be so forgiving then?

CHAPTER SIX

Malcolm should talk to Miss Etchingham. She had suggested their picnic, after all. It was the first display of initiative she'd shown with him.

Salford rode at her side instead, going on about the differences between Scottish and English fortifications. The woman didn't seem to care for Malcolm's conversational gambits, but her passion for architecture was apparent enough. She was arguing with Salford about something related to the Romans. They were so deep in conversation that it never occurred to them to ask Malcolm when the fort had been built.

Not that he minded. He had invited Miss Etchingham to Scotland, but it was her companion who attracted his interest. He reined in his horse, waiting for Amelia, who had fallen slightly behind their party. He shouldn't engage her in conversation — but tempting himself with the woman he shouldn't marry was surely better than listening to Salford's dissertation.

"Does your brother always talk about rocks like they're his firstborn children?" he asked when Amelia caught up to him.

She rolled her eyes. "Prudence is just as awful. She can't indulge like this in most circumstances. Her mother would lock her up forever if she knew Prudence was such a bluestocking."

"Then you aren't as enthralled by the clan's ruins as they are?"

There were few ruins on Malcolm's lands, but the fort rising above them was a picturesque site. With its missing windows and jutting crenellations, it was a broken crown above the rugged pastures where his clan scratched out their survival. Malcolm never thought of the architecture. He was always more consumed by who had lived there, and what they had lost.

Amelia's voice turned dreamy. "I am enthralled, but not by stones. Think what it must have been like to command such a place, or to conquer it."

"It was never conquered," Malcolm said. "But the Highlands were disarmed after Culloden and our defenses are falling back into the earth."

She gestured behind them, toward his sturdy castle on the other side of the valley. "Not everything here is crumbling."

"Perhaps the castle will eventually. But it won't while I am laird."

"So you won't lead an uprising and lose your castle?" she teased.

He snorted. "No. England's path is ours now. And I'll go there to save this place, even if London makes my skin crawl."

"Why would you want to leave such a place for London?" Amelia asked.

He paused to watch her navigate around a low-hanging branch. She would never win a race to Newmarket, but she was competent enough that he could relax.

"I don't want to leave," he said. "But the Highlanders aren't faring well. Most of the landlords care more for profits than people, and every year they evict more tenants to make room for sheep. And Parliament aids them at every turn. If my clan is to live to see another century in Scotland instead of America, they need me in London to advocate for them — for all of Scotland, if I can."

"You won't find many allies, my lord."

He sighed. He didn't want to think of alliances and political strategies. He would rather spend his days riding about his estate, meeting with tenants, smelling heather and gorse rather than coal fires and horseshit.

But his responsibilities didn't allow him the freedom to live as he wanted. "Perhaps no one in London cares about the Highlands. I cannot give in without a fight, though."

"Say what you will about Miss Etchingham's historical leanings," Amelia said, nodding toward the pair in front of them. "If it's a political wife you're after, she could write you entire treatises on what is happening here, if you gave her time to learn."

Prudence and Salford were deep in conversation, no doubt about some long-passed era. Whatever lack of interest held her tongue around him did not extend to Amelia's brother. Malcolm moved his horse closer to Amelia's, lowering his voice. "Miss Etchingham is accomplished, I'm sure. But I want a wife who can talk, and laugh, and feel something other than academic detachment."

A fly buzzed against his ear. He lifted his hand to brush it away. Amelia flinched away instead, as though she feared his touch.

He narrowed his eyes. "Is something amiss, Lady Amelia?"

She blushed, but she didn't apologize. "No. You should discuss your requirements with Miss Etchingham. Given enough time, you'll suit each other well enough."

"What if it's not Miss Etchingham I want?"

Amelia's hand tightened on her reins. Her mare mouthed the bit uncomfortably. "Then I wish you very happy with the next woman on your list."

Her voice was as cold as the great hall in winter. He wanted to be the fire that brought her back to life.

"There's only one woman on the list at present."

She reined in her horse, so quickly that he was ten yards beyond her by the time he came to a stop. He looked over his shoulder, turning slightly to keep her in sight. Her face was ashen, with all the pallor of marble under her crown of golden hair.

But her blue eyes were fierce as she nudged her horse up to meet him. "You brought Miss Etchingham here to marry, and marry her you shall," she said, in a dark, urgent voice. "Whatever you may think of either of us, I assure you that she is the one you want."

He wanted to touch her, to prove her wrong. But he couldn't do it here. "We both know what could have happened last night. Why would I give that up to marry a woman who barely speaks to me?"

She closed her eyes. Without the sharpness of her gaze, she suddenly looked vulnerable. "If you won't marry Prudence, find another. There are dozens of women in London who are better for you. I cannot entertain your suit."

"Do you not want to upset Miss Etchingham by marrying me? She and I were never engaged, and I don't even believe she likes me. There would be no scandal there."

When she opened her eyes again, she didn't look at him. Instead, she turned her gaze out over the countryside, across the estate he had vowed to save. "You know nothing about me, my lord. I've caused no scandals, but I'm not a witless porcelain doll. I have dreams of my own. Find a sweet girl who will be content to let you think for her. Your career will be better for it."

Her certainty shook him. But he couldn't agree that easily. "Meet me tonight," he said, knowing it was foolish to say the words even as they slipped through his lips. "Let's discuss this where we can have a proper conversation, not in the middle of a road. Earls should propose marriage indoors, at the very least."

That brought a glimmer of a smile to her face. "How very proper of you, my lord."

He had never felt less proper in his life. "Tonight?"

She didn't falter under the sudden command in his voice. She coolly stared him down, then looked up the road to where Salford and Prudence were disappearing around a bend.

When she turned back to him, there was mischief in her eyes. "The library, at a quarter to eleven. I trust that after our interview, this nonsense about a union between us will end."

She cantered away from him, up the final rise toward the fort where Salford and Prudence awaited them. He gave her a few moments' start before following her. She seemed so sure that they were ill suited — and perhaps they were. Ferguson surely had a reason for recommending Miss Etchingham over her.

Ferguson's disapproval made no sense. Amelia wasn't just more entertaining — she was the daughter of an earl, with a dowry large enough to compensate for any number of indiscretions. If he were marrying solely for status, Amelia was a better choice than Miss Etchingham, even without considering how her laughter heated his blood.

But Amelia's reference to her dreams gave him pause. The ton didn't appreciate women who thought of anything beyond the next social event. If her dreams were something that could harm his reputation by association, it could bode ill for his attempts to win allies.

A footman had taken his note to Ferguson that morning, as planned. It was a two-hour ride from Malcolm's castle to his friend's estate, but he could expect an answer by evening.

It couldn't be bad — but if it were, what would he do? His scowl was gone by the time they caught up to Salford and Prudence, but his conscience still vacillated. He needed to marry for the MacCabes, not for himself.

But for the first time, he wondered if the clan was worth the sacrifice.

*   *   *

The ruined fort was everything Amelia would ever want as a setting for something as cold and calculating as the proposed marriage between Malcolm and Prudence. She saw how she would write it: the innocent damsel sold into marriage to save her family, and the dastardly nobleman who intended to use her for his own gain.

In the crumbling courtyard, open to the sky, with all but the most tenacious bits of cobblestone consumed by grass and weeds, Amelia could almost believe that story.

She preferred the story to the sordid reality. If this were a book, Amelia had been cast as the evil seductress who might lure away her friend's sole chance at a match. Amelia didn't intend to stay in that role, even if it was hard to remember her goals when Malcolm's every word felt like a caress.

But Prudence wasn't doing herself any favors if she planned to marry Malcolm.

"Is the chicken to your liking, Miss Etchingham?" Malcolm asked.

There was an array of food laid out in front of them, nearly enough to feed the garrison once stationed there. Two footmen had brought the feast up ahead of them and spread the dishes out on a cloth, replete with china plates and cushions for the ladies' comfort. If this was Lord Carnach's style of courtship, it was lovely.

"Yes, the chicken is perfection, my lord."

Prudence's voice could hardly be heard, even in the shelter of the courtyard.

Amelia may have doubted Malcolm's intentions, but she had to commend him for pressing on. "Tell me, Miss Etchingham," he said, his voice soothing, "what is it that fascinates you about fortifications? Or must I call Salford out for boring you earlier?"

"Surely you love these ruins too?" Prudence asked, her disbelief shocking her out of the meekness her mother drilled into her.

Malcolm shrugged. "They are my clan's past. I must have more of a care for their future."

"But…" Prudence started. Amelia heard the passion in her voice. In the next instant, she caught herself. "But of course, Lord Carnach. Your devotion to your duty is exemplary."

"Come now, Prudence," Alex said, reaching for a bit of cheese. "I know you have a stronger opinion than that."

Only Amelia noticed the flicker of despair in her eyes. "My opinion matters naught. Perhaps Lord Carnach is right to stay so focused on the present."

Alex opened his mouth to argue. Amelia cut him off before the afternoon devolved into academics. "I'm sure Lord Carnach won't bite your head off if you tell him your thoughts," she said, trying to sound encouraging.

Prudence shaded her eyes with her hand and looked up at the sky. "I think us poor females are better suited to talk of the weather, don't you?"

Amelia snorted.

Malcolm threw himself back into the fray. "I trust you are more intelligent than that, Miss Etchingham. What do you see in these stones?"

Prudence cast her eyes around them, finally settling on Alex, as though she could look through him to the great ruined archway behind him. "The stones only tell bits of the story. I try to see what is missing — the colors they wore, the way they spoke, who they served, what they believed. Why build in the Highlands? Why defend this place above all others? That is what fascinates me, my lord — the hearts of men, not their busts carved in marble."

"You won't find much marble here," Malcolm said.

His words broke the spell. For a moment, the Prudence that Amelia knew had shown herself, almost as though she had forgotten where she was. But Malcolm's voice dragged Prudence's eyes away from Alex and locked the real Prudence away again.

"Of course. Forgive my ramblings, Lord Carnach. I was building castles in Spain."

"And populating them," Alex said drily.

Prudence flushed. "What use is a castle without people to live in it?"

Her tone was almost venomous — an undercurrent Amelia didn't understand. Malcolm smoothed over the awkwardness. "On that we are agreed, Miss Etchingham. May I offer you some of this excellent beef?"

The conversation turned away from stones, leaving Amelia to consider her options.

And really, she had none. Even if she wanted to marry, she couldn't let Malcolm risk a future political career on her, not when her secret writing life might someday be discovered — not when some part of her wanted it to be discovered. And she wouldn't take away what Prudence needed, even if Prudence looked more nauseated than enchanted when speaking to her prospective fiancée.

So after they had returned to the castle, Amelia laid a hand on

Prudence's arm and pulled her up to her chamber. She would question Prudence a final time, give her one last chance to abandon the thought of marriage. Then she would proceed with her scheme.

"Are you certain you want to marry Carnach?" Amelia asked.

Prudence shook her head. "It doesn't matter, though. He's nice enough to tolerate. I cannot afford another failed season on the marriage mart."

"But you can barely talk to him," Amelia protested.

"It's the anticipation, I think. I tell myself not to be nervous, yet when I see him, I dream of what might have been..." Prudence broke off, swallowing whatever that might-have-been was.

"Why have you given up on what you want?"

"If it was only the money, perhaps I wouldn't have," Prudence said, sitting on Amelia's dressing chair like it was a tumbrel taking her to the gallows. "But I don't have your fearlessness. And I can't keep waiting."

"You can still write your treatises even when you're married, I suppose," Amelia allowed, starting to pace.

Prudence threw her a strange look that Amelia couldn't interpret. "Of course. My treatises. Surely my nervousness about him will subside once I become more accustomed to him. And once we're married, it matters less if I slip and he discovers that I am an utter bluestocking — he can't divorce me for liking the Greeks."

A bit of her grin returned. Amelia knew what she had to do.

"Speaking of the Greeks — I found something in the library you should see."

"Shall we go now?" Prudence asked. "We've ages of time before dinner."

"No. It's better viewed in the moonlight. Tonight I'll retire from the drawing room early. Stay there when I leave so no one thinks anything, but come to the library at eleven and I'll show you what I found."

Prudence laughed. "Why all the subterfuge? Don't tell me you've found a treasure."

She thought of Malcolm's silver eyes. "After a fashion. I can't say more, though, or it will ruin the effect."

"Very well," Prudence said. "I know better than to argue when you have me in your coils."

Amelia kissed her cheek. "It will all come out all right in the end, Prue. I promise you."

It was a simple plan. Amelia would meet Malcolm, reinforce her refusal, and deliver Prudence to him instead. If Prudence didn't anticipate meeting him, she might not be so nervous.

Surely the moonlight would do the rest. And in the dark, it would surely be easier for Amelia to walk away.

CHAPTER SEVEN

In the end, he knew his duty.

If anything, dinner with his family had confirmed it. His brothers trusted him and his mother adored him. How could he tell them that he valued a woman over their well-being?

On the face of it, Amelia was perfect for all of them. She was beautiful, well spoken, possessed impeccable manners, and seemed to like his family. And Ferguson's reply to his earlier question, received right before the gong rang for dinner, didn't mention any scandals.

But the hastily scrawled script was all warning. *MacCabe — Do not marry the harpy. - F*

"Not" was underlined three times.

It was clear there was no love lost between Amelia and Ferguson. But they were two strong personalities — Malcolm could see how they might set each other on edge. Was Ferguson's opinion based on facts?

Malcolm had torn the note up and thrown it into the fire, cursing Ferguson's brevity. If there were legitimate grievances, Ferguson would have mentioned them. He suspected Ferguson and Amelia simply didn't like each other. Was Ferguson's perception of her more accurate than Malcolm's intuition?

More accurate than the desire that kept him on edge, eager for her footsteps in the hall?

His pocket watch read 10:43pm. He snapped it shut, then turned away from the French door at the far end of the library to regard the portrait of Ian MacCabe, the first Earl of Carnach. With his dark hair, grey eyes, and warrior physique, Malcolm bore an uncanny resemblance to his distant ancestor, although Malcolm's nose was slightly crooked from the brawl he'd gotten into with the twins the year before. Fighting after his father's wake was unseemly, but as a last bit of entertainment before a lifetime with the title, it had been vastly satisfying.

Ian was the one who started the tradition of marrying English brides. The strategy had given the MacCabes the connections necessary to avoid some of the worst assaults of the English monarchs. Of course, Ian had kidnapped his bride — a ploy that had its merits.

He grinned. The first countess had fallen in love with Ian before the week was out, if the stories were to be believed. He had no doubt Amelia would do the same with him, if she would only drop her armor long enough to give him a chance to win her.

But if he kidnapped her, Salford would likely kill Malcolm as soon as the ceremony ended. And if she truly hid something dangerous under her pretty face, Malcolm couldn't have her anyway. He was a peer of the realm, not a poet or a publican. Marrying for love — or lust, at least — was a pretty sentiment for the gossip rags, but it wouldn't feed his clan or keep the Highlanders from emigrating to America.

He would channel his ancestors' ruthlessness rather than their rebelliousness. He would rein in whatever madness possessed him when he was with Amelia and tell her that she shouldn't have come. After his guests left, he would go to London and broaden his search. And if he never saw Amelia — and the body that would never be his — so much the better.

The door at the other end of the room slipped open. He heard it shut again with a careful whisper and a soft click. Malcolm focused on the painting of the first earl, holding his stance as her almost silent footsteps drew closer. He knew he couldn't watch her hips sway toward him if he wanted to remember his intention to relinquish her.

Amelia stopped beside him, still silent. He looked down and saw her heeled slippers dangling from her fingers. "Did you think to sneak up on me?"

His voice was quiet, her answering laughter quieter still — but the thread of excitement woven through their voices was as clear as a battle cry shouted from a mountaintop. "The heels click too loudly on the wood floors in the passageway. You really must add more carpets, my lord. You can never host discreet house parties otherwise."

"I've never had cause to."

"Neither have I. You shall, though, when you enter the Lords. The ladies will swoon over you, and you'll be thankful for the carpets then."

He swung around to face her, leaving his ancestor as a silent observer to their game. "And will you swoon over me, Lady Amelia?"

She met his gaze. "You know I cannot, my lord."

His traitorous hand caressed her cheek, already disregarding Ferguson's warning and his own resolve. She wasn't a harpy. She was a goddess come down from Olympus just for him.

She pulled away. He followed, catching her wrist. "Cannot? Or will not?"

Her slippers dropped to the floor. "Both. We aren't meant for each other, Malcolm. You will marry Prudence, as you should. And I will retire to the country, as I should."

Her voice fought him, but she didn't struggle against his grip. "I won't marry Prudence. She wouldn't have me even if I wanted her."

Amelia glanced at the door. "She would…"

"She wouldn't," he said, cutting her off. "She might marry me to escape her mother, but that's not enough for what I require."

He raised her hand to his lips, brushing a kiss across her knuckles that said nothing of letting go and everything of possession. "I require wit, and charm, and a clever tongue. Not knowledge of Greek and a passion for marble."

Her fingers tightened in his grasp. "You need obedience, too, unless I misremember. Prudence is infinitely better at that than I am."

"But is Prudence better at kissing than you are?"

"I wouldn't know," she said. She looked down, wiggling the toes that peeked out from under her gown. Her toes sent a bolt of lust to his groin.

Then she looked up. "Marry her, Malcolm, like you're supposed to. And stop thinking of me."

He couldn't stop thinking of her. The part of him that was rock hard against his breeches knew what he wanted, even though his brain denied it.

He stepped closer, until he was inches from her, and his hand shot out to stop her when she tried to move away. "Yes, I invited her here with an eye toward marriage. But it's you I want, Amelia — and for your own sake, not because of the moonlight or the whisky or the dozen other excuses we made to ourselves this morning. Prudence could walk through that door with a hundred of the finest London whores and none of them could entice me more than you."

Amelia raised an eyebrow. "Is that supposed to be a compliment?"

Her voice was damnably cool, but she didn't make even the slightest attempt to pull away. He tilted up her chin. Her eyes were saying goodbye — but her lips were parted in what could only be a welcome.

"It is not a compliment. It's the truth," he said. "And if you haven't recognized that truth yet…"

He pulled her against him. She was stubborn enough to die before she admitted it, but he saw the stark longing behind her protective façade. Her eyes widened. Her mouth opened.

He didn't wait for her protest.

He kissed her, fast and thorough. He felt the war within her, the battle between the passion she craved and the vow she'd made. She clamped her lips shut, even though her body curled against him. But in that instant, he knew he would win her someday — even if he couldn't convince her tonight.

In the next instant, the door opened.

Disentangling was like fighting quicksand. Amelia pulled away with admirable speed, glaring daggers at him.

But speed couldn't save her. Prudence stood in the doorway, her face gaunt with horror in the light of the candle she held. There were no whores in her company — but Alex stood behind her, ready to detonate.

Malcolm would have preferred the whores. There was no time to wish Salford away, though. He was upon them in seconds. Malcolm moved in front of Amelia, ready to protect her. She tried to step between the men, but Malcolm thrust her back.

Salford raised his fist. Malcolm stood his ground. He deserved one blow from her brother, but would protect himself from the second.

The blow never came. Salford lowered his fist. He didn't stop scowling, though. "I'll spare you for now, Carnach. The ladies shouldn't see this."

"Don't stop on my account," Prudence said, shutting the door. "If you can handle Carnach, I shall take on Amelia."

As she advanced, Malcolm finally saw the spark that made Amelia and Prudence such fierce friends. That spark was suddenly something dangerous, an incendiary in a powderkeg.

"Prue, I didn't mean for this to happen," Amelia said.

"Neither of us want excuses, Amelia," Salford snapped.

Malcolm knew what he had to say. He perhaps even wanted to say it — but to her, not to her brother. The words felt odd in his mouth, like they were emerging into an ocean, cold and indistinct, ripped apart by the waves. "I will do my duty, Salford. Lady Amelia and I will wed as soon as the arrangements are made."

Amelia laughed, but the sound broke in the same ocean that threatened to drown him. "Nothing happened, Alex. Certainly nothing requiring marriage. If you and Prudence stay silent, no one in London need ever know."

Her voice was pleading. Malcolm didn't like it. "I wouldn't want anyone to take me for a seducer of innocents," he said.

"Have you seduced other innocents?" she asked.

"Of course not."

"Then Carnach only seduced you, Amelia?" Salford interjected. "That isn't a satisfactory answer."

"He didn't seduce me," Amelia said. Even from three feet away, Malcolm could hear her teeth grinding.

"And yet you're shoeless, in the dark, alone with him, and when we entered, he was kissing you."

"You and Prudence would have been alone in here if we weren't here," Amelia pointed out. "Would you have seduced her?"

"Prudence? Don't be absurd."

"Thank you, Salford," Prudence said.

Malcolm detected sarcasm in Prudence's voice, but Salford inclined his head, accepting her thanks as though she meant them.

"Still, nothing happened that merits marriage," Amelia insisted. "And to have you force it, when you were with Prudence quite late yourself…"

Alex held up a book, cutting her off. "Prudence said she had an errand in the library, and as we had been discussing architecture until five minutes ago, very properly chaperoned by our mothers, I offered to escort her. If you had been here alone, no one would have thought a thing of it."

"No one needs to think a thing of it if you will keep this quiet, Alex!" Amelia said.

Malcolm held up his hands. "Might we discuss this in the morning, when our tempers have cooled?"

Amelia whirled on him. "We won't discuss this in the morning because there is nothing to discuss. This may look suspicious, but it won't happen again."

"You've promised that before, Amelia," Salford reminded her.

"What the devil does that mean?" Malcolm asked, watching as Amelia turned red.

Prudence snickered. "Amelia will make such a wonderful political wife for you, Lord Carnach. So obedient, so proper…"

Amelia silenced her. "We all make mistakes, Alex. Don't hang me for mine just because you haven't gotten around to making your own."

There was dead silence. Salford stared at Amelia, assessing. Prudence looked at her feet, her thoughts seeming miles away. Malcolm wanted to know what Amelia's previous offenses were — but now that they'd been caught, he would have a lifetime to learn about them.

Salford was the first to blink. "I've made mistakes too, Mellie. After that business with Madeleine and Ferguson this spring…"

He paused. Really, the man was driving Malcolm mad by hinting at impropriety, then changing the subject. Malcolm knew Ferguson's marriage to Salford and Amelia's cousin was swift, but what was Salford's role in it?

Salford spoke again. "I won't threaten to send you away. Knowing you, you'd only enjoy it. But I can't ignore what I saw tonight. If Carnach doesn't agree to marry you, I'll find a way to ruin him without bringing you into it."

"I already said I will marry her," Malcolm said.

"And I already said I won't marry anyone," Amelia replied.

"And I said I would marry Lord Carnach, but apparently that doesn't signify," Prudence said.

Salford and Amelia both started talking at once, but the earl's stronger voice carried the floor. "You are better off without the bounder, Prudence. You deserve someone with a keen mind, not a rake."

She leveled a glare at him. "There are no men with keen minds in the ton, Alex."

Alex looked wounded. Amelia followed with another blow. "Do I deserve a bounder, then? Not a very brotherly sentiment, even from you."

"Enough," Salford snapped. "You've had every chance to live the life you want, and yet you risk it all far too often. Perhaps Carnach can control you where I've failed."

Malcolm could have told him it was the wrong thing to say. For someone so renowned as a collector, Salford really had the most inelegant way with women. Even Prudence winced, and she was not in Amelia's corner.

Amelia gaped at her brother. Malcolm felt a twinge of sympathy. Whatever she had done, she didn't deserve to be castigated for it in front of him.

"I won't have you talking to my future wife like that, Salford,"

Malcolm said, stepping toward Amelia and taking her hand in his. Her fingers curled lightly in his palm, devoid of their earlier passion, but she didn't evade him.

It was Salford's turn to gape. Finally he bowed to his sister. "I am sorry, Amelia. You know my words escape me when I'm in a temper."

She didn't respond. Malcolm squeezed her hand, lightly. She retrieved her fingers from his grip. When she finally spoke, her voice was frozen. "I won't forget, you know."

"I won't expect you to. Carnach, if you will wait on me in the morning, we can discuss settlements."

Amelia stooped to retrieve her slippers, then walked to a nearby footstool so she could sit and tie them on. Malcolm felt the chill emanating from her as she spoke. "At least promise that if Carnach and I don't suit, we may break it off."

She wasn't looking up, and so missed what Malcolm saw — the brief softening of Salford's face before he answered. "Divorce is out of the question. But you needn't marry for a few days. If you truly don't suit, I won't force it."

Her resulting smile was strangely triumphant. Malcolm ignored it. They suited, at least physically. And not even a deaf man could miss the heat of their banter. If the scandals Salford hinted at were truly awful, she was exactly what he didn't need in a bride. But was it worse to take her anyway, or risk Salford's wrath just as he was trying to build influence in London?

Amelia looked up and met his eyes. Her smile was positively wicked. He could read the thoughts behind it. Even though his honor was at stake, he gave her a wicked smile of his own.

She would try to escape him — to prove they weren't compatible.

And the devil within him was eager to prove her wrong.

CHAPTER EIGHT

Amelia was irate, aggrieved, enflamed — she could list adjectives for days, and probably would when she next sat down with pen and paper.

But she was also guilty. And ashamed. She would find a way to escape this engagement, no matter how intent Malcolm and Alex were on arranging it. But could her friendship with Prudence survive?

She dragged her eyes away from Malcolm's smile and forced her clumsy fingers to tie her slippers. "Shall we go to our rooms and leave the gentlemen in peace?" she asked Prudence when she was done, as though it were any other evening, as though nothing between them had changed.

"Can I bring my book with me, or do you plan to steal that too?"

Amelia winced. She heard her brother stifle a laugh, but she was done with him for the night. "I didn't mean for this to happen, Prue. Carnach kissed me, not the other way around."

Prudence raised an eyebrow.

"It's true," Amelia insisted. She was starting to panic, but she tried to keep the tremor out of her voice. "You're welcome to him, if you still want him."

Malcolm glared at her, but Prudence shrugged. "No, Alex is right.

I need a man whose intellect is keen enough to recognize the woman in front of him for what she is. None of the men in my acquaintance qualify."

She had, with one statement, comprehensively insulted them all. Amelia would have applauded, if only because Prudence had finally found her voice, but Prudence had already turned toward the door.

Alex frowned as Amelia rose to chase after her. "Are you sure you should follow her, Amelia? She doesn't seem like herself."

Amelia snorted. "She's right. You don't know her at all. If I can't apologize now…"

She trailed off and dashed after Prudence. Prudence was the slowest to anger of all of them. But once her temper ignited, it burned everyone in its path. When the flames died, her heart would be so hardened that Amelia would never be admitted again.

Prudence was walking fast, nearly running, but Amelia's longer stride caught her. She grabbed Prudence's arm just as they reached the great hall. "Prue, I'm unbelievably sorry."

Prudence whirled around, wrenching her arm out of Amelia's grasp. "Not here, you ninnyhammer," she hissed.

There was no one about, but the great hall was so cast in shadows that a dozen footmen could have hidden in the alcoves between the high, mullioned windows that lined the longest wall. The giant double doors were barred and locked, their iron fittings ominous in the moonlight. Amelia shivered. The ancient room bore down upon her, chilling her heart.

In five hundred years, how many forced marriages had happened here?

Probably more than she wanted to know of. But she wouldn't let herself be the next one. And she certainly wouldn't lose Prudence's friendship over it.

"Fine," Amelia whispered. "Your room or mine?"

Prudence didn't answer. Amelia followed her across the great hall and up the stairs to the guest wing. But when she tried to follow Prudence into her room, Prudence blocked her.

"I have nothing to say to you. You have nothing I wish to hear."

Amelia crossed her arms. "If you don't let me in, I'll start discussing this so loudly that we're both ruined," she threatened. "As there's only one earl downstairs to marry, we shouldn't risk it."

"There are two earls downstairs, if you count your brother," Prudence said mulishly. But she stepped away from the door and let Amelia in before her.

"If you want Alex, you should have him — although why you would marry such a prig, I've no idea," Amelia said, standing awkwardly in the center of the room as Prudence removed the pins that held her hair in place. "This is the second time in less than six months that he's forced a woman under his care into marriage."

"Madeleine wanted to marry Ferguson, if I recall," Prudence said, dropping pins one by one into a little ceramic dish on top of her dressing table. "From what I saw in the library, you and Carnach will rub along together quite tolerably. 'Rub' being the appropriate word, of course."

For a moment, when Prudence grinned at her own jest, it was just as it always was between them. But then Prudence remembered what Amelia had done, and the smile disappeared.

Amelia twisted her fingers. Her cracking knuckles were like icicles breaking off in the silence. "I didn't go to the library to kiss him, you know. I planned to throw the two of you together so you might discover some sort of attraction."

Her friend ignored the excuse. The last pins came away, and

Prudence's hair fell to her back. It was waist length and wavy, and the firelight added a golden edge that no one in society ever saw when it was contained by caps and chignons. Prudence shook it free, then savagely started brushing.

Amelia winced as Prudence tore at one of the tangles. "Shouldn't you wait for the maid?"

"I'm quite accustomed to brushing my own hair. The maid has enough work as it is," Prudence said. Each stroke crackled with static. "Without Carnach to rescue us, I may become a lady's maid myself."

"Surely it won't come to that."

"No. I would try for a governess position first."

She set down the brush and bowed her head for a moment. The curtain of hair obscured Amelia's view, but she heard the distinct sound of a sniffle. Amelia reached for Prudence's shoulder, tentatively, but Prudence shrugged the hand away.

"Why did you do it, Amelia?" Prudence asked, finally turning to face her. "I thought you didn't even like the man."

Amelia paused. The words that always came so easily for her were frozen someplace, blocked and inaccessible. How could she explain an attraction she couldn't understand and didn't want?

Finally, she leaned against Prudence's bed. She stared down at the slippers that had ruined her. If only she'd worn them in the library, she might have been able to sway Alex. "I don't like him. And I didn't want to kiss him. Whatever came over us in the library was madness, nothing more. It was like…like lightning, and I was the only tree on the plain. It struck me hard, and I couldn't move away from it in time."

"You never use hackneyed phrases like that — you must be overset," Prudence observed. Then her eyes narrowed. "Is that why you wanted to turn me against him today? So you could have him for yourself?"

"No!" Amelia exclaimed. "No. You know I don't want to marry."

Prudence examined her face. "I know. But you're not as immune to men as you pretend to be. And when this one came along, offering kisses, you didn't think a thing of hurting me."

Amelia cringed. "That's not true. I tried to stop him."

"That's not what it looked like when I arrived. How far would you have gone with him?"

"It was just a kiss! Nothing more happened — nothing more will happen, if Alex comes to his senses."

Prudence pulled her hair tight against her scalp with both hands. In her grief and anger, she looked like a Fury ready to render judgment. "It's not just a kiss with you, Amelia. After all the years you've kept yourself guarded, a kiss means you truly feel something for him."

Amelia shook her head, denying. "It could have happened to you instead, if you had been there instead of me. I thought if you met him tonight…"

"What, that lightning would strike me instead?" Prudence asked. "Lightning will never strike me again. I'm more likely to marry mad King George than I am to feel that attraction for someone else."

Amelia squinted at Prudence. She had dropped her hair, but somewhere under it, there was a secretive look in her eyes that Amelia had never seen before. "'Again?' When did it strike you before?"

Prudence shook her head and pointed to the door. "Go, Amelia. I need to decide what I can tell Mother about my failure to make this match, and I cannot think when I want to slap you."

"I am sorry, Prudence. I will find a way to make this up to you."

"How? By hiring me as your governess?" Her laugh was bitter, so bitter that Amelia could taste it on her tongue. "I'll thank you for not trying to help me ever again."

She turned away and started slamming the drawers of her chifferobe open and shut, as though looking for answers. Amelia wanted to say something, anything, but what good would it do? Either Prudence needed more time for forgiveness — or forgiveness would never happen.

So she left, closing the door softly behind her before seeking out her own room next door. Through the wall, she heard Prudence's angry rummaging stop. Prudence would be beyond her incandescent rage by morning. But the next phase, the cold, unforgiving phase, might never end.

Amelia's eyes burned. She hitched herself up onto her bed, lay down, and stared at the ceiling. She didn't want to wake her maid, not after Prudence's declaration, but she needed Watkins to help her out of her gown. The endless row of buttons down the back wasn't designed to be undone alone.

It didn't matter. She was unlikely to sleep. She needed time to think, before sunrise, before facing Prudence, or her brother, or Malcolm, again.

Malcolm. Why didn't she think of him as Carnach, or the earl, or "that dreadful man"? Something had happened between them that changed her. She stubbornly clung to calling it lightning even though Prudence had mocked her use of the phrase.

The ceiling above her bed was too dark to see. The curtains were closed against the moon and the wind, and the only light came from the embers of the banked fire opposite the bed. In the dark, alone, Amelia still couldn't admit to herself what she knew to be true.

Malcolm's touch enthralled her. His kiss left her weak-kneed and even weaker willed. But she wouldn't examine why she felt that way, after a decade of closing herself off from the attentions of men. It was safer to say it was a brief flare of insanity and leave it at that.

She sat up to pull off her slippers, then slid off the high bed just long enough to remove the pins from her hair and turn the covers back. She no longer wanted to think. She wanted to sleep, to pretend that she would wake up in the morning and Malcolm — *Carnach* — wouldn't be signing the settlements that would make her his.

Her dress would be hopelessly crushed, and she didn't relish the notion of sleeping in her stays, but it was better than feigning serenity with her maid. Amelia crawled back into bed. If she didn't wake up from this nightmare, she would need a plan.

As she curled on her side, she smiled grimly. Her mind already raced with alternatives. She excelled at plans. Her plan to put Prudence and Malcolm together had failed.

But Amelia Staunton never failed twice.

*   *   *

Drawing up the settlements was easy. Laughably easy, really. A solicitor would finish the formalities, but the negotiations were more civil than anything said in the library the previous night.

Malcolm hadn't felt civil when his hands were running over Amelia's body, or when his mouth devoured hers. And he certainly hadn't felt civil when they were interrupted — or when that kiss turned into a proposal she seemed determined to evade.

But daylight required civility, and smearing a patina of respectability over the sordid reality of their engagement. Malcolm still didn't feel civil, but he could fake it.

Salford sat on the other side of Malcolm's desk, making notes in a ledger. If Malcolm achieved the political clout he wanted, he would need to accustom himself to odd backroom negotiations, the kind done with no witnesses and an undercurrent of threats.

There was nothing seedy about the Earl of Salford, though. He was reputedly a shrewd negotiator in the antiquities world. Malcolm suspected there were few people who ever claimed an advantage over him. He wasn't the type to suffer fools or fall victim to a scam. So when Salford named a figure for Amelia's dowry that would have set the fortune hunters salivating, Malcolm raised an eyebrow.

"That is more generous than I expected, under the circumstances," Malcolm said.

Salford leaned back in his chair, utterly comfortable in Malcolm's study despite the subject matter. "I want to see her settled happily."

"She wasn't happy last night."

"Then you must convince her to be," Salford said. "Give her time to become accustomed to a new routine, and Amelia can be comfortable anywhere."

"Comfortable" didn't mean "happy," but Malcolm didn't point that out. "What were you hinting at about Amelia's past last night?"

Salford didn't tense a single muscle, but his dark eyes sharpened. "Nothing. I was angry and spoke out of turn."

"I can't have a wife who will embarrass me," Malcolm warned.

"She won't. Nothing she's done has been reproached. It's the suitors around her who have been problematic. Really, I should thank you for taking her off the marriage mart so that I no longer have to entertain offers for her hand."

Malcolm steepled his fingers under his chin. "That isn't quite as safe as I would like."

"Take her or leave her," Salford said, his voice turning to ice. "But if you leave her, I'll ruin you more comprehensively than any rumor could."

Malcolm didn't respond well to threats. He felt his blood rise, like a fox backed into a corner, and his muscles prepared to attack. But his battle-mad ancestry was more of a hindrance than a gift in modern politics. He gritted his teeth and willed himself to take a breath.

When he spoke, his voice was deceptively calm. "If the lady will have me, I will gladly do my duty. But I won't force her. And if you would, you're not the man I've heard of."

It was dangerously close to a mortal insult. The answering tic in Salford's jaw said the man took it as such. "You don't want to make an enemy of me. But let me assure you that I have Amelia's interests at heart, perhaps more than she does."

"Amelia seems the type to make up her own mind."

Salford's laugh was genuine. "That she is. She also won't change it. A bit of advice, Carnach — convince her that she loves you, and she'll follow you to the ends of the earth. If you fail, neither of you will have a moment's peace until one of you is dead."

Malcolm knew how to seduce a woman. Love was another matter. He'd sought to arrange a marriage based on the bloodless mutual respect that would serve his political interests, not the passion that would distract him. "You've set a Herculean task, Salford."

"No worse than the Augean stables," he replied, referencing the myth he no doubt knew by heart. Salford paused, staring at Malcolm as though he, like Prudence, cared about hearts and minds instead of ancient artifacts and cold stones. "Mind you, I've not forgiven you for this, and I shan't forget it. But Amelia can be stubborn. If you make every effort with her and she still rebuffs you, I won't force the issue. The ton may ruin you for jilting her, but I won't."

Malcolm narrowed his eyes. "What changed your mind?"

Salford shrugged and began gathering his documents. "You haven't pled your case. I would have shot you if you'd tried to weasel out of this." He rolled a sheaf of papers and slid them into his document case, looking utterly serious. But when he looked up, Malcolm was surprised to see him grin. "Amelia will either plead with me until I give in, or she'll find another way to extricate herself. She will not go gently into the marriage you both deserve. If she succeeds, I can't punish you for it if you tried your best to fulfill your obligation."

"I thank you for the warning," Malcolm said drily.

Salford rose. "She is attracted to you, from what I could see, even if she denies it. For my part, I believe she'll be happy married to you — happier than she ever would have been living in my house for the rest of her days. I trust her dowry is enough inducement for you, if you can find a way to manage her where I have not."

Malcolm inclined his head, noncommittal. Salford took his leave with a jaunty wave. The man had the air of one relieved of a great burden, like Atlas suddenly freed of the world. The kiss in the library could have been swept under the rug if Salford hadn't pressed the issue.

It seemed a bit too convenient now, if Salford's mood could be believed. Malcolm thought Amelia was lovely, but Salford was glad to hand over responsibility for her and Ferguson had warned him against her. What was the truth about her personality?

After Salford left, Malcolm sat behind his desk again. He'd come to love the study in the year since his father's death. It still felt wrong, sitting behind this desk. Most days it felt like his, but occasionally he would find a bit of old sealing wax or a scrap of paper covered in his father's handwriting, and the grief would suddenly cut as fresh as it had the day they'd lowered his coffin into the ground.

It had all been too quick — the cold that suddenly turned to pneumonia, the moment his breath stopped, the flicker of pain on the doctor's face before he reached down and closed those sightless eyes.

The speed with which everyone started calling Malcolm laird.

Malcolm picked up the stone paperweight on his desk, worn smooth by generations of earls who had toyed with it. Legend said the first laird had pocketed it when they dug the foundations for the keep, and it stayed on the desk as a talisman. When Malcolm held it, he felt the weight of the clan and the granite strength of his obligation to them.

His father had kept them intact by isolating them. But the factories in the south and the plantations abroad would someday destroy them. They'd survived Flodden Field, Dunbar, even Culloden, but they wouldn't survive the changing economic landscape unless he saved them. The march of progress could not be stalled, not by guns and not by his father's brand of benevolent *laissez faire*. Malcolm would take up the cause where his father hadn't — he would not be the earl who saw their clan destroyed.

Could he save them with Amelia at his side? He didn't deny that she tempted him. She had a beautiful body and a quick wit, a combination he couldn't refuse. But if her brother was so eager to be rid of her, could Malcolm manage her well enough to meet his needs? He couldn't sacrifice his clan for her, no matter how lovely she was.

If she cried off, though…

There was a part of him — not just between his legs, but somewhere in his gut as well — that wanted to bind her to him. But she was too independent for his dominance and too accustomed to having her own way to cleave to his side. Perhaps it was for the best if she left him.

His smile turned feral. He would show her just a bit of his baser nature. If she ran back to England at the first sign of his lordship, he would bid her farewell — even if he doubted she would leave his thoughts as quickly as she could leave his castle.

But if she didn't run, he would keep her to save both their reputations. And he would seduce her so comprehensively, so cunningly, that she would never think to betray him.

CHAPTER NINE

"There's nothing to be done for your dress," Watkins said, surveying the creases in the silk.

"You may have it," Amelia said, pouring a cup of chocolate from the pot Watkins had brought her.

"You should have called, my lady. You must have been uncomfortable in your stays all night."

"I was up too late with my letters," she lied. Watkins looked at her skeptically, and Amelia wondered what rumors were circulating among the servants. She didn't ask, though. It was better to pretend nothing had happened, even if the fact that she'd slept in her dress would likely be dissected and mulled over in the servants' hall.

In retrospect, she should have called for Watkins, no matter how late the hour. Even if the dress didn't stir gossip, she had been uncomfortable sleeping in it. Sometime just after dawn, she had debated cutting herself out of the dress just to remove her corset, but it wasn't a risk she would take with a penknife. Instead, she gave up her bed and threw back the curtains, letting the sunlight stream in and clear away the cobwebs of her half-awake dreams.

As she expected, she hadn't slept well, but she had come up with a plan. The plan wasn't comprehensive enough to repair her friendship with Prudence. But there would be time enough for that if she returned to London unwed. Her first priority was breaking her engagement. It was preferable to end it quietly, before the mothers were informed. If that didn't happen, though, she wasn't averse to creating a bit of scandal to save Malcolm and herself from a lifetime of woe.

Lifetime of woe. She liked that line, enough to evade Watkins's efforts to repair her hopelessly tangled hair and reach for a pen and ink. Watkins was accustomed to her mistress's eccentricities, and Amelia didn't keep her waiting above a minute as she noted the words.

There was a bright spot in all of this — the castle and her narrowly avoided marriage would surely inspire her next book.

Watkins had nearly tamed Amelia's curls when someone rapped on the door. The door opened before Amelia responded. Her heart had hoped it was Prudence, but she was disappointed.

"Mother," she said, her mouth dry as she stood to kiss her. She blindly reached for her second cup of chocolate, but her favorite beverage was made for indulgence, not fortitude. "You're awake rather early."

The tiny web of lines around Augusta's blue eyes crinkled in concern. "Do you have a moment, dear?"

It was phrased as a request for Watkins's ears, but Amelia knew she had no choice. She told Watkins to await her summons, then watched as her mother shut the door.

"I would offer you chocolate, but I've finished the pot. We can ring for tea if you like?"

Augusta shook her head and gestured at the chair by the fire. "Shall I take the chair? I would have waited until you were dressed so we might have this chat in comfort, but it cannot be delayed."

Amelia closed her eyes. If her mother knew, there was no hope of dissuading Alex and Malcolm quietly.

Her mind was already racing toward alternate plans, but she forced herself to focus on her mother. She didn't have her cousin Madeleine's acting talent, but she could weave a story out of nothing. It would have to be enough.

"Please, sit wherever you like," she said. She perched on her dressing stool, glad that the window was at her back so the sunlight wouldn't reveal everything on her face. "What do you wish to discuss so urgently?"

"You know why I am here," Augusta said, leveling a stare at her.

She knew the general subject — but what had her mother really learned? "You've talked to Alex?"

"No. He's been closeted in Carnach's study all morning. Lady Harcastle is most distraught, though. She said you and Carnach have decided to wed. And then she stopped speaking to me."

Amelia paused, searching for the right words. "I am sorry Lady Harcastle is angry."

"Mary isn't the girl I knew thirty years ago. Perhaps we wouldn't be friends if we'd only just met." Then she caught herself. "Never mind about Lady Harcastle. What happened last night?"

"Carnach offered for my hand," Amelia said, as casually as if this was any other proposal she intended to refuse. "But I am not sure we would suit."

"I recommend deciding that you will suit," Augusta said, her voice a smooth sheath over hardened steel. "If this offer came in the middle of the night and Alex is already involved, I can only assume the worst."

Amelia flushed. She shifted her unbound hair off her neck, suddenly warm. "It wasn't the worst, Mother. Alex and Prudence found us in the library, and…"

Augusta cut her off. "You know as well as I do that appearances matter more than facts."

"But no one needs to know!" Amelia cried. She glanced at the door and lowered her voice. "It was a kiss, nothing more. If Alex and Prudence say nothing, the ton needn't find us out."

"You kissed him? She's likely to feel betrayed at that, dear — and I can't say I blame her. I feel sorry for her, in fact. Do you trust such a secret in her hands? If she's as angry as Lady Harcastle, either one of them could be quite dangerous. If you don't marry Carnach, Lady Harcastle will surely ruin you, even if Prudence does not."

Augusta was even more blunt than Amelia when the situation warranted, and Amelia winced. "I didn't intend to betray her. I was trying to help her."

Her mother sighed. "Believe it or not, I am not angry with you."

"You aren't?"

"No." She paused, and her grin was wry when she continued. "Mind you, I think a lesson to correct your meddling is long overdue."

"That seems uncharitable," Amelia muttered.

"And I'm sure Prudence doesn't feel charitable toward you either. But you can make the best of this. Carnach is a worthy match for you. If you haven't considered it yet, you should give a thought to your future."

"I have given thought, Mother. I've told you time and again that I've no wish to marry."

"I know. And I let you persist in that while Madeleine also remained unwed. Funny, that — I despaired of ever seeing either of you married, and you've managed to trap yourselves without any assistance at all."

Amelia scowled as her mother chuckled. But Augusta pulled herself together and continued. "Perhaps I should have been harder with you both and encouraged you to marry sooner. But I did so enjoy having you at home."

"It's a shame you're encouraging me to marry a Scotsman, then

— you may never see me again."

"Carnach wants a political career — you'll be in England often enough," Augusta said, waving the overblown concern aside. "And I shan't live forever. You might prefer to marry Carnach than be dependent on Alex."

That gave Amelia pause. Malcolm's kisses were an undeniable benefit over her current status.

But Alex didn't watch her closely enough to guess about her writing. Malcolm was too observant by half. He wouldn't want her harboring secrets. Life as a spinster bored her — but it gave her freedom in the ways that mattered to her.

She couldn't say that to Augusta. Her mother didn't know about her novels. She thought Amelia was merely a dedicated diarist and letter writer. "Carnach and I aren't meant for each other," Amelia repeated firmly. "Will you speak to Alex and stop this?"

Augusta tilted her head as she looked at her. She was still beautiful in her early fifties, far from the death she warned Amelia of — but in that moment, she looked tired, and Amelia's heart wrenched.

"Never mind," Amelia said before her mother could speak. "I shall find Alex myself. You needn't worry. We will settle this and return to normal."

"This is normal," Augusta said. "All children must leave the nest. I've been lucky to have you this long, but perhaps this is a sign that you should take the next step in your journey. It's not right that you still live with Alex rather than having a house and family of your own."

Amelia's position in front of the window meant the light illuminated everything on Augusta's face — including the tears forming in her eyes. "Are you all right, Mother?" Amelia asked.

Augusta dashed at the tears with her hand. "I'm just melancholy at the thought of losing you, as much as I think it's time. But Carnach could be good for you if you give him a chance. He reminds me a bit of your father, actually — trying so hard to be dutiful when you can see he just wants to run amok."

Amelia laughed. "You can't trick me into liking him by claiming he resembles Father."

Augusta's tone sharpened. "Promise me you will try, Amelia. Promise you won't scheme your way around him without letting him talk to you."

Her mother knew her too well. Amelia intended to find a way out, and she wouldn't let Malcolm convince her otherwise. But even though she couldn't make such a promise without a good-faith effort to fulfill it, the stark, urgent concern in her mother's voice gave her no choice.

"I promise," she said.

Her mother's shoulders sagged. "Good. Good," she repeated, as though her conviction was enough for both of them.

"I can't promise I'll love him, though. Not like you and Father."

Augusta's mouth twisted. "Your heart may yet surprise you."

Amelia didn't say anything as her mother came over and smoothed back her hair. Amelia suddenly felt like a child again — and she wished she could stay like that, without the momentous changes being negotiated for her in Malcolm's study.

Augusta smiled as her hands warmed Amelia's cheeks. "Start as you mean to go on, dear. You have a good heart — let him see it."

Her mother left her then. Amelia slid slowly from the footstool to crumple on the floor, still bound in last night's ruined silk. She buried her head in her arms and focused on her breath. She willed everything else away — the warmth of the sun on her back, the stays still digging into her ribs, the errant curl tickling her neck, the moisture slowly streaking over the fading sensation of her mother's hands on her cheeks.

Amelia exhaled and let the breath skim over her bosom. In that moment, in a ball on the floor of a castle hundreds of miles from home, she realized she was alone. Not the quiet solitude she occasionally craved — the isolation of one banished and wandering in the wilderness. Madeleine was married, she'd ruined things with Prudence, she wasn't ready to forgive Alex, and her mother...

Maybe her mother was wrong. But would Augusta forgive her if Amelia abandoned her engagement?

Her inhale turned to a sniffle. She didn't want to be alone, but she had comprehensively mucked up so many relationships. Her mother claimed Amelia had a good heart, and perhaps she did. But a good heart and a bad temper were still too volatile for most. And no matter how guilty she felt after, she never seemed to learn. It would be better if she didn't let Malcolm marry her. He seemed eager — but when he learned that she would never be the obedient chit he needed, he would regret his attraction to her.

She steeled herself, forced herself to wipe away her tears, and sat up straight against the stool at her back. She already had a plan. The money from her writing would support her in comfort, if not opulence, even if Alex never gave her a penny of her dowry. Madeleine was married and Prudence hated her, but she could still set up her own cottage someday.

It had been a lovelier vision when her friends had been beside her. But it was better than giving herself to Malcolm, then waiting for the day when she said the wrong thing, was too direct, too witty, too sarcastic, too independent, too *everything* to keep his affection.

She had promised her mother she would let Malcolm talk to her before she schemed. That trumped anything else. She had too much honor to break a promise so blatantly, even if she wanted to.

But her promise said nothing of lowering her defenses — or of staying when Malcolm came to his senses and tossed her away.

She would dress, go downstairs, and write like it was any other day. And when the time came, she would talk to Malcolm. But she wouldn't show him her heart — or let him win it.

CHAPTER TEN

He found Amelia in a small salon in the main wing, between the music room and the library. In the odd hours between breakfast and luncheon most house parties were dull, and theirs was no exception. Salford had left for the village to post his letters. His mother and Augusta were huddled in the drawing room with their embroidery and their whispers, and Lady Harcastle was in her room with her vapors. Graves reported, with a disappointed sniff, that Miss Etchingham had demanded a horse and a groom after breakfast and gone for a ride. That meant Amelia was somewhere in the castle alone, and it didn't take long to track her down.

She had her back to the open door. The sunlight from one of the tall windows turned the blonde curls escaping from her chignon into a fuzzy halo. Her gloves were off, and her fingers were stained with ink. She was a messy writer, then, even if she usually seemed polished in public. She bowed her head over her quill, and her hand hovered above the paper. Her hesitation struck him as melancholy — a feeling he suspected she didn't give in to often.

Malcolm knocked on the doorframe. "May I have a word, Lady Amelia?"

Her head snapped up. She stared ahead for a long moment, out the window to the Highlands beyond, as though gathering her reserves. It was only a moment, but it was enough to verify his suspicions.

Amelia would not easily accept the future their kiss had doomed them to.

She turned to greet him. "What an unexpected surprise."

It wasn't an invitation. He walked in and shut the door. "You needn't pretend with me. And you aren't surprised to see me."

Her eyebrows rose as he closed off the rest of the house. "Should we be together unchaperoned, my lord?"

"What can they do? Force us to marry?"

She grinned, a momentary crack in her armor. "We have made a muck of things, haven't we?"

Malcolm wasn't so sure. Seeing her smile and the corresponding light in her blue eyes made "muck" seem like the opposite of what had occurred. "It wasn't in either of our plans, I'm sure."

"You can end it with Alex. Simply tell him you won't have me." She turned back to her paper, dismissing him.

He rounded the table and stood in front of her, blocking the light and casting a shadow on her writing. She made a show of gathering the papers together and rapping them against the table to straighten them, all without looking at him, like he was a peasant awaiting her favor.

This time, as his annoyance rose, he let it take the reins. When she finally looked up at him, he regarded her insolently, with a slow, roving perusal of her face before settling on the bounty of her breasts. "You suit my hands, if nothing else. My mouth too, if we're being honest."

When he glanced back up to meet her eyes, they were widened in shock. She stared at him for a breathless moment, and his lips curved as he continued. "Now why would I tell Salford that I won't take such a bonny lass?"

He rarely used Scottish colloquialisms; his mother was English, as were his grandmother and most of his other female ancestors, and he didn't feel the same affinity for the language as he did for the land. But Amelia didn't know that, and she glared at him. "You need more than a 'bonny lass' as a wife," she said, her voice dripping with sarcasm.

"Never say you'll be my mistress instead? You would be skilled, I'm sure."

Her voice turned to ice. "I am not that kind of woman. You do yourself no honor by saying such things."

She was right. But honor was what told him he needed to give her a chance to break this off, even if he wouldn't be the one to let her go.

Malcolm shrugged. "We have decades to learn everything about each other. I must start as I mean to go on."

Something flickered in her eyes. "I received that advice as well."

"However, if you truly think we wouldn't suit…"

He waited for her to say the words. She dropped her eyes from his face, in a move that seemed demure — until he realized she was examining him just as outrageously as he had done. Her gaze caressed his jaw, his throat, lingered over his shoulders, then dropped precipitously toward his groin. He felt himself stirring, and he shifted his weight onto one foot. She smiled, the same insolent grin he had given her.

Truly, she was a devil. And he had never gotten so hard from just a look.

"No, we wouldn't suit, my lord," she said, as cool as a spinster at a Bible study. "I require more than a 'bonny lad,' as you might say."

"I'm hardly a lad." She snickered, and he realized that he'd taken offense when he should have responded to the sentiment rather than the insult. "And anyway," he continued, "if you believe we wouldn't suit, you should tell Salford. If you are willing to destroy your reputation to be rid of me, then our courtship is at an end."

"If this is a courtship, I would hate to see the wedding," Amelia muttered. He raised an eyebrow at her, and she flushed before returning to the subject. "So you want me to cry off and leave you looking for all the world like a man who tried to do his duty?"

"I'm not the one who wants to stay unwed."

She dipped her pen in the inkwell and drew a lazy curlicue on the top sheet of paper. "And if I don't ask Alex to let me leave you?"

Her hand continued to move across the paper, and he wondered how much of her dowry would go toward keeping her in parchment. "You know I won't. Salford would destroy me. Even if he didn't, a man who jilts a woman is blackballed. I would never outlive it."

"Are you staying engaged for my reputation? Or because you don't want a scandal?"

The ground shifted under him when she looked up. "I am marrying you for both our reputations."

Her mouth compressed.

"And don't mistake me," he added quickly. "I am not unhappy with this state of affairs. I'd just as soon marry you as anyone."

"How romantic."

"What else would you have me do? In any event, Salford and I drew up the settlements this morning."

That made her well and truly angry. "Alex already agreed for me? You never even asked me if I would marry you."

"Do you want me to ask you to marry me?"

She drew a vicious *x* through her curlicues. "Don't be absurd, Lord Carnach."

He leaned over her table, planting his hands on either side and looking her directly in the eyes. "You are the only one who can end this. If you don't, we will marry, whether you like it or not."

She didn't back down. "You cannot force me to like you."

"Did I say anything about liking each other?"

Amelia sat back at that, crossing her arms as she regarded him. "If we are forced to live together, it would be more pleasant if we enjoyed each other's company."

There was something about her defiance that made him give her fair warning, even though he couldn't break things off. "I'm not seeking a wife to enjoy," he said. "I'm seeking a wife who will obey me, host the right parties, and provide an heir. If you prefer enjoyment, the offer of becoming my mistress still stands."

Her arm twitched as though she was tempted to do him violence. Instead, she stood abruptly, planting her hands on top of his and leaning in just as he had done. "If I become any man's mistress, it won't be yours. But I can't cry off, not if I want to remain in society."

Their eyes locked together for an endless minute. With their mouths so close, and Malcolm's manhood still painfully hard, he almost, almost dipped in to kiss her.

And, God help him, she looked ready for him.

But a knock on the door broke them apart, and his hands missed the warmth of hers on top of them as she jerked away. "I am not suited for obedience, so you'd best talk to Alex yourself," she hissed, every *s* becoming harsh in the silence.

Then she called out for the person to enter, not letting Malcolm get the final word. He turned toward the window. His servants were loyal, and nearly all were distant relatives, but it still wouldn't do to be seen sporting an erection with an unwed woman, betrothed or not.

It wasn't a servant. It was Prudence. "Lady Amelia, my mother and I are leaving today," she declared, wasting no time on greetings.

"Are you sure it is safe to travel alone?"

"I've nothing a highwayman would wish to steal."

"Do not sell your safety so lightly, Prue."

Malcolm finally heard a note of distress in Amelia's voice. When Prudence responded, he flinched for both of them. "You may call me Miss Etchingham," she said. "My mother and I shall be safe enough. I found your brother in the village and he agreed to escort us as far as Edinburgh. We will take a stage coach from there."

"A stage coach?" Amelia asked. "Are you sure you cannot wait until we all return to England?"

"You won't be returning to England until your husband takes you there," Prudence said venomously.

Malcolm finally turned toward the women. They confronted each other like generals before a pitched battle. The ice in the room had frozen his desire. "Lady Amelia will not return to London as soon as she would like, but you are welcome to stay as long as you wish."

"Stay here? And watch both of you settle into connubial bliss?" Prudence laughed, but it wasn't pleasant. "I'd sooner be run through by a highwayman. I shall return to London, where I belong. Many happy returns to both of you, I'm sure."

Prudence turned toward the door. Amelia's hand reached out to stop her, but Malcolm watched it fall before it could close the distance. Her hand dropped, and he heard her sigh.

Prudence was out the door before he called to her. "Miss Etchingham, another moment?"

She kept walking.

"Stay here," he ordered Amelia, ignoring her huff of protest. He followed Prudence, catching her in a few strides.

"What do you require now, my lord? You surely don't need two wives."

The bitter twist of her mouth made him feel a kick of guilt. "I am sorry for everything, Miss Etchingham. My actions to the contrary, you are a lovely woman. You deserve better than to be treated thusly."

She looked over his shoulder, toward the open door of the sitting room. "Thank you, Lord Carnach, but I believe I know how to apportion the blame for this sad affair. I trust you and Lady Amelia deserve each other."

He thought back to their confrontation, still not sure whether he wanted to throttle Amelia or kiss her breathless. "Perhaps we do. I am still sorry, though. Would you and your mother allow me to hire a post chaise to take you from Edinburgh to London? You shouldn't bear the cost of this trip."

Prudence lifted her head, as proud as any queen. "I do not accept charity, my lord."

He sighed. "Consider it an apology."

The war between pride and expediency played out on her face. In the end, the attraction of a private coach over a crowded public conveyance won. "Very well. We shall be ready to leave after luncheon."

He bowed to her. Prudence dropped the barest curtsey before making her escape. He frowned as he watched her go. If she had displayed this much fire when they were first introduced, would he have found Amelia so tempting?

It was a stupid question. Even now, when Prudence felt wronged by both of them, his thoughts turned toward how Amelia would survive the loss of her friend, not how Prudence might fare without his offer of marriage.

He heard Amelia walk up behind him. "It was good of you to offer the coach," she said.

There was a respect in her tone that he hadn't heard before. Gratitude, too — and the way it softened her voice warmed him. He could drown himself in her voice if it always sounded like that.

But losing himself to the pleasure Amelia could give him was not his plan. "I thought I told you to stay in the sitting room," he said.

Her voice turned from the soothing warmth of a hearth to the scalding heat of a forge. "And I told you that obedience isn't one of my virtues."

"Then it seems we're at an impasse."

"Indeed," she said.

He wanted to kiss her, to break through her shields. But he couldn't give in to every desire to kiss her, not if he wanted to stay focused on the duties that had made him seek a wife.

So he walked away instead. But before he left, he took the last word. "The choice is simple, darling. Break off our engagement, or I'll see you at the altar."

CHAPTER ELEVEN

Hours later, after dinner, Amelia paced up and down the drawing room. The teacart had arrived five minutes earlier, but she was the only one there to enjoy it. Augusta and Louisa had abandoned her.

She'd nearly begged them to stay. She had thought all afternoon about how she might drive Malcolm away, and she knew she would have to do something truly scandalous to get him to break the engagement. It would be easier to do something shocking if their mothers weren't there to watch her.

But being alone with him carried a different risk. If his effect on her didn't wane, it would be hard to pursue her plans and not be affected by the desires that came with their sparring.

So when Augusta had kissed her on the cheek, Amelia grabbed her hand like a child. "Surely you aren't leaving me unchaperoned, Mother?"

"If he misbehaves, hit him with the fire poker," Augusta said. Louisa smothered a laugh. "But I trust it won't come to that."

"The man is debauched," Amelia protested. She flushed when Louisa arched an eyebrow, but she didn't relent.

"You are already engaged, and you'll wed as soon as Alex returns from Edinburgh. I see no harm in leaving you alone. If anything, the more time you spend together, the less likely it is either of you can cry off."

Amelia kept her arguments to herself. Her mother was firmly in the marriage camp, and she wouldn't be swayed unless one of them killed the other. Even then, she'd probably prefer the murder to come after the wedding.

Amelia knew she was being unfair, but she didn't care. She also knew it would be safer to retire before Malcolm emerged from the dining room with his brothers, but she wouldn't run to her room like a chastised child. "Start as you mean to go on" was the refrain of the day. She couldn't let him grow accustomed to her retreating after every battle.

If only Malcolm would listen to reason and agree to break their engagement. She couldn't be the one to break it off — if Lady Harcastle wanted to ruin her for taking Prudence's would-be husband, the only hope Amelia had was for Malcolm to take the blame.

She sighed. It was too much to expect that he would, particularly since she knew she wasn't perfectly innocent. He wouldn't let himself be blackballed, unless marrying her was worse than the consequences of jilting her. And even if he did, Amelia's reputation would still be in tatters — Lady Harcastle would surely tell everyone she knew that Amelia had been caught with Malcolm in the library.

She halted her pacing by the teacart and refreshed her cup. If she told Malcolm about her writing, would it horrify him enough to force his hand?

She'd mulled over it all day. Logically, a politician couldn't have a wife writing romantic novels, particularly the satire she had written the previous spring. Malcolm was a logical man. If she told him, he would see their unsuitability instantly.

But what if he didn't back down? If they married, she and everything she did would become his property. By law, she would cease to exist in her own right — and he could forbid her to write, or legally destroy every page she wrote. Or he could confiscate all her income from her writing, since it wasn't part of the pin money in her marriage settlements. She would be even more dependent on him than she was on Alex.

And if he knew about her writing, he would watch her far more closely than Alex ever did. Any dream she ever had of being recognized for her writing would die the moment he put his ring on her finger.

She'd never have any hope of freedom after that.

Amelia sipped her tea, which had become more of a sweet sludge as she'd absentmindedly dumped five lumps of sugar into the cup. It was a shame she couldn't discuss this with her mother. Augusta had uncanny insight when it came to men, and she could have helped Amelia snare any man in the ton if Amelia was so inclined. She would undoubtedly have a number of suggestions for Amelia's current situation, but they would all be appropriate for salvaging the engagement rather than destroying it. And Augusta didn't know about Amelia's writing either. If Amelia did escape this marriage, she needed somewhere to go. Telling her mother might cost her the only refuge she had.

The door opened and Malcolm entered. He regarded her for a few seconds from the doorway before shutting it and strolling toward her.

"Where are your brothers?" she asked. Her own brother had left for Edinburgh with Prudence and Lady Harcastle and wouldn't return for four days, but Duncan and Douglas lived in the castle, and Alastair often took his dinner with the family.

He shrugged. "Duncan and Douglas are doubtlessly off making some kind of mischief, and Alastair is likely praying for them. Where are our mothers?"

"They retired for the night. I doubt they will drink ratafia again soon."

She offered him tea, but he refused. When she sat, awkwardly, as though it could calm her nerves, he threw himself down into the chair across from her and withdrew a flask from his jacket.

"Do you really not care for tea?"

Malcolm took a long drink from his flask. "I am practicing for the ton. I haven't been to London in an age, but it wouldn't do to fall down drunk at White's."

It was true that most English gentlemen drank to excess, particularly at parties that Amelia had never been reckless enough to attend. But practicing for the ton seemed unlikely. "If you don't desire tea, I shall take my cup and leave you to your practice."

"You should practice too," he said. "If you handle your ratafia as poorly as your mother, you'll never survive the salons I need from you."

Her lamentable temper perked up at his words. "I know nothing of politics, nor do I care to. All the ratafia in the world would not make me conversant in the issues you are pursuing."

"You are pretty enough that men won't mind your ignorance," he mused, almost to himself. "With you at my side, you can attract them and I'll talk to them."

The temper she'd tried to restrain escaped its leash. "I have more to do with my days than being kept at your side."

"Keeping you where I want you will be my right in less than a week. If you are so unhappy with this match, there is still time to end it."

"Are you asking me to leave?"

He laughed. "Nay. You may not like it, but I've made my bed, and I'm very much looking forward to lying in it with you."

She blushed. "That's not a reason for marriage."

He seemed to catch himself when she said that. His tone sobered. "No, it's not. I'll need you to be a proper wife. If you can't do that and wish to break our engagement, I won't chase after you."

Amelia slumped back into her chair. Even if Malcolm would not come to fetch her, her mother would still be disappointed if Amelia ran off of her own accord. Amelia needed more of a reason than "he won't come after me" to give to Lady Augusta — particularly when she was already compromised. By the time Lady Harcastle reached London and spread word of her behavior, she'd be truly ruined. If Malcolm jilted her, there was the slimmest chance she might be saved — but if she jilted him after being compromised, no one would ever receive her again.

Malcolm laughed — but this laugh was warmer, almost like a caress. "You almost look disappointed, darling. Do you want me to chase after you?"

"Hardly," Amelia snorted. "But even a lout such as you should recognize that we are not well-matched."

"No, we aren't well-matched," Malcolm agreed. "I have been tricked into marrying an on-the-shelf harridan, and you want a man you can keep in your pocket."

She saw red. "Or you are an autocratic barbarian with antiquated notions of marriage and a woman's place within it, while I have been deprived of all the freedoms I have guarded so carefully."

Malcolm held his hands up in mock surrender. "You know me so well. We are not suited at all. But given how much you hate me, I wonder why you waited to take tea with me tonight?"

"If I did not take tea after dinner, I would be as ill-bred as you are."

"I shudder at the thought of you becoming any more ill-bred. Unless kisses in the library are now all the rage for polite young ladies' reputations?"

"Now that, my lord, is really too much, since you share the blame," Amelia said.

Malcolm grinned. "Aye, I do." His accent, barely noticeable before, broadened as he swallowed another measure of whisky from his flask. "And I think you are still here because you want another one."

"Never," she sputtered.

"Very eloquent, darling."

Amelia balled up her fists and counted to ten. "I was not waiting to see you. And I am not your darling," she finally said, icily calm.

"Methinks the lady doth protest too much."

"Shakespeare? I would have expected you to quote a drinking song, but not the Bard."

"I do like to read, you know. Even autocratic barbarians need some entertainment."

"I would think you more likely to entertain yourself in the pub."

He shrugged. "When every person in that pub depends on you for their livelihood, wasting an evening getting foxed in front of them loses its appeal."

"I am about to depend on you for my livelihood," she retorted. "Will you continue to get foxed in front of me?"

He looked down at the flask in his hand. "I've drunk more in the last three nights than I have in the last three weeks."

"I don't think it's advisable. Look at the trouble it caused in the library," she said primly

He took a long, deliberate swallow from his flask. "Nagging already, darling?"

She stood abruptly. The part of her that had softened earlier when she heard the loneliness in his voice hardened again at the reminder of what she would become. "This has been a delightful evening, but I suddenly find that I have the headache. If you will excuse me?"

Malcolm grabbed her wrist as she walked past and pulled her

across his lap. The shock of impact drew a gasp from her lips and she struggled to rise, but he held her fast.

"Let me go, Malcolm," she ordered.

"Always so demanding," Malcolm said, setting aside his flask. "Things would be so much more pleasant if you would only say, 'Yes, Malcolm,' like a good wench."

"Why should I want things to be more pleasant? The sooner you tire of our engagement, the sooner I can go home and resume my real life."

Malcolm's grip relaxed, but Amelia was too mesmerized by the sudden dark look in his eyes to make her escape. "So that's your plan, is it? You want me to tire of you?"

She stiffened in his arms. "You will tire of me anyway when I fail to host your precious salons. I would make a better bargain if I escape before you drag me into a political game that I have no intention of playing."

"I may regret having you as a hostess, and I have already tired of your sharp tongue." The words cut, even though he only mimicked hers. But his next statement snatched her breath away. "I also know how that mouth feels against mine. And I cannot promise that I will ever tire of that, or the other charms your body offers."

His voice lowered into the seductive growl that had been her downfall. "And I didn't kiss you in the library because of the whisky. I kissed you because I wanted you enough to risk everything else. I was a fool — but when you're in my arms, at least I'm a lucky fool."

Amelia was suddenly, painfully aware of his chest, unyielding under her hand as she tried to shove him away. The tight muscles of his arms encircled her, as strong as any knight who'd claimed a maiden in the castle before.

None of it scared her. It wasn't until she saw the desire turning his eyes silver that she felt a glimmer of fear. Not fear for her safety, though.

Fear that she wouldn't remember to leave.

"I should go to bed, my lord," she said shakily.

"I will let you go if, for the next five minutes, you only say 'Yes, Malcolm,'" he said, his voice low and tightly controlled.

"Mal..." she started to say.

"Either say, 'Yes, Malcolm,' and I let you go, or say anything else and I will lock us both up in the tower for the night. Do you understand?"

Amelia paused. It felt like a lifetime as their gazes locked together. There would be absolutely no hope of escape if she spent an entire night with him — and as she feared, she no longer quite remembered why escape was necessary.

"Yes, Malcolm," she finally said.

Malcolm smiled, then bent down to claim her mouth. His lips were firm and hot against hers as he shifted her to a more accessible position in his lap, twisted so that she was facing him. The searing jolt of connection was just as intense as that night in the library, but the undertone was darker, more dangerous — and more exciting.

And this time she parted her lips without thinking, already mindless in his arms. She gasped as he invaded, reveled in that first moment of contact when their tongues intertwined and the heat from his mouth swept into her very core.

He lifted his hand and swept her hair back, strewing pins across the drawing room floor. Her hair tumbled down around her shoulders. His fingers twined through her curls, gently pulling her closer as his tongue delved deeper into her mouth.

She clasped her hands around his neck and tugged him closer.

There was no room for strategy, for concern about winning or giving in — just the heat of his mouth and the need to prolong the delicious feelings building within her.

As though he could read her thoughts, he pulled away, and she could not stop her moan of annoyance. He grinned, then pressed a line of kisses across her jaw and down her neck. She arched back, sensitive to his caresses, the momentary annoyance forgotten as he moved lower still. Just as he kissed the hollow of her collarbone, however, he pulled back. "Do you want me to untie your bodice?" he asked.

Pride warred with desire. She opened her eyes, her gaze meeting his. He looked like Lucifer offering her the world, daring her to fall.

"Yes, Malcolm," she whispered.

His lips claimed hers again, rewarding her obedience as his fingers found the ribbons of her bodice. He tugged quickly and the dress fell open, revealing her chemise...another tug, and she was bare before him.

He pulled away from her mouth, staring at her breasts as though to memorize them. She flushed hotly as his head descended. He started where he had left off, kissing the hollow of her throat, then moving down, leaving a moist trail of kisses as he moved slowly, slowly across the expanse of creamy flesh. He circled her left breast, spiraling inward, getting ever closer to his goal as she arched toward him. She wouldn't ask for what she wanted, but her body begged.

His mouth finally closed around her nipple. She shuddered. The warmth spread, radiating from his mouth and into her core, sending delicious pulses through her belly to the sensitive areas beyond. He clasped her gently between his teeth, then sucked away the fleeting pain, swirling his tongue around the hardening nub.

Just as every bit of her focused on that one point of connection, just as she lost herself in his mouth, he pulled away and took a shuddering breath. "Do you want more?" he asked hoarsely.

She didn't hesitate. "Yes, Malcolm," she said, in a voice that was almost a sob.

He lavished the same attention on her other breast, kissing, biting, sucking, until the sensations threatened to overwhelm her. She entwined her fingers in his hair and guided his mouth back to her lips.

This time, she was the aggressor, the longing for something she couldn't name fueling her as she entered his mouth and claimed his tongue. Her body throbbed, and she pressed closer to him, unsure of what she wanted but sure he could help her find it.

Without breaking their kiss, Malcolm shifted her in his lap so that her legs were slung over the side of the chair. Through the hot, airless haze of their kiss, she felt his fingers skimming up her calf, sliding over her stocking and garter. He continued higher, tracing his fingers along the sensitive flesh of her inner thigh.

She drew in a shocked breath. His hand rested there, branding her with his fingers. "Do you want me to continue?" he asked.

She knew she should stop him. She could pretend she was an early Christian martyr, and risk death for maintaining her virtue against the barbarian onslaught. But the need he had stoked demanded satisfaction — and when she said, "Yes, Malcolm," her voice was heavy with desire instead of obedience.

Perhaps he heard her desperation. His exploration turned bolder. Reclaiming her mouth, he kissed her back into surrender — then slid his fingers higher to rest in the slick folds at the juncture of her thighs.

The feel of him there, in her most private place, should have filled her with dread. But she couldn't quite bring herself to remember why she should run. And then, as he grazed a knuckle against the nub hidden within her curls, her delicious shudder of response erased all thoughts of fleeing.

He dipped a finger down to her entrance, and he chuckled against her mouth when he found the moisture there. "You're wet for me, aren't you darling?" he asked.

She couldn't respond. He didn't seem to expect it, instead focusing on whatever torment he planned for her. He slid his finger back up to her aching clitoris, and his intentions became apparent. With her own moisture to smooth his movements, the pleasure intensified, building into a need more desperate than anything she'd experienced before.

As his fingers intensified their strokes, her body throbbed. Her breasts were swollen, her breaths were ragged, and her skin would catch fire if he didn't end his torture. And all the while, the pressure continued to build, driving her towards a cliff she was all too eager to leap from if she could just find the precipice.

He held her there for an endless minute. She moaned and writhed against his hand, until she thought that he intended to keep her like that forever. Then he whispered in her ear, "Do you beg me to let you come?"

She was too far gone to care about her pride. "Yes, Malcolm…oh, please, anything," she said, turning incoherent as she sobbed her need into his chest.

He stroked her harder then, sliding a finger into her wetness. His invasion was enough to push her over the edge. She screamed, and he kissed her again to swallow her cries. A shudder wracked her, so intense she thought she would break from it, and she fell limp into his arms as the dam of her need burst and the hot tide swept her away.

When the last of the tremors faded and she could think again, she opened her eyes. Malcolm's hand was still resting in her curls, his fingers sifting through them as though he were petting a prized cat. The sight of his strong, lean fingers contrasted so starkly against her pale thighs made her shiver again.

She looked away from the hand that possessed her. She shifted in his lap to pull away before he could stoke her desire again. She felt the heaviness of his need against her derriere — and then she felt, rather than heard, Malcolm's groan, just as he roughly pushed her back. His eyes were still silver, but darker, like a stormy sea, and his body was rigid with barely-suppressed need.

"Obedience wasn't so difficult, now was it?" he said, his voice harsh.

Amelia stiffened, his tone and her sudden embarrassment splashing cold water on the remnants of her longing. And even though she should have been glad that he stopped before they risked a pregnancy, she felt inexplicably close to crying.

She pushed his hand away and rolled off his lap. For one awful moment, she thought she might fall, but she managed to stand on shaking legs and smooth her skirts before attempting to retie her bodice. She couldn't bear to look into his eyes for fear she would find mockery there — but from the way his hands clenched on his legs as she straightened her dress, he wasn't nearly as calm as he sounded.

There was nothing to be done about her hair, but she would rather have every single servant see her in this state than spend another moment under his silvery gaze. "I believe my five minutes have passed," she said, stalking to the door without awaiting an answer.

She managed to make it all the way to her chamber before the tears started to fall.

CHAPTER TWELVE

The next morning, Amelia slashed through another paragraph of drivel. The story, which was so promising when she worked on it in London, had come completely undone in Scotland.

Perhaps that was the inevitable consequence of living a Gothic romance instead of writing it. How could she care about Veronique's predicament when she was also trapped in a remote castle, doomed to a marriage she didn't want?

She was being dramatic again. She'd been at her desk in the downstairs salon since shortly after dawn, breaking only when her maid had pressed chocolate and a bit of bread upon her. Her best words usually came in the morning, but after another fitful night — and the shame of her encounter with Malcolm — it was little wonder that sunrise didn't bring her muse with it.

If she were forced to become the hostess Malcolm demanded, she would rarely see the dawn unless she returned to their house as the sun came up. What would her muse do then?

The sound of laughter in the hall brought her back to the present. She laid aside her pen and pulled on her gloves, concealing the ink stains in preparation for callers. Perhaps fifteen minutes with whoever had chosen to visit would refresh her. Most social calls in London made her want to stab out her ears with a butter knife, but any distraction was welcome when it felt like the well from which her words came could produce nothing but buckets of dust.

She pasted on her best smile and opened the door. The first face she saw didn't belong to a stranger — it was almost as familiar as her own.

"Madeleine!" she exclaimed, nearly toppling her cousin as she embraced her. "Whatever are you doing here?"

Madeleine, now the Duchess of Rothwell, laughed as she returned Amelia's affections. "I've never seen you so happy to be interrupted."

Amelia pulled away, holding Madeleine at arm's length as she examined her. "Our visit hasn't been quite the holiday I expected."

She didn't mention Prudence, but she didn't have to. Madeleine shook her head, mock reproof mingled with an undercurrent of something real. "We heard it all from Prudence yesterday. She and Alex stayed the night with us en route to Edinburgh. Ferguson made the estate sound like a tiny country house, but it's more like a grand manor, albeit in need of decorating. You and Carnach must come for a visit after the wedding."

Madeleine's chatter about her new husband's house didn't disguise the underlying sentiment — that Amelia's wedding was already a *fait accompli*.

"Why are you so sure we will marry?" she asked.

Madeleine rolled her eyes, then spoke over her shoulder. "Ellie, I told you she wouldn't be eagerly planning the nuptials."

Behind her, Ellie Claiborne, the widowed Marchioness of Folkestone, stepped out of the drawing room. It was her laughter Amelia had heard earlier, a fact she realized when Ellie chuckled at Madeleine's comment. "I agreed with you, if I recall," Ellie said. "I wouldn't have left my bed for this visit unless I thought the story behind the engagement might be worth it."

Ellie pretended to stifle a yawn, but her blue eyes were bright with humor. Amelia embraced her, too. Ellie was Madeleine's new sister-in-law, and her red hair proclaimed her relationship to Ferguson and to the Scottish clan their mother descended from. Amelia hadn't met her until Madeleine's involvement with Ferguson several months earlier, but Ellie had quickly become one of her favorite people.

"Did you say Prudence stayed with you? Are they still at your house?" Amelia asked.

Her voice was casual, but it didn't fool her friends. "We asked them to stay, but Prudence insisted on pressing on this morning," Madeleine said. "We hadn't thought to impose on Lady Carnach's hospitality until the end of the week at least, especially since we just saw you when we parted ways four days ago. But when Prudence arrived on our doorstep, then left just as suddenly…"

Madeleine trailed off. Ellie steered Amelia into the drawing room. Lady Carnach was there, spooning tea into the teapot near the fire, while she and Augusta continued what sounded like a heated discussion of the merits of Brussels lace over domestic handicrafts. Ellie's half-sisters, Lady Maria and Lady Catherine, stood on the other side of the room, their identical profiles framing a window as they murmured to each other about the view.

Amelia didn't know the twins well, nor was she fully comfortable with Lady Carnach despite the woman's enthusiasm for welcoming Amelia into her family. But she loved Madeleine and Ellie — and she was sure she didn't want to hear their opinions on her marriage.

They would definitely have opinions. Madeleine had been friends with Prudence just as long as Amelia had, and the three had dubbed themselves the Muses of Mayfair years earlier. It was a nod to their artistic passions — Amelia wrote novels, Prudence studied history and art, and Madeleine longed to be an actress. Ellie was a painter and had joined more recently, but her personality meshed perfectly with the other women.

The Muses had supported each other through everything. But which side would Madeleine and Ellie come down on now that Amelia had caused a rift with Prudence?

As Lady Carnach passed around cups and cakes, the talk stayed inconsequential. It was like any number of at-homes in London, light and meaningless, words dissolving like meringues as they sipped their tea. Amelia watched the clock, but when the usual quarter hour had passed, Madeleine, Ellie, and the twins made no move to leave.

It was foolish to hope they would. The house Madeleine was now mistress of was nearly two hours away by carriage, too far for a short call. And while they weren't well acquainted with Lady Carnach, their claim on Amelia made a longer call acceptable.

Amelia tried to head it off. As soon as she finished her tea, she set aside her cup and stood, abandoning her position between Madeleine and Ellie on a settee. "I really must return to my letters. If you are still here at dinner, I shall see you then."

They wouldn't stay for dinner. It was too dangerous to drive home through the hills after dark. But Madeleine caught her hand before Amelia could escape. "Who are you writing to so urgently? Everyone you care for is here."

Amelia glared at her. Madeleine knew Amelia wasn't writing letters. But her jest trapped Amelia more efficiently than any plea for her company, since Amelia couldn't explain herself in front of her mother.

So she sat, ungrateful for the diversion she had previously wanted, and answered in monosyllables when the conversation turned to her.

She wasn't proud of her behavior. Given the choice, though, she would rather forestall the inevitable conversation about her engagement, and what she had done to Prudence, than be accommodating to her friends.

But inevitable was the right word. When Augusta and Louisa stood, Madeleine and Ellie stayed seated.

"I am sure you have much to reminisce about," Lady Carnach said cheerfully, "and little use for two old birds flitting about you. Lady Salford and I shall walk through my garden while the weather is fine, but I do hope you'll stay as long as you like. Perhaps you will take luncheon with us?"

Madeleine nodded. "We would be delighted, unless Ferguson wishes to leave as soon as he and Carnach finish their discussion."

"They will be at it for some time, I've no doubt," Louisa said. "Carnach has missed Ferguson — or Rothwell, I suppose I should say. I wish you both much happiness, your grace."

Madeleine had only recently become a duchess, but even though the title still startled Amelia, the role suited her. She was as gracious with Lady Carnach as if she had been born to the role. "Thank you, Lady Carnach. You must return the visit if the wedding arrangements permit us to beg your time."

Louisa beamed as she accepted the invitation. "Of course, Duchess. And if you want more refreshments, please don't hesitate to ring."

"Do you have a music room?" Ellie interjected. "Lady Catherine and Lady Maria would appreciate the practice, as the instruments at Ferguson's house are sorely out of tune."

"We wouldn't want to be so rude as to leave you alone," Kate said quickly.

"Nonsense," Ellie said, with a smile that bared her teeth. "We shan't miss you, I'm sure."

It was very nearly an order, but Louisa was too polite to comment on it and the twins too well bred to cause a scene. "Of course, Lady Folkestone," Louisa said. "And may I say it is lovely to welcome you to Scotland again after all this time? I remember your mother and miss her greatly."

Ellie's eyes flickered. "Thank you, Lady Carnach. Perhaps I shall visit the area more regularly in the future."

Louisa smiled, then ushered the twins toward the music room. Augusta followed, closing the door behind them.

"Now, Amelia," Madeleine said, moving off the settee to stand by the fire, "what the devil have you done?"

"I am shocked at your language, your grace," Ellie said, laughing as she took up the spot by the teacart and poured herself another cup.

"You and your brother share the blame for my language," Madeleine retorted. But her gaze had never left Amelia's face. "Why did you fix your attentions on Carnach? You knew what the match would mean for Prudence."

Amelia was glad she'd abandoned her cup, or she might have shattered it against the floor. "I didn't fix my attention on Carnach. When have I ever done that?"

Madeleine tapped her fingers on the mantel. "That is the same question I had when Prudence told her story. And yet you are engaged and she is returning to London with nothing."

"I was trying to help her," Amelia said through gritted teeth.

"The same way you tried to help me?" Madeleine asked.

During Madeleine's involvement with Ferguson last spring, Amelia's efforts to help her had resulted in a horrible conversation with Alex — and the same threat of marriage that Amelia now faced. "I was sorry for betraying your confidence then, and I still am."

Madeleine's green eyes were sharp. "And yet you interfered with Prudence as though you still feel better suited than any of us to manage our affairs."

Amelia spread out her hands. "Do you think she'll forgive me?"

The pause was ugly.

Madeleine finally sighed. "Prudence did say she didn't care at all for Carnach. If anything, she seemed relieved not to be marrying him."

"As well she should be," Amelia muttered.

Madeleine scowled, but she continued without haranguing Amelia again for her meddling. "Lady Harcastle is something else entirely," she warned. "She was utterly venomous about you — so venomous that I would have asked her to leave if there were any inns within an hour of our house. Perhaps Prudence will forgive you, but as long as she lives with her mother, she likely won't be allowed to see you."

Amelia moved to the teacart to freshen her cup, letting the silence lengthen as she poured. When her cup was full, she tried to lighten the mood. "I am trying not to be dramatic, but doesn't this seem like a story I would write? A heroine in a remote castle, friendless and alone, about to be forced into marriage?"

Madeleine laughed. "You should add a ghost. And possibly a ruined abbey."

"I wish that was all it took," Amelia said, taking her tea back to her seat. "At least if I were writing this, I could give myself a happy ending."

Ellie cleared her throat, so daintily it almost went unnoticed, and yet so demanding that Madeleine and Amelia both turned to her. "While the idea of writing a novel about this is diverting, you are missing the most important questions," she said.

"And what are those?"

Ellie sipped her tea, pausing as though her throat still bothered her. But her charisma was such that no one spoke until she set her cup in its saucer. "Question one: what drew you to Carnach when so many other suitors have failed? And question two: when you marry him, what will come of your writing?"

Amelia snorted. "Can I add a question?"

Ellie nodded graciously.

"Question two is invalid, as I shan't marry Malcolm. I would replace it with how I can make things right with Prudence."

"You may add Prudence as question three," Ellie said. "But I predict you shall marry Carnach. You already call the man by his Christian name — surely an indicator of passion."

Amelia blushed. Ellie sat in the very chair where her last encounter with Malcolm had occurred — the one that lodged his name on her lips and burned his touch on her skin. "Passion and marriage are very different," she said weakly.

"Are you blushing, Mellie?" Madeleine demanded.

"Of course she's blushing," Ellie said. "She knows I'm right."

Amelia stood abruptly, setting her tea on the table beside her and balling her hands at her sides. "No more questions. If you won't help me, my time would be better spent alone."

"Do you really not wish to marry him?" Madeleine asked, her tone softening.

"Why would I?" Amelia asked, pacing as she usually did. "I can't write if I marry him."

"I redirect you to questions one and two," Ellie said.

They had sounded like a jest, but Ellie's tone was utterly serious. "I don't understand," Amelia said, still pacing.

"Why are you attracted to him? And how can you write while married? Solve those questions, and I vow the rest will work itself out."

"That's easy for you to say," Amelia scoffed as she halted by Ellie's chair. "No one is forcing you to marry."

Ellie's voice turned cold. "Not anymore, but I have been in your shoes, and with far less attraction between us. Better to make your marriage on your own terms than run from the man if you genuinely want him. Don't let your fear confuse you."

"I'm sorry, Ellie," Amelia said, dropping back into her seat on the settee. Ellie's marriage had been arranged a decade earlier, and if the marquess hadn't died, she'd still be trapped. "I spoke without thinking."

Madeleine stepped forward to sit at Amelia's side. "The damage is done, Mellie. You might even find you like marriage if you let yourself enjoy it."

Madeleine still had a newlywed's glow — but then, she had loved her husband well before their wedding. Amelia didn't care for Ferguson, but he and Madeleine were perfectly suited.

"I won't find what you and Ferguson have," Amelia said.

Madeleine patted her knee. "Try. If you kissed him in spite of Prudence's situation, I'm convinced there's something there."

Ellie made her throat-clearing noise again.

"Do you need more tea?" Amelia asked acerbically.

Ellie grinned. "That obvious, was I?"

All three laughed. For a moment, Amelia felt that with their support, she could get through anything — either marrying Malcolm, or leaving him.

But the mood was lost when Ellie stopped laughing. "Amelia, even if you don't love him, you should know something else. There have been rumors in London."

"Rumors of what?" Amelia asked. "Lady Harcastle couldn't have possibly spread word of my indiscretions yet, and you journeyed north with us. What could you have heard that we did not?"

"It isn't Malcolm. It's your writing."

Amelia's optimism collapsed. "What are they saying?"

Ellie's voice was soothing, but serious enough that Amelia didn't relax. "No one has said anything about you. But your last book was so pointed in its satire that only a member of the ton could have written it."

"They've said that for months," Amelia said. "No one has suspected me."

"But this time — you do remember that you skewered Lord Kessel?"

"I had to have a villain, and he's a good one. He deserved it after his horrid attempts to marry me last year."

"Well, Kessel was in his cups at a soiree I attended the night before we left London, and someone called him Lord Grandison after the name you gave him in the novel."

Amelia laughed. "I never thought the men would read it."

Madeleine snorted. "You wanted the whole ton to read it so they'd stop speculating about Ferguson's sanity. You shouldn't have risked it."

"I had to, if only to make amends to you," Amelia said. It had been her attempt at an apology, and Madeleine had appreciated it at the time despite the risk.

"You succeeded, but it has a life of its own now," Ellie interjected. "Kessel vowed to find the author and horsewhip him, then transport him for slander and libel. Apparently the definition of those terms and the usual sentence escaped him," she observed drily. "But the threat remains. He's offered three hundred pounds for information leading to the author."

The sum wasn't a fortune. It wouldn't tempt Ellie, for instance. But if anyone who needed funds knew her secret, she would face the choice of buying them off — and likely having to pay them forever — or letting them tell Kessel and hoping he wouldn't believe them.

"Did anyone come forward that night?" Amelia asked.

"The usual round of people trying to collect, but none mentioned you. If you are lucky, he will find some other person to hang for it before anyone suspects you."

"Why didn't you tell me before?"

"I didn't see a serious threat. Only the four of us and Madeleine's coachman knew of your writing, so there was no one to betray you, and no need to worry you. But now that Prudence has, if you'll allow me to judge, a somewhat legitimate complaint against you…"

"You think she would sell my secret?" Amelia asked, disbelieving.

"She wouldn't," Madeleine declared.

Ellie sipped her tea. "I've seen more betrayal than either of you. Nothing surprises me."

Amelia shook her head. "I agree with Madeleine. Prudence hates Kessel almost as much as I do. I think I'm safe. Madeleine, you haven't told Ferguson, have you?"

Her cousin took offense. "You could trust Ferguson if I told him, you know."

"Have you?" she demanded.

Madeleine scowled. "Yes. He was saying again that you're a harpy, and I thought he might be nicer if he realized he had you to thank for urging the gossips on to a topic other than us."

"You didn't," Amelia said.

"I'm sorry, but I cannot keep secrets from him. He won't tell Carnach, though — you can be sure of it."

Amelia sighed. "We do have a way of giving up each other's secrets to try to save each other, don't we?"

Madeleine looked into her teacup. "Let's hope Prudence doesn't take a leaf out of our book."

They were silent for a moment. Amelia wouldn't dwell on Prudence, though. Her friend would nearly be to Edinburgh by now, and no apology she could write would catch her before she reached London — particularly if she didn't want to read it.

Amelia smoothed away the frown on her face. "I do hope Ferguson keeps his vow. Malcolm must never know about my writing. If I marry him, I won't let him put an end to my endeavors."

"You won't be able to write if you lose your link to your publisher," Ellie warned. "Now that Kessel has an incentive to learn your identity, you cannot be as straightforward as using Madeleine's coachman to deliver your manuscripts and pick up your payments."

She wouldn't have anything to publish for a few months if she maintained her recently glacial pace. "By the time I choose to publish again, I'm sure the furor will have died."

None of them looked convinced, but Amelia was grateful when they let the topic drop. Madeleine changed the subject to Ferguson's Scottish estate. Amelia made all the right noises, but her thoughts kept slipping back to her writing — and to Malcolm. If he married her just before her secret was discovered, he would be a laughingstock.

She wanted acclaim and recognition — but with Kessel hoping to destroy her if he could learn her name, acclaim was a dream she might never realize. She had always hoped, perhaps vainly, that someday the climate would change, that a gentlewoman could take credit for her writing without fear of scandal.

But if her plan to avoid marriage failed, she wasn't the only one who would be touched by any scandal her writing created. If Malcolm didn't cry off, she would have to bury her writing identity so deeply that no one could ever unearth it.

And she would have to hope that, despite everything, Prudence let it stay buried.

CHAPTER THIRTEEN

Malcolm had retreated to his study with his breakfast that morning, in no mood for Amelia's patently obvious attempts to avoid the inevitable. He hadn't slept well, even after taking himself in hand to relieve the arousal Amelia had caused. That she was the only woman in his fantasy as he came annoyed him as much as it spurred him on.

He wouldn't be the one to leave. And if she stayed, he wanted more than bits of forced obedience between periods of open war.

But even though he wanted to put her avoidance to an end, there was no use in chasing after her — she would reconcile herself to their marriage eventually, and he had other duties to attend to. So he spent the morning behind his desk, rereading weeks-old copies of *The Gazette* and *The Times*, making notations of which lords held which positions on the issues of the day. The news was light in September, with Parliament not yet in session. But he owed it to his clan to know the battlefield before he approached it.

The battle wouldn't be easy. There were only sixteen Scottish peers in the House of Lords, voted in every session from the far larger Scottish peerage. Their limited influence had been forced on them with the Act of Union, when England had dictated terms to make sure Scotland would always be under her heel.

Malcolm could take a seat in the House of Lords despite the restrictions, due to his subsidiary English title, Viscount Leybourne. But most aristocrats, even those whose lands were in Scotland, held no love for the Highlands. Despite the war against America, few cared whether the entire population of Scotland left for those shores. All that mattered was profit — and most landlords could make more money from sheep than they'd ever earned in rent from their tenants.

When Graves tapped on the door, Malcolm ordered him away without looking up. Graves ignored him. "His grace the Duke of Rothwell," the butler announced, unusually stiff with formality.

"Don't say you won't see me, MacCabe," Ferguson said, striding to the desk and clasping Malcolm's hand before Malcolm had fully risen from his chair. "I spent two hours with my sisters to reach you. The least you can offer is a drink."

Malcolm gestured him into a chair and walked to the cabinet for a decanter and two glasses. "Your letters sounded pleased about your reconciliation with your family. Has something changed?"

Ferguson rolled his eyes. "You've only brothers — you cannot possibly understand. They can go on for thirty minutes about ribbon, of all things."

Malcolm eyed the man's elaborate cravat and impeccably tailored jacket, more commonly found in the exclusive clubs of London than in any precinct of the Highlands. "You aren't unfashionable yourself."

"I long ago reconciled myself to the backward fashions of the Highlands, but I don't have to lower myself to meet them."

"Wouldn't you be better occupied by something other than spending two hours tying your cravat?" Malcolm asked, handing him a glass.

"I am such a genius that I require only one hour to tie my cravat,"

Ferguson said with a sniff.

Malcolm laughed at Ferguson's mock conceit. "I appreciate your willingness to take a few moments out of your daily rituals to attend to me, your grace."

"Please, I'm still Ferguson to anyone who matters. And I wouldn't dream of neglecting you when you're in such a coil," Ferguson said, sipping his brandy with an appreciative grin. "I do hope your plans to rid yourself of your fiancée will break me out of my boredom."

"Who says I intend to break my engagement?" Malcolm asked, leaning against the edge of his desk.

"I've known you for nearly three decades and cannot think of a single time you let yourself be forced to do something. You surely have a plan."

Malcolm swirled the brandy in his glass. The nutty aroma slid through him as he contemplated his answer. Ferguson was right. Malcolm didn't respond well to force.

"Perhaps I'm not unwilling to marry her."

Ferguson snorted. "You would have been better off with Miss Etchingham."

"No. She was nice enough, but she didn't show an ounce of spirit until the end."

"She had gallons of it at my house yesterday. A woman scorned is a sight to behold."

Malcolm sighed. "I know she feels wronged, even if an engagement was never formally discussed. But there's something about Amelia that makes me think I could take over the world if she were at my side."

Ferguson arched a brow. "I never thought you would seduce an innocent for political gain. You may yet surpass my schemes, MacCabe."

"No, you remain the greatest schemer in the Highlands," Malcolm said. "But my time with Amelia has complicated matters."

He told Ferguson about his encounter with Amelia in the library, including Alex's threats and Amelia's desire to break the engagement, but leaving out last night's interlude in the drawing room. Rather than sympathizing, or even disapproving, Ferguson laughed.

And laughed some more.

"Really, Ferguson, I don't see what's so amusing about this," Malcolm said through his teeth.

Ferguson wiped his eyes, still chuckling. "Ever since you inherited, you've tried to accomplish your duties to the letter. Marrying the right woman was so important to you — and now you've made a cake of yourself with the one woman I told you to avoid."

Malcolm ran a hand through his hair. "I knew better, but she was just too damned appealing. Far more appealing than the prim Miss Etchingham. What is so wrong with Amelia that you tried to warn me off?"

Ferguson sobered. He considered his words carefully, and when he answered, there was a reticence that Malcolm rarely heard from him. "Amelia has everything required to make a brilliant match, but she jealously guards her spinsterhood. Did you hear of *The Unconquered Heiress*? It came out in the spring and caused a sensation among the fashionable set."

Malcolm nodded. "I read it."

"I didn't take you for a romantic."

"I'm not," Malcolm said. "But with you in England, there was little else to do when I wasn't working, unless I wanted to listen to the twins' carousing and Alastair's moralizing. And my bookseller in Edinburgh said I should read it if I plan to go to London."

"Do you remember the plot?"

"Of course. It was good, if a bit overdramatic."

Ferguson snorted. "Of course it's dramatic. It's based on your fiancée."

Malcolm's eyes narrowed. "Don't tell me she was actually kidnapped by a dastardly Italian."

"No. Her reputation is fine, even if I think she is a harpy. But you should ask her about the book."

"That 'harpy' is about to become my wife. I thank you for watching your tongue.

Ferguson toasted his apology. "Forgive me. She tried her best to keep me and Mad apart, and I admit I'm biased. But the fact remains that Amelia has gone out of her way to avoid marriage until now. She is not an easy target. And she is so renowned for it that the entire ton will be gossiping about how you won her — and watching for any sign of discord."

Malcolm moved to the chair across from Ferguson, offering him the decanter before topping off his own glass. "If I win her, is she worth the fight?"

Ferguson stared into his glass as though he could read the future in the depths. "From what Madeleine has told me, she isn't conventional, MacCabe. I've only known Amelia a few months, but I'm confident she isn't what you were looking for in a wife. She won't be a china doll you can dangle from your arm at parties, then put away until you need her again."

He paused. Just as Malcolm thought he meant to end with that scathing indictment, Ferguson continued, quieter, almost to himself. "But if marriage has taught me anything, it's that one unconventional woman at your side is better than the prettiest china doll at your feet."

They fell silent, each nursing their brandies. From the secretive smile on Ferguson's face, Malcolm guessed there was a side to the new Duchess of Rothwell that would shock the ton.

Amelia had secrets too, though he hadn't learned them yet. But were her secrets worth the risk, if it gained him a partner like her?

When they finally stirred, Ferguson drained his glass. "I'll back you whatever you decide, MacCabe. Ask her about the book, though. You shouldn't marry with secrets between you."

"I'll ask," Malcolm said.

"Good. And if you want to make any last attempts to drive Amelia to jilt you, I'm your man."

"You are always scheming, aren't you," Malcolm observed.

"My blessing and my curse," Ferguson replied.

"No wonder you hate Amelia — you're two of a kind."

Ferguson scowled at that. "I'd call you out if I didn't think your wedding will be a bigger punishment than my sword."

Malcolm laughed and tossed off the contents of his glass. As long as Amelia's answers to his questions about *The Unconquered Heiress* were suitable, he didn't want to give her up.

He couldn't throw her aside anyway. But he was driven by more than just his reputation. He wanted her to come apart in his arms again, as she had done the night before. He wanted to feel her under him, over him, around him — and not just in the moments when she forgot that she didn't want to marry him.

He had tried warning her away the day before. He'd shown her the autocrat he could be, and she'd met him eye to eye. He had compelled her obedience, if only for a few moments, and she hadn't jilted him.

She hadn't admitted it yet, but she *would* marry him eventually — neither of them had any other choice. But if he seduced her properly, branded her with passion until she was driven by the same lust that fueled him, perhaps she would go the altar willingly.

He hadn't planned to marry for passion, and he couldn't let it distract him. But if he had to marry Amelia, they might as well enjoy each other.

And he would start tonight. If a moonlit library had been enough to overcome her reserves, he knew just the activity that would set her heart racing and send her straight into his arms.

"You're looking rather evil, MacCabe," Ferguson observed.

Malcolm grinned. "That's high praise, coming from you." He paused a moment, thinking over his plans for Amelia's seduction.

Then, throwing caution to the devil, he asked for Ferguson's help. "Do you mind if I borrow some sheep?"

CHAPTER FOURTEEN

"Something wrong with your dessert, Lady Amelia?" Malcolm asked her as she sat next to him at dinner that night. "I know it isn't as good as last night's effort."

She was confused for a moment, not remembering anything of the previous evening's dinner — until his slow grin reminded her of what they'd done in the drawing room afterward. She raised her chin. "I don't particularly care for any of the desserts you've offered."

He scooped up a bit of custard with his spoon. "That sounds like a challenge. I am happy to keep looking for offerings that will pique your appetites."

"You will find me hard to satisfy, my lord."

He smiled. "I don't doubt it. But I'm not one who will give up."

Down the table, Amelia heard her mother sigh. It didn't sound like censure, though. It sounded more like nostalgia.

Amelia watched Malcolm finish his custard. He savored the dessert, taking his time with it, finishing every last bit of it. She suspected that, if he'd been given a different life, he might have been a hedonist — driven by pleasure, rather than duty.

More like his brothers, perhaps. Douglas and Duncan had kept the party laughing all evening with tales they'd heard in the pub the night before. It wasn't a conversation she would have heard in her London circles, with rules that prevented talking across the table and taste levels that confined the conversation to safe, boring topics.

But the MacCabes had fully welcomed her and her mother into their fold. Her marriage still loomed over her, but in the moments when she forgot about it, she realized that she wanted to stay in Scotland, in this castle.

She wouldn't go so far as to say she wanted to stay with this man.

Malcolm leaned back in his chair, taking his wine glass with him. His fingers curled around the stem, and he looked at her over the rim of the glass as he sipped.

There was still pleasure in his eyes. If they could have passion between them, rather than cool civility and political constraints, would marriage be so bad?

Lady Carnach stood at the end of the table. Malcolm and his brothers stood too. Amelia set aside her napkin. Would Malcolm join her in the drawing room later, as he had the night before? Would she wait for him — or would she run, and try to think of a way to escape a marriage that she increasingly knew was inevitable?

"By all means, dears, there's no need for you to retire," Lady Carnach said. "I believe I shall go to my room."

"Shall I escort you, Mother?" Malcolm asked.

She nearly snorted. "I've lived here for nearly thirty-five years. I suppose I can find my room one more time."

He offered his arm to Amelia's mother next, but she also refused. "You young people should continue to socialize," Augusta said, pulling her gloves on after rinsing her fingers in the bowl of water at her plate. "It is unconventional, but you are practically married, after all. And you'll be glad of these quieter hours together when you're deep in the

London season."

Malcolm's brothers immediately claimed other commitments — Alastair with his sermon for the next day and the twins with some cousins at the pub. That left Amelia and Malcolm staring each other down in the medieval expanse of the MacCabe dining room.

In any other circumstance, she would have been enchanted. Unlike the family wing, the dining room had been carved out of the original remnants of the ancient castle, and its provenance showed in the stone walls. Faded tapestries covered the walls between the narrow windows, dampening the echoes and adding a bit of color to the endless swathes of grey. The giant fire blazing in the hearth added warmth, while the iron chandelier suspended over the table cast ominous shadows on the diners.

She ignored the appeal of the room, trying to stay focused on her thoughts, trying to find where her heart intended to guide her. At least some time alone with Malcolm might reveal his strategy. Despite everything he'd said before of obedience and duty, he'd been so solicitous at dinner.

Almost like he was wooing her.

"Would you prefer tea, darling? Or something stronger?" he asked, taking his chair when everyone else had left.

Definitely like he was wooing her. Where was the autocrat he had shown her the day before?

"I'll drink what you drink," she said.

"Graves, two glasses of whisky and the teacart."

She was sure Graves noticed her impropriety, even if his master didn't. He bowed stiffly, with either arthritis or apoplexy.

"We can separate if you prefer, my lord. Perhaps everyone else had the right idea by retiring early."

"No, I've a better idea. Come to my study and I'll show you."

She shook her head. "I really should write my letters rather than spend time with you unchaperoned."

"Daylight is for letters. Evening belongs to conversation. You will disappoint Graves if you show no interest in social engagements."

"It is too late, my lord," Graves said as he brought two glasses of whisky from the sideboard. "I shall go to my eternal rest regretting that I could not prevent this union."

Amelia would have fired a servant who spoke like that, but Malcolm laughed as he stood and offered her his arm. "Ignore him. The man is a genius at running the staff and the wine supply, but our lack of proper entertaining has dulled his social graces."

More like destroyed than dulled, but Amelia held her tongue. She took Malcolm's arm. He palmed the whisky glasses in the other hand. "Graves, send the tea to my study. No poisons, if you please."

"Your staff is unconventional," Amelia remarked as they left the dining room.

"You haven't seen the rest of the clan. Graves was reportedly a paragon of propriety when my mother hired him from England thirty years ago. But I'm sure his service to us has ruined him for other employment."

"Does your clan have such a bad effect on all who join it?"

They reached his study and Malcolm opened the door. "You can ask my mother. She doesn't seem so bad for it. Although perhaps she would disagree — she no longer cares for London, after the freedom she's had here."

He ignored the seat behind his desk and set the glasses on a small table nestled between two chairs by the fireplace. The chairs were covered in supple chestnut leather, inviting a man to lean back into their depths.

The room was exactly what one would expect of a gentleman's retreat, with hunting trophies interspersed between the books and paintings lining the walls. It didn't have the personal effects and antiques that littered her brother's study — but then, Malcolm had only been the earl for a year, while Alex had inherited a decade earlier.

Malcolm gestured to the chairs. "Will you sit?"

She remained standing. "What do you want, Lord Carnach?"

He angled his head, the picture of innocence. "What do you suspect me of wanting?"

"Don't be obtuse. We've sparred like rival statesmen since the moment Alex found us in the library, and now you've suddenly stopped. Why?"

Malcolm crossed his arms. "Do I need a reason?"

"You should have ended this by now. Why haven't you ended it?"

The question hung in the air like a dangerous blizzard rolling down from the Grampian Mountains. It stayed suspended as Graves tapped on the doorframe, arranged the teacart near the chairs, and muttered something about shameless hoydens before closing the door.

She made eye contact with Malcolm all the while. The answer to her question lurked in the grey depths, just barely visible under layers of nonchalance. She suspected that she knew what it was — and that there was an answering sparkle in her eyes, if Malcolm peered as deep as she had.

But she wouldn't name it until he did. She wouldn't give it the space it needed to grow from a spark to a bonfire, either. Her voice was cold as she reminded him of her question. "Why haven't you ended it?"

He still watched her as he picked up his glass. There was something about his perusal of her over the rim that awoke the need within her — a need he could stoke with just a look.

Her breath seized. She suddenly didn't care for why, just whether — whether he would touch her again, whether this time she might touch him too.

His glass clicked against the wooden table and pulled her back. "I haven't ended it for the same reason you haven't," he said.

She tilted her head up and looked down her nose. "Neither of us wants to be the one who risks ruin to break this off, but if you were a gentleman, you'd take the blow."

Malcolm laughed. "The 'gentleman' argument won't work, darling. And that's not why we're still here."

"Then why are we here?"

Her voice was a whisper, barely audible over the popping fire, utterly removed from the strong, demanding tones she usually used to escape suitors.

His voice had all the confidence hers lacked. "We want each other. On some level, we need each other. Neither of us can say goodbye until it's out of our systems."

She shook her head. If she were a child, she would have covered her ears. She started to, unconsciously, but he came forward and clasped her hands in his.

"Don't fight it, Amelia. You know it's true."

His hands were warm, even through her gloves. They were also hard — but the hardness of a support beam, not a prison wall.

"What shall we do?" she asked.

He lifted her hands to his lips and brushed a kiss across her knuckles. "I've thought of an option, but you may not like it."

"If you say we should marry, I'll poison your tea myself."

"Bloodthirsty wench — you can be the Borgia to my Caesar and we'll rule the world together," he said, the grin on his face and his mixed time periods drawing out her laugh.

"I rather fancied myself a Scheherazade."

"The power behind the throne? Or do you intend to tell me stories until I free you?"

"Both," she said, twining her fingers through his.

"A thousand and one nights," he mused. "And here I thought I could only ask you for one."

"One night for what?"

He kissed her fingers again. "One night to exorcise the passion between us. If you still want to leave at the end of it, then I'll cry off. But I wager one night won't satisfy us."

She pulled away. "You're mad."

"Not mad, brilliant."

"Mad," she emphasized. "Mad to want me, mad to even suggest this. You've already seen my passion. But you've said yourself you need propriety."

"Propriety can hang. And you're more proper than you claim you are."

The lingering heat of his touch felt like a brand on her ink-stained fingers. If he knew of her writing, he would never find her proper again.

"I'm not proper, Malcolm. I'm really not."

"Does this have something to do with *The Unconquered Heiress*?" he asked.

The floor dropped out from under her. He sounded curious, not angry — but how could he only be curious, if he knew what she had done? Had Ferguson spilled her secret?

"Did Ferguson tell you about that?" she asked.

"He only said I should ask you about it. The heroine does seem to resemble you."

She tried to keep her voice steady. "It's a satire of the ton. Why someone chose to make me the heroine, I don't know."

His face was still open, trusting. "I know why. You have more personality than any woman I know — in the book, you leap off the page."

His praise sent a swift jolt of satisfaction through her, but she couldn't acknowledge it. "You read the book?"

"Hasn't everyone?" he asked. "So if you are holding out on marrying me because of whatever the truth is about what happened between you and Lord Kessel, you should know I don't care at all."

In the book, Lord Grandison, the character she'd modeled after Kessel, killed his first wife, then abducted the heroine and tried to force her into a marriage. It was a darker version of real life — Kessel's wife had died in childbirth, but he had not been subtle in his attempts to gain Amelia's hand. It was only after Alex had prevented Kessel from dragging Amelia onto a balcony at a party that the baron's "courtship" stopped.

"Nothing happened with Lord Kessel. He wanted to marry me. I refused. And Alex didn't try to press me into it, unlike his rather enthusiastic willingness to toss me into a marriage with you at the first sign of trouble."

Malcolm's eyes narrowed. "How close did Kessel come to forcing the issue?"

"Not close enough that you need to worry," she said. "I don't love him, if that's what concerns you."

He snorted. "Unless the writer got your character utterly wrong, I guessed you didn't love him."

"No, that bit's right. But still, Malcolm, the whole ton knows about it. And they also know I'm headstrong, impulsive, prone to meddling, and all sorts of other unfortunate attributes. Don't marry me if you don't want to be saddled with that."

They'd stood throughout the conversation, rivals sizing each other up before making the first move — but Amelia saw on Malcolm's face the moment he decided to go in for the kill.

"Have you slept with a man in the last three months?" he asked.

Her jaw dropped. "Of course not."

"Good, no cuckoos in my nest. Any secret children? Bigamist marriages? Radical politics?"

"No."

"Gambling debts? Penchant for spirits?"

"I don't gamble, and you drink more than I do."

He grinned and retrieved his whisky, lifting it in her honor. "Then you're proper enough for me. Now, will you give me one night?"

It was a challenge phrased as a request. If she refused, they'd still be at an impasse. Their wedding was only four days away. He seemed perfectly willing to go through with it — which meant her only choices were to cry off herself, or use this night to prove their unsuitability.

"What will you do with your one night?" she asked.

"You will need to change your clothes. And trust me."

CHAPTER FIFTEEN

Amelia took his bait. He had known she would. Her desire for freedom was even stronger than her passion for him — giving her the chance to use the latter to win the former was a challenge she couldn't refuse.

While she went upstairs to dress, Malcolm waited in the great hall. He flung himself into one of the chairs at the long, immovable table that had stood on the dais for centuries. The great hall was empty, but in a few days it would host the feast for his wedding.

He leaned back in his chair and looked up at the coat of arms and crossed swords hanging on the wall above him. His wedding feast was yet another step on the path all his ancestors had taken. With a woman like Prudence, it would have been civil enough. But with Amelia...

With Amelia, it would be something else entirely. He wouldn't be able to stay cool with her. Every time she laughed, she unleashed the man he might have been, if the yoke of an earldom hadn't settled on his shoulders.

Malcolm swung his feet up and rested them on the table. He needed to stay focused. She was destined to be his wife. And she would remain his wife, even when the passion inevitably cooled and duty took its place.

But it would be nice if they were happy on their wedding day, even if love was too much to ask.

And even if love was too much for him to offer. He liked her better than he planned to like his wife. But the deep, soul consuming love that poets wrote about — he couldn't give her that. He had to save it for his land and remember what mattered most.

He scowled up at the sword on the wall. He would have preferred to fight his enemy on a battlefield. A decisive battle, ending in one party's destruction, would be so much easier than fighting the forces currently remaking his country. This shadow war, played out in Parliament and the papers, would take him a lifetime to fight — and he couldn't let himself be distracted from it.

But he couldn't live like a monk, either. If he had to be distracted occasionally, Amelia was the woman he wanted in his bed. And he would prove that she wanted it too. She needed laughter and adventure — not the bleak, boring days of a spinster.

A moonlit ride and a bit of larceny, previously arranged with Ferguson, would surely appeal to the strong desires she tried so hard to control. Tonight, he would show her everything he could give her.

And if she took it, he was sure their marriage was one battle he could win.

*   *   *

Watkins was in Amelia's room, knitting as she normally did while waiting for Amelia to return. But the covers weren't turned down, and Amelia's dark blue riding habit hung in place of her nightrail.

"Are you riding with his lordship?" Watkins asked, jumping up to take Amelia's shawl.

"I don't know what I am doing. He said you knew — that he had arranged it with you before dinner."

"Yes, my lady." Watkins's cheeks were red. "I hope you don't overheat in the velvet, but he wanted the darkest habit you own."

It was hideously improper. Amelia fidgeted with the cameo at her neck. "No, Watkins. I should retire."

The maid pursed her lips, but she had never been as open with her mistress as the Scottish servants were with Malcolm. It had never occurred to Amelia to ask Watkins's opinion on anything other than this hairstyle or that reticule, but something — the castle, the wine at dinner, the earl awaiting her favor — made her reckless. "What do you think, Watkins?"

Watkins dropped one of the riding boots she had started to put away. "I beg your pardon?"

"What should I do?"

Watkins paused, weighing her words. "I think it's romantic, my lady. His lordship seems nice, nicer than most, and you are engaged to him. Wouldn't it be lovely to sneak away for a ride?"

The maid's voice held a wistful note. Amelia felt suddenly, horribly ungrateful. She didn't want to marry — but her choices were still more numerous than those of most women of any station.

She couldn't give her choices away to someone else; life didn't work like that. But she could make the most of them.

"Very well. I shall go," she said.

Watkins beamed. "I will have you ready in only a few moments, my lady."

It took longer than a few moments, but not much. The buttons on her pink silk evening gown were difficult, but Watkins worked quickly to undo them. She helped Amelia into a heavier petticoat, and then

Amelia stepped into her full riding skirt. She watched in the mirror as
Watkins fastened the gold frog clasps on the military-style riding jacket,
wishing she knew why she was dressing for an outing when she had
assumed they would stay inside.

She remained silent as her maid removed her pearl-tipped hairpins
and quickly braided her hair. Watkins wrapped the braids around
Amelia's head, securing the braids to her scalp before covering them
with a dark blue bonnet. This was all so absurd — and yet, she was so
curious about what Malcolm intended that she couldn't back down,
even if she knew it would be safer to evade him.

After Watkins guided her feet into her riding boots and handed
her the black leather gloves, Amelia took her riding crop from the
maid's outstretched hand. "Did the earl have any other instructions
for you, Watkins?"

The maid smiled. "My lord said not to wait, my lady."

Outrageous. But their supposed engagement made Watkins think
this was a display of love, not a scandal. Perhaps the castle and the
MacCabe staff had addled her wits too. Amelia left her to straighten the
room, tapping the riding crop against her leg as she walked down the
hallway toward the stairs to the great hall. Her thoughts were suspiciously
vacant, as though she couldn't pin any of them down long enough to
examine them.

Perhaps she knew that if she thought for more than a second
about what awaited her, she would run. But would she run away from
Malcolm? Or would she run to him and demand whatever he offered?

When she entered the great hall, Malcolm rose from his chair on
the dais. As he walked to meet her, his dark greatcoat swirled around
him. He hadn't changed, but the coat over his severe black trousers and
Hessian boots matched her dark attire.

"I was beginning to think you might not come," he said, taking her arm.

Her fingers curled lightly over his coat. "I was beginning to think I shouldn't have. I must say riding was not the entertainment I assumed you were offering."

He gave her a cheeky grin as he led her out the doors to a pair of waiting horses, held in place by a yawning groom. "I'm sorry to disappoint your wicked desires, darling."

Amelia sniffed, feigning offense even though her grin gave her away. "May I ask what you intend for us to do tonight?"

Malcolm tossed her up into the saddle, then leapt onto his own horse and gathered his reins. He dismissed the groom and waited until the man had rounded the side of the castle in the direction of the stables before answering her question.

"I thought you should see more of the estate than you have so far. And there's no better way to introduce you to it than through one of the oldest traditions in the Highlands."

"And what would that be?"

"*Reiving*," he said with dark smile as he dug his heels into the sides of his stallion.

Malcolm almost reached the top of the steep hill leading down into the village before she managed to nudge her horse forward. From what she knew of Scotland, raiding, or *reiving*, had been stamped out by the English decades ago. Malcolm was so bound by duty — why would he still practice the sport?

She didn't ask, though. Instead, she focused on the fierce, illicit thrill of riding out into the night. The moon was mostly full, and Malcolm held them to a pace that allowed them to see potential obstacles in the dim white light. Stars twinkled in glorious swaths across the sky.

She liked London well enough, but she was glad to be away from the gritty soot and endless noise.

She glanced over at Malcolm. Had every previous MacCabe looked so commanding? With the moon casting a glint in his silver eyes, he looked like he could lead an assault on the gates of hell, smiling in the face of the devil himself.

Amelia shook her head hard, trying to clear the visions. Her inner thoughts were incorrigible. And she needed to stay focused if she wanted to discover why Malcolm was doing something as out of character as conducting a nighttime raid.

"Where are we going?" she asked after they passed through the village.

Malcolm held a finger to his lips. "Quiet," he whispered. "We will be in enemy territory soon. You can't risk our necks by talking loudly."

"If I promise to whisper, can you tell me where we are going?" she asked.

"We are stealing sheep."

"Why are we stealing sheep?" she asked suspiciously. "Surely you do not need the money."

Malcolm chuckled. "It's not about money. Scots lairds steal from each other for revenge, to send a message, or even to entertain themselves."

"Which of these noble goals are we pursuing tonight?" she asked.

"Revenge, of course. And a bit of entertainment."

"Revenge for what?"

"Someone spoke ill of you. And I'll have him know I don't allow such talk about my wife."

She frowned. "Who could have spoken ill of me? I haven't met any of your neighbors."

He turned off the road onto a smaller, rutted track. "You have. Our good friend Ferguson insists that you're a harpy. If he weren't a duke, perhaps I'd have murdered him for it. Stealing his sheep will have to suffice."

Amelia choked back her laugh and lowered her voice. "If I'd known we were stealing from Ferguson, I wouldn't have even bothered with dinner. We could have gone at once."

"You really are a bloodthirsty wench, aren't you? Maybe not a Borgia, though. You don't have the subtlety for poisons."

"Well, you seem to be more of a general than a politician," she pointed out. "Neither of us is precisely subtle."

They rode for half an hour, overtaking the occasional man walking home from the village. Everyone who greeted Malcolm called him "laird" rather than "my lord" — in this corner of Scotland, at least, the old traditions still held sway. And Malcolm seemed to know something about all of them, as though they were extended family rather than faceless tenants.

Eventually, they crested a small hill and Malcolm called a halt. A pasture lay next to the track they rode on, stripped nearly bare by the sheep huddled in the center of the enclosure. A low stone fence prevented their escape.

"Shall we jump it?" she asked.

Malcolm shook his head. "Not when you're on a horse you don't know and with little light to guide you. Wait a minute and I'll make a gap."

If she were a stronger woman, holding true to her plan to stay unwed, she might have taken offense at the sudden protective note in his voice. But the thrill of the escapade was weakening her. She recognized his intention then — this wasn't about revenge, or entertainment, or sheep. He *wanted* her to weaken for him.

But she couldn't resist an adventure that felt like something out of one her stories.

Malcolm slid off his horse to create a gap in the stones. He worked with the ease of a farm hand, piling stones to the side as though he opened and closed fences every day. Amelia wanted the hedonist she sometimes glimpsed in him, but she had to admit that his duties did have some benefits — watching the muscles of his shoulders ripple under his coat as he heaved the rocks aside was far more appealing than listening to some society dandy inhale yet another pinch of snuff.

When he finished, he jumped onto his horse, gesturing for Amelia to go through the fence ahead of him. She looked out over the dark field. She had seen sheep on her family's country estate in Lancashire, of course, but she had never tried to herd anything. Stealing sheep from Ferguson entertained her, but even with her enthusiasm, she wouldn't be a useful partner across any serious distance.

"Is no one guarding them?" she asked.

"No. Sheep are turned loose in the summer and someone moves them when they need a new pasture. But there are no serious dangers to the sheep. The wolves disappeared in this area centuries ago."

"How far do we have to take them?" she asked. She already envisioned accidentally driving the sheep off a nearby cliff. She didn't want to inadvertently murder them, even to get revenge on Ferguson.

Malcolm pointed at a fence in the far corner of the pasture. "This is the very edge of Ferguson's holdings, where his land abuts ours. If we move them through the fence into our pasture, I'll send a herdsman tomorrow to retrieve them and take them to the other side of our estate."

"Won't Ferguson be able to steal them back just as easily?" she asked as they rode across the pasture to the opposite fence.

Malcolm dismounted again and started pulling down a portion of the fence. "Have you met Ferguson?" he said. "He excels at business, but he knows nothing of sheep. He won't notice they're gone, and since he failed to mark them, he can't claim them. If he spent half as much time on his sheep as he does on his wardrobe, he'd be rich."

She laughed. Ferguson was rich beyond imagining, but the wealth came from his recent English inheritance, not his mother's Scottish lands. "I'm surprised you're friends with the bounder."

"Careful, darling. If you insult him, I might have to steal something from you as revenge too." He tossed another stone onto the pile, then flashed her a wicked grin. "Although I would likely start in your wardrobe. I'd burn all your prim day dresses if it meant I could see you in more gowns like the one you wore tonight."

Amelia blushed. He really was trying hard to charm her. But, heaven help her, she liked it.

When the fence was down, he mounted and directed her to circle the sheep. "This should be easy enough. Ferguson's new estate manager should have moved them several days ago — they're almost out of pasture. Once we get the first sheep to go through the fence and find better grass, the rest will follow."

Despite her misgivings, she warmed to the task quickly. Pulling one over on Ferguson was remarkably satisfying, even if she was sure Malcolm was doing it to seduce her. If she thought the loss of the sheep might harm Ferguson — or, more importantly, Madeleine — she might have felt a twinge of guilt. But the Rothwell holdings in the south were nearly rich enough to rival Devonshire — thirty sheep wouldn't break them.

With Malcolm occasionally calling instructions, they herded the sheep through the gap in the fence. It wasn't as easy as he'd made it sound, particularly since Amelia sat sidesaddle and was weighed down with yards of riding skirts. But there was something exhilarating about being outside, in the dark, engaged in an activity which her very proper upbringing hadn't prepared her for.

When the last sheep was through the gap, Malcolm started rebuilding the fence again. She didn't have a watch, but it couldn't have taken more than thirty minutes to move the sheep. They would be back at the castle before midnight. Would he say goodnight to her then? Or continue his campaign to break her resolve?

After he rebuilt the other fence, he looked up at her from the ground. "Have I offended your delicate sensibilities? Or did you enjoy yourself?"

"You know I enjoyed it," she said. "Thank you, Malcolm. Our one night was lovely."

If she was disappointed that they spent it stealing sheep rather than kissing, she hid it so well that even she didn't acknowledge it.

But Malcolm wasn't done. "There are still several hours of darkness, darling. And I intend to use every minute you've agreed to."

CHAPTER SIXTEEN

Malcolm's behavior confused her. When he was civil to her in the dining room she had thought it was another ploy, believing that his occasional flashes of autocratic behavior were his real personality.

But she had willfully blinded herself to the evidence. In the moonlight, the evidence spread around her for leagues. Every well-kept crofter's hut and carefully maintained fence showed how he cared for the people he both led and served. Even Graves, as dreadful as he was, was loyal, and Malcolm hadn't turned him away.

That night, Malcolm treated her like a partner. She'd never had a partner before. She'd had friendship and camaraderie, and her fellow Muses of Mayfair shared similar artistic ideals. But she had never worked with someone or shared their sense of purpose.

For the first time, she wondered if she had missed more of life than she had thought. Was solitude a fair price for independence?

When they reached the castle, Malcolm dismounted first and strode around to help her slide off her saddle. He lifted her free of the horse, and as he set her on her feet, his hands stayed firmly around her waist.

"Tell me what you want, Amelia."

The question surprised her, enough that she actually considered it. She wanted warmth, and adventure, and laughter — not the impersonal safety of a guest room. "I thought you had plans for us tonight?"

It was the closest she intended to come to an invitation. He was either obtuse or stubborn, because he didn't accept it. "That's what I want. What do you want?"

His hands on her waist burned through the velvet. She'd never thought of hands as heavy, but the weight of his touch rooted her to the ground. His eyes were that melted silver color again, warm and demanding even in the dimmest light. He looked like he wanted to kiss her.

"Why do you care what I want?" she asked.

He shook her, just a bit, just enough to make her wonder why her body thrilled at his touch when he could so easily break her. "Stop turning this toward me. I want you. You know that. But I also want you willing. I won't have your passion at night and your hatred in the morning."

"I don't hate you," she said.

Malcolm grinned a little at that. "I don't hate you either. Marriages have survived with less."

He did kiss her then, just the briefest graze across her lips, so quick she didn't realize what was happening until he'd pulled away. "Then if you don't hate me, does that mean I have your passion?" he asked.

He was intent on making her confess it. She'd rather let him be the aggressor in their seduction, if only so she wouldn't feel like she was giving up. It wasn't fair to him — but when was life ever fair?

"Your touch is not unpleasant," she allowed.

A lesser man would have been wounded. He had the audacity to tweak her nose. "You'll have to do better than that, darling."

Her horse started to move away from them on the drive, and Malcolm let go of her to retrieve the reins. When he had both horses in his grip, he turned back to her. With his eyebrow raised in silent question, he looked like a king disguised as a groom — strong, confident, and utterly in command.

But he wouldn't command her into his arms — at least not tonight. She had to take that step alone, if she wanted it, and trust that he would catch her.

"Will you keep me out here all night for my answer?" she snapped, not ready to confess.

He jerked his head to the side of the castle and the stables beyond. "I must tend to the horses, since I sent the grooms to bed. If you want me, wait for me in my chamber. If you don't, hide in your room. I shouldn't be more than half an hour."

"And if I am not waiting for you? Will you call off the wedding?"

His mouth turned grim, betraying the warrior concealed beneath the words that promised her a choice. "No."

It was abrupt, harsh, final. "I thought you wanted me willing?" she said.

"In bed, yes. But you're utterly compromised and I'm the one who did it. By the time Lady Harcastle reaches London, I'm sure the length of Britain will know that you're ruined. The ton won't accept me if I abandon you, and even if they did, I couldn't live with myself. So it's time to cut bait, darling. You *will* marry me."

She took a deep breath, inhaling the scent of heather and the cooling leather of their saddles. She wanted to run, to deny him, to preserve everything she'd so desperately fought for.

But she also wanted him. And her breath came out as a sigh when he finished his declaration. "You will marry me," he said again, as though he didn't think she'd understood. "But the kind of marriage we will have — that's a choice."

"You would consent to live in separate houses?"

She didn't necessarily want to, but she had to know. Her horse nickered in protest as his hand tightened on the reins. "Separate counties, if you like. You can have a marriage of convenience, although you must attend certain functions. And give me an heir or two, of course. I'll take them and raise them, so they won't interrupt your precious letter-writing."

He'd struck hard, in more ways than he realized. She was too careful to reference the letters, but his statement about children surprised her. "You would take my children away from me?"

"Our children," he said. "Any court would give me custody. But it doesn't have to be like that. We can share a house. I'm certain the pleasure we'll find there will more than make up for the lack of sleep."

She laughed at his playful leer. "Such a noble offer, my lord."

He made an elaborate bow. "I only make promises I can keep."

She hesitated. In some corner of her heart, she knew she had already lost. There was no way out that she could see — and if she was trapped, she would rather be seduced by the reiver than ordered about by the autocrat.

He noticed her hesitation and pressed his advantage. "You can have all the pleasure you've denied yourself, Amelia. You don't have to be locked away with your letters for the rest of your days. If you come to me tonight, I'll show you. If you don't come…"

He trailed off. Their eyes met. She saw the hunger in his, and wondered what he saw in hers.

He kissed her, swiftly, suddenly, not waiting for her answer. She molded herself to him, wanting him to accept her kiss in lieu of the words she couldn't say.

But he wouldn't give her that escape. He broke away, his breath ragged with the effort.

And when she tried to kiss him again, he stepped back. "If you don't come to me tonight, I'll try again. But only if you ask me. Don't test my patience, darling."

He led the horses away, leaving her standing in the drive. She walked slowly toward the stairs. The gravel crunched under her feet, matching the echo of his steps as he strode into the night.

She knew what she had to do. But how would Malcolm react?

*   *   *

She paced, turning small circles in the area between the fireplace and the bed. It was what she did when a plot in her manuscript led her straight into a wall. This felt like those moments writ large, a trap that had engulfed her rather than her characters.

Malcolm wasn't a trap, to be fair. He was an unexpected fork in a road she thought she'd mapped to the end of her days. A week ago, her road led to her own cottage in Sussex and a life spent covered in ink and blotting sand. Tonight, the road offered a partner and a life spent covered in Malcolm's kisses.

If she had the courage to pursue it.

But what took more courage? Staying on the path she'd planned for against all of society's expectations, or setting off on a new path, one that society would expect her to embrace? She had given everything to her writing, sacrificing companionship for art, comfort for the threat of ruin. Was Malcolm an even bigger risk, or a cowardly escape from the life she'd built herself?

Amelia forced herself to take off her hat and gloves and sit by the fire, but she couldn't stop twisting her fingers in her lap. These questions were useful when plotting a story, but if she thought of her life solely in terms of logic and the structure of a perfect plot, she would go mad. Logic told her to leave him before she was hurt — or, more likely, before she hurt him.

When she heard footsteps in the hall, she stopped breathing. Her logic reared up within her, told her to flee when she heard the doorknob turn, made one last attempt to stop her...

But when Malcolm strode through the door, scanned his room, and finally let his eyes rest on her, logic lost. All she could say was, "Malcolm, I want you."

He was on her an instant later. She'd barely risen from the chair when he dragged her into his arms, his lips meeting hers before she had a chance to take a breath. It wasn't polite, this kiss — it was demanding and hungry, and all those other indelicate feelings a spinster wasn't supposed to have.

She discovered she didn't want polite. She moaned against his mouth, and when he opened his lips, she was already waiting for his tongue to claim her. She wrapped her arms around his neck and pulled him closer. He slid a hand under the curve of her buttocks and lifted her, angling her toward him, leaving only her toes to graze the carpet. She felt the length of his erection between them, and maybe it should have frightened her, but she felt a fierce kick of pride. She'd caused that — and with this man, she wanted what it offered.

Her life always came back to words, but for once, she couldn't track her observations as they happened — her words found it impossible to keep up. Within the swirling heat of their kiss, she registered impressions, like the stubble of his shadowed beard abrading her hand as she caressed his jaw. The wild taste of his mouth, whisky mixed with the barest trace of salt. The low growl in his throat as she nipped his lip — the answering thrust of his tongue as he deepened his claim.

Cool air skimmed her skin as he hiked up her skirts. The little breath she still had rushed out of her lungs as he broke their kiss to scoop her up into his arms, and she instinctively wrapped her legs around his waist. The bulge in his breeches jutted dangerously close to her most private place, drawing all her attention to the throbbing between her legs.

"Please, Malcolm," she whispered into his neck.

He shifted her up, even closer, and kissed her again. He was slower this time, almost gentle — almost polite.

But not quite.

One of his hands cupped her derriere, pushing her hard against him, and the slower pace of their kiss let her feel everything else. His scent worked its way through her, the tang of his sweat, the heady combination of leather and exertion. She should have felt dirty, should have wanted the pale, perfumed skin of a London gentleman instead of Malcolm's callused hands stroking her waist.

She didn't want a gentleman. She wanted him.

And she wanted him *now*.

"Please," she said again, more demanding this time.

He pulled back just enough to see her clearly. His face was almost impassive, a statue carved out of granite, and she might have thought that he was unaffected by her. She'd gotten better at seeing into the depths of his eyes, though. And in the flickering firelight, she saw how much he wanted her, too.

"I didn't think you would be here," he said.

She exhaled. "I didn't think I would either."

He paused. She saw some battle play out over his face, so quick she might have missed it had she not been dying to understand his thoughts. The consequence wasn't what she expected.

He set her on her feet.

Her skirts fell around her. The velvet settled in heavy folds, suddenly feeling like a tomb in which her desire would be buried alive. She must have gaped at him, because his hand came up to tap her chin and shut her mouth. His thumb slid across the corner of her lip, and he almost leaned in to kiss her again.

She would have accepted it. But at the last moment he pulled back. "Are you sure you want me?" he asked.

She was dazed by his kisses, too dazed to understand what he was driving at. "I'm here, aren't I?"

"I know you want me now. But I don't want you hot one minute and cold the next. I'd rather have a marriage of convenience than come to your room every night wondering whether I'll get the whore or the nun."

"That's not nice."

He shrugged. "This could just be another strategy on your part. If it's not a trick, then tell me what you want — show me what you want. But if you can't stomach the thought of sharing my bed every night, then get out."

She was out of her depth. Usually she was the one who saw five steps ahead. But while she was scheming her way out of their engagement, Malcolm had been planning for their inevitable future together. So when he demanded her view of it, she didn't have any logic ready.

All she had was instinct.

And instinct told her to jump.

She bridged the distance between them and twined her fingers with his. "This isn't a trick. I want the pleasure you promised me, Malcolm. And I want it tonight."

CHAPTER SEVENTEEN

Amelia held her breath as she waited for Malcolm's response. She had never done anything so brazen. But knowing that he wanted her — not her dowry, or her bloodlines, but *her* — was enthralling. She would see where that desire led.

And if he hurt her, or broke her trust, she could still find her way back to her original path.

He was tightly wound, a grim warrior surveying his captive. Or maybe he was the captive and she was the warrior queen, able to grant mercy if he pleased her. She glimpsed every story between them in that moment, read the web of tangled roles, felt the shifting balances as he regarded her. He took a step toward her, lifted her again, and she sighed against his ear as he cradled her in his arms.

But when he set her on the edge of the bed, he didn't join her. "If you claim you want pleasure, I await your command," he said.

His eyes were hooded and his thoughts were unreadable as he stood before her. She looked away from his eyes, down the slightly crooked nose, the tight lips, the firmly sculpted chin, to the broad shoulders and chest below.

She threw her lot in with the devil. "Take off your jacket," she ordered.

He raised an eyebrow but complied, shrugging out of the tightly fitted jacket and tossing it on a nearby chair. His shoulders were just as wide in his linen shirt as they were in his jacket — no tailor's artifice was responsible for the way she swallowed at the sight of him.

Then he waited.

"Do I really need to ask for everything?" she said, her cheeks already flaming as she struggled to articulate her desires.

Malcolm grinned then, and even though his smile disappeared almost as soon as it arrived, it gave her heart. "This is your adventure, darling, not mine."

"Very well, then," she said, hoping her blush would die. "Remove your cravat and your waistcoat."

Malcolm did as he was instructed, slowly, leisurely, with nothing to hide. His long fingers slowly untied the starched linen cravat, slipping it loose from his neck and letting it slide to the floor.

His eyes met hers as he began to unfasten his waistcoat, and her breath caught. He seemed to be daring her to continue — but could she handle what she asked for?

She broke away from his gaze and watched as each button came free. He threw the waistcoat to join the jacket on the nearby chair.

"Your shirt next," she said, feeling a thread of heat uncurling deep inside her.

He didn't bother with the ties that held the shirt closed. He tugged violently at the neckline, tearing the cloth as he pulled the shirt over his head. She watched the muscles of his stomach ripple as he lifted his arms to pull the shirt off. She had to clasp her hands to stop herself from reaching out and skimming her fingers across the flat planes of his belly.

Malcolm dropped the shirt to the floor and ran a hand through his tousled hair. The warrior look was back. "Should I guess what you will demand next?"

His breeches couldn't conceal the bulge of his manhood. He wasn't as unaffected as he pretended. She heard it in his voice, too — he was dangerously close to taking over, to forgetting his vow to make her say what she wanted.

The devil inside her urged her in a different direction.

She wanted to watch him strip completely, but the need to touch him was too great. "Kiss me," she demanded, grasping his hand and pulling him toward her. Closing her eyes, she lifted her face to meet his.

He grazed the tip of her nose.

"Kiss my mouth," Amelia clarified, gritting her teeth.

Malcolm chuckled, then cupped her face with his hand. His lips claimed hers, and she felt the shock of connection where her lips were still swollen from their previous kiss. She wrapped her arms around the back of his neck, willing him closer. But while the kiss held all the heat and promise of their earlier kisses, he made no move to deepen it. He stayed tightly in control, even when she tentatively ran her tongue across his closed lips in silent invitation.

Finally, she pulled away. "You really won't make this easy for me, will you?"

He almost looked contrite, but his eyes were smug. "I'm merely giving you what you want."

There was something undeniably alluring about having him follow her orders. But if she had to stop every minute to issue further instructions, she doubted she would find fulfillment.

She switched tactics. "What would you do if a courtesan asked you to pleasure her? Would you know what to do?"

"Of course," he snorted. "But…"

She cut him off. "Then that's what I want. I want you to pleasure me like that."

"I thought my reference to whores offended you," he said, his harsh tone warning her to stop.

Amelia pushed ahead. "You piqued my interest. You may begin at your leisure."

He eyed her darkly. His expression, so controlled a few moments earlier, was suddenly feral, and she shivered as he pulled her against his chest. The bed still supported her, but just barely. He seemed to like having her reliant on him for support.

But she reached that point again where thought was difficult, and then motivation and machinations didn't matter. Where their last kiss was soft and restrained, this kiss was hot, wet, maddening. He ran his hands over her hair, still pinned tightly to her scalp. His roughness as he loosened hairpins, then braids, only increased her need. Her fingers pressed into his bare shoulders as her golden curls tumbled around them, urging him closer.

He broke away. Her lips parted on a silent question. He shook his head. "I will give you what you asked for," he said. It sounded like a warning as his fingers deftly unfastened her riding jacket. "And you had best not change your mind, because it is too late for me to stop."

He flicked open her jacket, pushing both the jacket sleeves and the thin straps of her chemise over her shoulders. Her arms were trapped by the fitted fabric, but he didn't wait for her to remove them. He untied the neck of her chemise and shoved it down, freeing her breasts and staring at them for one endless moment before kissing her again.

She kissed him back, driven on by the heat building within her. She wanted to touch him, and she struggled against her jacket. He shook her shoulders, just a bit, just until she gave up her efforts and left her arms bound up in velvet.

When she was still, he slowly slid his hands over her tightening nipples. This time, she didn't protest as his lips moved away from hers, didn't try to free her arms. She guessed his destination, and she watched his progress through heavy lids as he swept a trail of kisses down to her breasts.

He slid a hand down to her ankle, skimming his fingers up her calf, tickling them across the sensitive flesh behind her knee, and finally caressing the curve of her derriere. Without breaking the kisses he was bestowing on her bosom, he shifted her and eased her skirts past her hips. She drew a shocked breath as her bare bottom met the cool silk coverlet, then moaned as his mouth abandoned her.

He tugged her skirts above her waist, the yards of velvet pooling on her belly and baring her to his hungry gaze. Ignoring her sounds of protest, he pushed her back to rest on her elbows, knelt before her, and draped her legs over his bare shoulders.

"Malcolm, I don't..." she started to say, but her words fled as his lips found the nub of pleasure hidden beneath her curls.

The arousal caused by watching him undress was nothing compared to the sudden conflagration sparked by this new onslaught. When she cried out, his kisses turned rougher, until every stroke of his tongue was a teasing torment, holding her on the brink of release.

She urged him closer, arching back into the bed, her muscles tensed and trembling with need. But instead of pushing her over the edge, he slowed down, languorously licking and suckling between her soft folds.

He continued this pattern for endless minutes. A few strokes of his tongue on the center of her pleasure would send her to the brink — until he pulled back, kissing her inner thigh or swirling slowly around the outer edges of her opening, leaving her panting with frustration. Then he would start again, stoking the fires within her, until all of her thoughts were consumed with the need to leap over the edge.

Finally, she could take no more. "Malcolm, now," she demanded, wrapping her legs around him as her desire overcame her.

As though he had been waiting for her command, he intensified his assault, flicking his tongue rapidly across her core, and she screamed as she shuddered in climax. The tide as she came took her somewhere beyond thought, to a moment of perfect, endless silence.

She fell back on the bed, breathless, melting, her legs slipping off of Malcolm's shoulders as he pulled away. She slowly came back to earth, still trembling with the aftershocks, and opened her eyes to see Malcolm standing above her. He gave her a self-satisfied grin. She'd lost herself for a moment, but he had found her, and she thought the gleam in his eyes looked almost devious.

They regarded each other for long moments. Malcolm watched her with the intensity of a predator readying for the kill. Amelia couldn't resist him even if she wanted to — and with the memory of his mouth still on her flesh, she thought she might never resist him again.

"Are you satisfied?" she asked.

His laugh was pained. "Hardly. But I trust that you want me."

Her gaze dropped to his crotch, still rock hard under his breeches. "I'm not convinced you want me, MacCabe."

She'd never called him that. He arched a brow. "What proof does the lady require?"

Amelia shrugged out of her jacket, leaving her upper body bare as her chemise fell to her waist. Malcolm watched, his eyes narrowing as he sought control, and she pulled him down into another kiss. It was brief, but she found his hunger and the shocking taste of herself on his lips.

She broke it off, then repeated his words. "If you want pleasure, I await your command."

*   *   *

He wanted her. By God, he wanted her. He wanted to plunge into her, bury himself in her warmth, feel her clench around him as they both came. Or feel her lips wrap around his cock, her tongue a glorious torment. She was on his bed, half dressed, offering it all to him.

He wanted to take it.

His hand was already moving toward his buttons when he stopped himself. He hooked his thumbs in his breeches. "I want you. But I can't have you."

Her eyes flickered. "I thought…"

She stopped. She swallowed, hard, and slowly tugged her chemise up over her breasts. "I misunderstood, my lord."

The ice was back in her voice. He pulled her up into his arms and crushed her against his chest.

She tried to pull away, but she couldn't break his grip. He skimmed a hand over her cheek, used it to push her tousled curls back behind her ear. Holding her there, he leaned in and growled, "I want you, Amelia. I want you everywhere, in every way."

She shuddered against him, leaned in to rest her forehead on his shoulder. She still wasn't talking, though.

He brushed a kiss on her neck and felt a tremor of her reaction. "Amelia, understand. If we were married, nothing would stop me from taking everything you offer. But you're still a lady. I won't risk leaving you with my child until we're safely wed."

She stroked his chest, letting her hand rest over his pounding heart. "I'm half tempted to shoot you."

His lips curved as he moved lower, pushed her chemise aside to kiss her shoulder. "Save your bullets for after the wedding — it will take an army to get me out of your bed then."

She laughed, the ice melting. "I'll ask Alex to add militia expenditures to the settlements."

"Consider it done, my lady," he said, nipping her earlobe with his teeth. She arched against him, her laughter turning breathy.

He didn't want to stop. And for a few moments he didn't. He let himself kiss her, let his tongue have what his cock could not, and it was both pleasure and torment. No matter what else happened between them, this — this pleasure, this need, this connection — was real.

Finally, he broke it off. She moaned in protest, but he had to retreat. The pressure in his balls wouldn't let him stop if he didn't end it now. "No more, Amelia. I'm dying."

"You deserve to, if you leave me like this," she said, breathless.

How many other women in the ton felt like that? For all that Amelia wasn't what he'd sought when thinking of marriage, he was glad that he hadn't gotten what he wanted. He thought back to Alastair's comment about finding pleasure in duty.

With Amelia, it was impossible to tell where duty ended and pleasure began.

"Four days, darling. Our wedding is four days from now. We can survive until then."

He wasn't sure he could, and Amelia's face said the same. But that dark look was in her eyes, the one his seductions momentarily expelled, the one that always came back. "How can I know it will always be like this between us?"

"You can't," he said, his impatience sparking. "No one can see the future. But I can guarantee that if you walk away, you will never find anything like this again. Better the devil you know, darling."

She closed her eyes.

He waited. There was nothing else, short of force, that he could do to convince her to give up her fantasies of evading their wedding. He wasn't so noble that he wouldn't use it. Alex would never let her leave Scotland unwed if he knew what had happened tonight. But there was still time to let her make this decision on her own. And he would rather have her think she had chosen freely than hate him for making that choice for her.

Finally, she opened her eyes, leveling them on him. He felt another jolt of lust. Her gaze was direct, challenging — the meeting of an equal, not the submissive frailty of most debutantes. He wouldn't mind her submission, but the challenge she presented made him ache for her.

"You negotiated the settlements with Alex," she said, her voice clear and steady. "But I want to add my own terms."

"You couldn't be better provided for. The settlements for your widowhood are extremely generous. I will show you what we agreed to, if Alex hasn't yet."

She waved a hand at that. "I trust both you and Alex know how to arrange finances. I don't care about the money."

"Then what do you care about?" he asked.

Amelia paused, and he saw her struggling to decide something. His fiancée still had secrets. Would she share them now?

"I know you need a political wife," she said when she finally spoke. "I don't mind attending parties, and I will do my best to host whatever you wish. But socializing is not what I want to do with my life. If you promise that I can use my days however I choose, I will marry you without complaint."

"What do you want to do with your time?" he asked.

"What I've always done — read, write letters, visit with my friends," she replied.

Her voice was light. But then, her request seemed light. Most aristocratic wives spent their days engaged in precisely those activities, without needing special dispensations from their husbands to do so.

He didn't let on that she had aroused his suspicions. "I'm not a tyrant, darling. If you want to visit your friends when we are in town, I won't stop you."

She looked up at him, her eyes flickering back and forth across his face as she tried to read his intentions. He hoped he looked supportive, not curious. Whatever she saw must have satisfied her, because he felt her relax, just a little, in his arms.

It wasn't much, but it was enough to make him wonder.

"Is there anything else you wish to agree to before the wedding? Anything you should tell me?"

Amelia looked at his feet. "As we discussed, I don't have any secret children or scandalous former lovers. You'll find me quite boring, I'm sure."

It was an adequate answer, even though she hadn't specifically said that she had nothing to tell him. He let it go. It wasn't like him to leave a thread dangling, but whatever her secret was, it wasn't anything that would excuse him in the eyes of the ton — or his own conscience — if he jilted her.

So he laughed instead of questioning her further. "Never boring, Amelia. Whatever awaits us, it won't be boredom."

She smiled up at him, and his suspicions were temporarily buried. It was enough to have her in his bed. Theirs wasn't a love match and might never be, if his duty to his clan occupied him as much as it should. But they would still find pleasure together.

And if love didn't grow between them — he told himself that lust would surely be enough.

CHAPTER EIGHTEEN

Amelia survived until the fourth day — but only just. In the moments when her mother, and then Madeleine and Ellie, left her alone, the solitude that usually helped her to temper her emotions gave her too much time to think. Her thoughts oscillated wildly between excitement and escape, between eagerness for Malcolm's touch and fear that her attraction to him would destroy her.

As the carriage carrying her to the church lurched on the rough road, she thought it wasn't so farfetched that he might be her doom. She had behaved like an utter wanton when he demanded it, needing only the slightest encouragement to ask for the pleasure she'd always denied herself. When she awoke the next morning, safely tucked into her own bed after sneaking across the length of the darkened castle, she was ashamed that he had stopped when she had not. If he hadn't pushed her away, she would have ended the night in his bed, beyond all reasonable thought, and no longer a virgin.

Tonight, her first night as Malcolm's countess, her virginity would likely be gone. Malcolm wouldn't refrain again, not when he watched her for the past three days like a rebel readying an ambush. But she hoped she maintained her reason. She couldn't afford to give away her sanity, not if she wanted to remember who she was and what she really wanted from her life.

Madeleine interrupted her brooding. "You're frowning, Mellie. What is the matter?"

Amelia gripped the strap affixed to the wall as the carriage jolted on another rut. "We should have ridden to the church. This road is abominable."

"Is that all that bothers you?" Madeleine asked.

"Of course not," Amelia snapped. "If I recall, you had nerves on your wedding day and I didn't press you about them."

"Likely because you were hoping I would give in to them and toss Ferguson aside," she retorted with a laugh.

"I will allow that I was not precisely charitable about the Duke of Rothwell's pursuit of you," Amelia said. She continued over Madeleine's snort. "But I do see the depth of your feelings for him. It made your wedding day a joy rather than a burden."

She and Madeleine were in a carriage, their last moments alone before Amelia's wedding. Amelia's mother and Lady Carnach had gone ahead, as had Ellie, Ferguson, his sisters, and Malcolm's brothers. They would be waiting in the church, or the kirk, as the MacCabes called it. And Malcolm would be there too, ready to claim the rest of her life as his own.

She shuddered, just a bit, but Madeleine saw it. She reached out and took Amelia's hand. "Are you sure you see Malcolm as a burden?"

Amelia wasn't sure, but she couldn't keep thinking about it if she wanted to walk down the aisle without bolting. "What will be will be, Madeleine. My fate is tied to him whether I like it or not."

Madeleine didn't respond. Amelia stared out the window. The Highlands were a fairy tale — hills and crags covered in vegetation and drenched in mist. It was raining on her wedding day. She tried not to take it as an omen.

"Do you love him?" Madeleine asked, squeezing her hand.

Amelia sucked in a breath. "I barely know the man."

"I didn't know Ferguson above a fortnight before he offered for me, but I already knew I would love him."

Amelia pulled away from Madeleine's grasp. "Not all of us are so blessed, Maddie."

She was prevaricating, though. It was true she barely knew Malcolm. All the little facts, like what pudding he preferred, whether he liked to hunt, and where he bought his boots, were a complete mystery to her.

But she knew he was a good man. And she knew he could win her heart with nothing more than a quirk of his grin and the occasional moonlit adventure. She had never believed someone could scale her barricades so effortlessly. The thought of falling for him, of losing her heart and giving him everything, scared her more than anything else.

She wasn't eager to see the church, but at least their arrival ended Madeleine's questions. Through the window, the church loomed, ancient and imposing. Flowers arced over the doorway, dripping slowly onto the stone steps. Alex waited under the arch, ready to escort her.

Amelia willed a smile onto her face. She was nervous beyond belief — but no one in the church, least of all Malcolm, would see her fear.

*   *   *

Malcolm stood at the altar, feet firmly planted, hands clasped behind his back. The raucous laughter of his cousins and connections in the pews behind him filled his ears, making him wish they had eloped instead.

It would have been easy to elope. Any other parish in the area would have sufficed. Scottish marriages were easier to obtain than English ones, without the nonsense of reading banns or procuring special licenses.

Still, he didn't like standing in front of his clan, hearing their carousing, and knowing he hadn't done his utmost to fulfill his duty to them. Amelia would do as his countess — she was now the only woman he could imagine in that role — but she wasn't the cool political bride he had intended to give his clan.

He just had to hope they wouldn't all pay dearly for the ill-advised kiss that forced them into this.

He cast a sidelong glance at Duncan and Douglas, who leaned against the wall on the right side of the sanctuary. They were flashing hand signals at each other. From their devious grins and the direction of their stares, he suspected they were making an utterly scandalous wager about the availability of Ferguson's twin sisters.

Malcolm sighed. His brothers were free to marry whomever they wanted. But he should have followed his duty, not his cock.

"Second thoughts?" Ferguson murmured from his place at Malcolm's side.

"Is it that obvious?"

Alastair, standing in front of them, looked up from the sermon he was reading to himself. "You look ready for an execution, not a wedding."

Malcolm jerked his head back at the gathered throng. "Our relations are ready for an execution as well. You could have made a fortune on the ceremony if you had brought meat pies to sell them during my beheading."

"That might have been adequate recompense for the flock of sheep I'm missing," Ferguson mused.

Malcolm laughed. "You should be more careful with your livestock. You've a duchess to support now."

"I don't care for sheep nearly as much as you do, it's true," Ferguson said.

Alastair snorted at the jibe, then tried to look pious.

"If you won't care for your estate, you might at least look out for your sisters," Malcolm said, nodding toward Duncan and Douglas.

Ferguson looked over, and his smirk turned to a scowl. Malcolm laughed again. Really, if he could have this with Amelia — the conversation, the comfort, the humor — he would be a happy man. Add in her luscious body, and he would probably die from pleasure long before his clan noticed that he hadn't been particularly dutiful.

And if marrying her was a mistake…

It couldn't be a mistake.

But if it was…he would enjoy the mistake as long as it lasted. Knowing Amelia, if their marriage was bad, she would find a way to escape long before he needed to send her away.

He heard the inner door of the church bang against the wall as someone threw it open. He turned and saw young Angus MacCabe, the son of one of his fourth cousins, run in through the open door. "The ladies are here!" he shouted.

Alastair picked up his prayer book, trying to compose himself.

Duncan signaled something to Douglas, who laughed aloud — then stopped abruptly at a glare from Ferguson.

And Malcolm's blood turned to ice. In a few moments, Amelia would be his. And with her came a whole world of possibilities.

He said a silent prayer that she would be capable of seeing them.

*　　*　　*

Amelia waited in the carriage as her brother helped Madeleine out of it and escorted her into the church. Madeleine laughed at something Alex said as he opened the door, and Alex's answering smile was the first bit of happiness she'd seen on his face since before he found her and Malcolm in the library.

He had returned from Edinburgh the previous day, saying nothing about Prudence other than that he had found a post chaise to take her safely to London. Amelia didn't deserve a message, but the lack of one fed her guilt.

She drew in a breath and wiped her hands on her skirts. The gesture didn't alleviate the clamminess inside her gloves. She picked up her bouquet, a dramatic clutch of white hydrangeas that stood starkly against the icy blue silk of her newest dress. When she'd purchased it in London before the trip, she hadn't intended for it to be her wedding dress, but it was an appropriate nod to the blues that featured prominently in the MacCabe colors.

Alex strode over and opened the carriage door again. "Ready, Amelia?"

He reached up and plucked her out of the carriage, setting her down carefully to avoid any puddles that would soak through her slippers. She was grateful that the rain had subsided to a drizzle; when she took off her pelisse and handed it to a servant standing near the door, her dress still looked dry.

She held out her arm for Alex, but he didn't offer his to her. Instead, he pulled her into a hug. "I wish you very happy, Amelia. I hope you know that."

All morning, her eyes had stayed dry — but Alex's gruff tone was enough to wet them. "I know, Alex. I hope you find your happiness too."

He shrugged, then squeezed her again before stepping back. "With you and Madeleine settled, perhaps I shall."

"As though we held you back. I rather think it's your books that keep you unwed, not Madeleine and I."

Alex started to ruffle her hair, but she yelped and he remembered not to muss her hairstyle. "We all have our passions, do we not?" he said.

He didn't know about her writing. For the first time, though, she wished she had told him. His duty had made him stuffy, but he had never discouraged her. If anything, until Malcolm came along, he had been more accommodating than any other guardian she knew.

She wondered again why he had been so quick to make her marry Malcolm, particularly when he knew just as well as she did that Prudence needed the match. But the start of her wedding wasn't the time for confessions or confrontations.

She lightened her tone. "Perhaps Madeleine and I should force you to marry, since you've done all the honors so far," she teased.

Alex had the grace to laugh. "If you find the woman who equals either of you, send her my way."

She took Alex's arm and let him lead her across the vestibule toward the inner sanctuary door. Amelia hadn't intended to marry. But she would walk into the church like she wanted to be there, like she had no doubts at all about this union. She owed it to her family. She owed it to Prudence.

She owed it to Malcolm.

They paused long enough for someone to open the final door. Her hand tightened in the crook of Alex's arm; the other made a fist around the flowers she carried.

When Alex escorted her into the church, suddenly walking faster than she could ever be ready for, she felt like she had been dumped into another time. The crowd was positively medieval, boisterous and enthusiastic, more like fairgoers than the stern, somber Presbyterians she had expected. She knew the MacCabes belonged to the Church of England, but even in the south, she had never seen a church with such an air of raucous celebration.

If this was a fair, she was the main event. Alex half-dragged her up the aisle. She looked straight ahead to the man who waited for her. She felt like a jouster without a horse, moving inexorably toward her foe.

Not her foe. Her husband.

His gaze was hot and heady as she approached. If he had looked like a rebel planning an ambush before, this was the moment when his efforts bore fruit. As Malcolm took her arm from Alex, she felt the unbreakable strength of his grip — and the restraint as he brushed a kiss across her knuckles, then stopped himself from doing anything else.

She smiled at him. Then she realized her smile was genuine, which only made her smile more.

Amelia was afraid — no, terrified — of what marriage meant.

But if she had to stand in front of an altar, Malcolm was the only man she wished to stand there with.

"You are the most beautiful woman I have ever seen," he said.

She thought Ellie and Madeleine, standing just behind her, were both prettier than her, but the way Malcolm looked at her made her believe it. For a moment, it was just the two of them. If it could always be just the two of them, perhaps she wouldn't be scared. A life with him, and without any other social ties, sounded almost perfect.

"You are quite handsome yourself, my lord," she replied.

"Not the most handsome man in all the land?"

She laughed. "You are, but I wouldn't want it to go to your head."

He grinned at her. Her stomach settled into place. When Alastair cleared his throat, she stood beside Malcolm, somehow relaxed and nervous all at once.

The ceremony passed quickly. Later, she wouldn't remember most of it. She remembered their vows, though. And when she looked at Malcolm directly, their eyes focused only on each other as he held her hand.

He was a more polished version of the man she had first kissed in the library. His hair, while still longer than fashionable, was better controlled, and he had removed all trace of stubble from his face. The smoothness only highlighted the sharp, angular planes of his jaw, and even though his aquiline nose had been broken at some point in the past, he still looked entirely in command. She felt a brief thrill as he vowed to have and to hold her forevermore.

He was the first man she'd ever known who seemed capable of that vow.

Malcolm finished in a strong, steady voice, without a hint of regret. She managed to match his confidence. If she faltered a little over her vow to obey him, he didn't seem inclined to hold it against her. His lips twitched, and half the clan snickered, but his grip on her hand was reassuring.

When she finished, she thought she heard her mother sigh with relief, but she couldn't look away from Malcolm long enough to check. Taking the ring from Alastair, he slid it onto her finger.

"With my body, I thee worship," he said, amusement — and something else — evident in his voice.

He caressed the palm of her hand as he left the ring in place, and she felt a brief flare of heat. The gold band, its perfect square-cut sapphire surrounded by a circle of diamonds, seemed to carry a weight of cool foreboding, but she dismissed the thought. Bad omens were good for her stories, but they had no place in real life — not if she wanted to avoid turning her marriage into a Gothic horror.

The rest of the ceremony passed in a blur, until Alastair closed his prayer book and allowed his solemn façade to crack. "Welcome to the clan, Amelia," he said warmly, before raising his voice to address the crowd. "Ladies and gentlemen, I present to you the Earl and Countess of Carnach!"

The church erupted in cheers, as though they had witnessed a match born out of love rather than coercion. They grew even louder when Alastair said, "Malcolm, you may kiss your bride."

Amelia turned to face her new husband, and she caught a brief flash of some strong emotion lurking in his eyes before he reached out, tilted her face upward, and kissed her. The kiss was just as hot and intense as their first kiss, but something had changed. He tasted of peppermint rather than whisky. And this wasn't a seduction, but a possession. It ended almost immediately, but Amelia could still feel the heat of his mouth on hers.

She wanted to kiss him again. His silver eyes mirrored her desire. But there would be time for that — time for everything, now that their lives were intertwined.

As they walked back up the aisle, showered with cheers and laughter, she felt the first true crack in her heart.

And at that moment, she knew she was doomed.

CHAPTER NINETEEN

The wedding breakfast wasn't a small family gathering — it was a feast fit for a medieval laird, filling the great hall with every man, woman, and child within two hours' walk of the castle. The festivities spilled out onto the lawn, and the feasting looked ready to continue for another week.

Amelia wasn't sure she could last another hour.

She drummed her fingers on the ancient oak table, next to her nearly untouched plate. The breakfast — if one could call a meal of this magnitude a breakfast — had already lasted three hours, and the kitchen was still sending up vast platters of food. Perhaps she should have been more involved in the planning, if only to shorten the celebration.

To her left, Malcolm tilted a bottle of champagne into her glass. They'd said little at the table — but there was little they could say, sitting side by side at a grand table on the dais overlooking the hall, flanked by their families.

They hadn't said much in the carriage after the ceremony, either. Then again, it was hard to talk when their tongues were intertwined.

She stopped drumming her fingers and picked up the champagne. She hadn't wanted to marry him and didn't intend to obey him — and yet, when she kissed Malcolm, she forgot all that.

And if she was now obliged to share his bed, if she could give in to all her hidden desires with no repercussions — why did she have to wait another minute for him?

"You're blushing, darling," he murmured in her ear.

She sipped her drink, then looked sidelong at him under her lashes. "You would be too if you knew my thoughts."

She felt like a hoyden, but his lips curved into a smile that matched hers. "If you knew my thoughts, that pretty blush of yours would be permanent."

It was so odd to want him. The heat of it scared her. It shamed her, too. She wasn't ashamed to want him, but such base physical desires could utterly destroy her reason.

She could regain her reason tomorrow. She took another sip of champagne. "You won't find me easy to shock, my lord."

His hand slid down to her thigh, and the weight and heat of it seared through the silk. "And you won't find me easily satisfied."

She turned to face him fully. Time compressed in that moment, froze them for endless seconds. At the very end of her life, in her final moments, she would remember the hunger in his grey eyes, the sensual curve of his lips, and the way he wanted her — her, not titles or dowries or political machinations. In that beginning, at the creation of their world, the need and longing that flared between them overwhelmed everything else.

That morning, she didn't know whether the longing would transform into love, or fade into apathy. She just knew she had to see where it would end.

He stood before she realized what he was about, then swooped down and plucked her from her chair. She reached for his arm. He dipped and slung her arm over his neck, picking her up and cradling her to his chest.

"Malcolm," she exclaimed, "you're mad."

He kissed her forehead as his clan cheered. "It's something of a tradition here. Unless you aren't done eating?"

"Very well," she said, suddenly feeling like her prim London vocabulary had no words for what she felt, to ask for what she wanted.

Malcolm knew, though. Her spine was rigid as he carried her through the hall. The ribald suggestions shouted by the clan discomfited her. But she relaxed against his chest after he cleared the stairs to the family wing.

"A strange tradition, don't you think?" she asked.

His hand caressed her hip. "I thought so, but now I see the appeal. The first earl kidnapped his bride, and it ended as a love match. Carrying you off is supposed to be good luck."

"You haven't conquered me, you know," she said.

Malcolm paused just long enough to kiss her. "I will."

She should have been insulted, but his smug, confident grin as he strode toward the end of the passageway made her want to kiss him again. "Perhaps I shall conquer you instead."

He shouldered open the door to his bedchamber and kicked it closed behind him. "You can try any time you like, darling. But today — today I have plans for you."

He dropped her onto the bed, and she squealed as she hit the mattress. The sheets had been turned down by an expectant servant, and the drapes were shut. Malcolm left her sprawled inelegantly on the bed and went to the window to fling back the curtains.

"What are you doing?" she asked, coming up on her elbows.

He fiddled with the ties to hold the curtains back. The rain had stopped, and a bit of sun strayed through the glass. "I have to see you,

Amelia."

She felt a brief twinge of nerves. What if he didn't like what he saw? "I don't think that's necessary."

He opened the next set of curtains. "Do you know how your hair gleams in the sun, Amelia?" he asked. "In candlelight, it looks like spun gold. But in the middle of the day, it looks like an angel's halo. If the rest of you is that heavenly…"

He trailed off. She swallowed hard as he turned to run a slow, roving gaze over her body. Sprawled on his bed, her legs spread and her breath shallow, she did feel conquered — and he hadn't even touched her.

She lifted her hand toward him, inviting him with her body since she couldn't find the words. He took two steps, sat on the edge of the bed, and brought her fingers to his mouth.

"I'm going to make you feel, Amelia. I'm going to hear you scream my name. And whether you wanted to marry me or not, by the time you leave this bed, you'll never again doubt that we were made for this."

She shuddered. She already felt. All the emotions she'd always kept in check were inches away from breaking through her last defenses. She wasn't ready to let them out. The panic clawed at her, telling her he couldn't see everything, that she couldn't let him get that close.

Then he kissed her.

The panic didn't die, but it retreated just enough to let her kiss him back.

He must have felt her tension. He pulled away. "Are you ready?" he asked.

It nearly undid her. The thread of sensual promise was still there. But when was the last time someone had been concerned for her? Not about her, but for her?

"I'm…" She took a breath. "I want to be. But I — it's —"

She was incoherent. Amelia Staunton was never incoherent. Perhaps as Lady Carnach she would never have the right words again. That thought made the panic bubble up again.

His hand was gentle as he smoothed a bit of hair away from her face. "It will be all right, darling. I will always make it right for you."

She nodded just the tiniest bit against his hand. "I am ready," she said.

It was only a partial lie.

The smile she glimpsed before he kissed her again was joy overlaid with barely concealed need. She forced herself through her fear, let her body take over, gave herself permission to wrap an arm around his neck. She pulled him deeper, welcomed him into her mouth as her other hand stroked his cheek.

His hands were already lifting her up to fumble with the buttons of her dress. He couldn't undo them all, though, not in their current position. She swallowed his sigh as he pulled away from her mouth.

"Should I call my maid?"

"I doubt my esteemed ancestor called a maid." His grin was devious. "Turn over."

She hesitated.

"Trust me," he said.

Amelia did trust him, at least with this. She turned over, lying flat on her stomach. Her dress tangled around her legs and she pillowed her head on her crossed arms. Being unable to see him and unaware of his intentions should have scared her.

Instead, it added a new dimension to her need.

She felt him slide closer, until the muscled flesh of his hip and thigh pressed against her side. Her hair was still up, but he made quick work of that, tugging out her pins until he was able to sift her hair through his fingers.

"Are you an angel or a devil?" he asked, whispering the question through her golden curls.

She shivered. He brushed her hair away from her neck, revealing the buttons he'd already undone.

Then he slipped the next one free. It only revealed her chemise, but he kissed her there anyway. Then the next button — and another kiss.

Her dress had forty buttons.

She counted as he moved lower. She never knew how many buttons there were, but as he pressed a kiss into the curve of her back, just above her derriere, she didn't think she would ever ignore how her dresses fastened again.

Eventually her dress was fully opened. She felt the fabric gaping to bare her to him. But her stays and chemise still thwarted them. He unlaced her quickly, flicking the stays apart.

Then he whispered another question against her ear. "Do you care about your chemise?"

She shook her head. The beginning of that gesture was enough. He impatiently brushed away the curls that had fallen against her neck as she'd trembled under his kisses. Then he ripped open her chemise.

The sound was barbaric, echoing through the room. Her elation matched it.

"God, Amelia," he breathed as he slid his hand down her spine. He kissed the hollow of her back again, right where his hand caressed her whenever they walked together. The curious mix of seduction and possession made her writhe against the covers.

"Please," she gasped, clawing into the sheets as he nipped her with his teeth, then sucked against her skin.

The languorous exploration turned into ravenous hunger. She

wanted to touch him, was desperate to kiss him. She turned over without prompting, then sat up and slid her arms out of her dress. Her stays fell around her and she tossed them aside.

Her ruined chemise still offered some protection. She stopped, hugging an arm around her chest. "Are you not going to undress?" she asked.

He was half-reclined against her. Instead of moving to disrobe, he hooked a finger under the hem of her sleeve. "You've already bade me to undress before you once. It's time to repay the favor."

She was maddeningly aware of all the layers between them — chemise, dress, stockings, and slippers, not to mention everything from his cravat to his buckled shoes. She was eager to see him, to feel whatever he had promised to make her feel.

Theoretically, they didn't have to rush. They were married now. They could stay in this bed as long as they liked.

Amelia didn't want to think in terms of decades. She wanted him fast, before her logic overruled her. And she knew just how to spur his seduction.

She rolled away from him, off the bed before he reached for her. When she stood, she let her dress pool at her feet. She kicked off her shoes next, then reached up under her chemise and untied her garters, giving him a generous view of her bosom as she bent down to pull the stockings free.

She stepped to the side, leaving her clothes huddled on the floor. Malcolm leaned up on his elbow, stretched out on the bed. His eyes were intent on her fingers as she bent to grasp the lower hem of her chemise. She could have stepped out of it, too, but the hoyden hiding within her urged a different tack.

She lifted her chemise, closing her eyes as she felt the cloth clear her legs, then her belly, then her breasts. His breath turned sharp, and she heard him shift on the bed. As her chemise slid over her face, she grinned.

Her grin turned into a laugh as his arm suddenly wrapped around her waist.

He kissed her, stealing away her laughter. She tugged at his cravat. He unbuttoned his jacket, then his waistcoat, pulling away from her only to shed the tight garments and leave them on the growing mound of clothes. His shirt was next, jerked out of his trousers and pulled over his head, leaving his chest as bare as hers.

Amelia grazed her fingers across his torso, feeling the planes of his muscles and the odd dip over his pelvic bone that was so different from her own soft flesh. He groaned but didn't stop her as she fumbled with the fastenings of his trousers, suddenly clumsy. He held his hands on his hips, daring her to continue.

He was nearly as chiseled as any ancient statue, but he wasn't cold — he was heat, and velvet, with a surprising amount of dark hair leading down his belly toward the opening she worked to unfasten. And when she finally succeeded, when his trousers fell open and the bulge she'd felt but never seen finally sprang free, she realized she'd been misled by all those statues.

He was enormous, far larger than anything she'd seen erect in marble. He jutted up toward her, the purpose obvious, but she didn't see how he could possibly fit.

"This will never work," she said, stepping back until her knees hit the bed.

Malcolm laughed as he discarded his shoes, trousers and small clothes. "My pride thanks you. But it will work."

He tipped her onto the bed. She scooted back toward the pillows and he grabbed her ankle. "We will fit," he said again, "but only when you're ready."

"I thought I was ready, but now..."

He kissed her thigh, then moved lower, kissing her knee before moving toward her foot. "You're still too composed, darling. I want you to need me so badly that you can't think about anything else. Then you'll be ready."

It didn't take long. Her thoughts were already fleeing before his onslaught, her defenses shattering with every advance of his clever tongue. He murmured compliments against her skin. Every word felt like a charm binding her to the bed, tying her to him.

With him, she believed the words. In his gravelly voice, layered with lust and awe, she heard how desirable she was. When her legs opened for him and he grinned up at her with his dark hair falling into his eyes, her last thought was that here, now, she finally wasn't alone.

Some endless time later, he found her mouth again. She quivered under him, had been quivering for what felt like hours, and she moaned as his hand fondled her breast. "What are you thinking of?" he whispered.

"You," she said, pulling him back against her lips.

His hand slipped between her legs and found the slick moisture there. "Now you're ready," he said.

"Are you?" she asked.

His laugh, short and pained, was answer enough. His fingers stroked, teased, until her breath turned ragged and her back ached from arching so high to meet his touch.

"Malcolm — please, Malcolm," she moaned as he pulled just out of reach.

He moved over her and positioned himself so that his manroot grazed her sex. He was slow and careful, and she felt his control as he pressed forward an inch, then another. The pain was sharp at first, but it dulled as she stretched around him. She felt deliciously full, just short of discomfort, like he was a feast and she had gorged herself on him.

He shifted within her. The movement stroked some hidden part of her she'd never known of before. She gasped as he retreated, then gasped again as he plunged into her. He filled her completely, and with every stroke she craved the next one, absolutely desperate for the one that would hurl her over the edge.

When it finally came, her mouth opened in a silent scream as her body disintegrated. There was nothing left of her but the place where their bodies joined, no feeling but the fire that consumed her, no breath to say his name.

She shuddered. She felt him stiffen, heard him grunt as his seed spilled into her womb. He collapsed onto her, his breath hot and harsh against her ear.

When the bits and pieces of her body came back together, she realized she was holding his hand. His fingers pressed her wedding band against her skin, just as his body held her firm against the bed.

When he rolled off her, she didn't think — she curled into his arms, stroked a hand across his chest, and fell asleep. Her ring and his muscled chest were the last things she saw.

And in the haze of her midday dream, she saw castles and coronets instead of cottages and quills.

So when she awoke later to find Malcolm ready for her again, she obliged — if only so she wouldn't have to think of what her dream meant until her logic returned to save her.

CHAPTER TWENTY

14 October 1812

It had been two weeks since her wedding day, and Amelia still felt illogical. She knew what it felt like to live in a dream — the feeling came over her whenever her writing flowed through her fingers like blood onto the page, wrung out of her with every breath.

But in her old life, the dreams used to fade when she stopped writing and spent time with her family. With Malcolm, she always felt on the verge of some dream world, tumbling headlong into his eyes when he gave her one of his heated looks, abandoning all thought to fall into his arms.

It was most disconcerting. Amelia Staunton never behaved like this. Apparently as the new Lady Carnach, her behavior had changed as irrevocably as her name.

Malcolm sat next to her now, whipping a two-seat curricle up the drive toward Ferguson and Madeleine's estate. At least beside him, she couldn't look into his eyes. She could pretend that she was still capable of feelings beyond arousal, or contemplating events beyond the next day.

When she did think of the future, the path that presented itself — hostess, mother, widow, dowager — scared her. She wouldn't dwell on it today, not when the weather was so perfect. They'd chosen a sunny day for their visit, warmer than usual, with just a hint of clouds in the distance. It was safer to embrace the moment and ignore the rest. As long as she and Malcolm stayed in Scotland, she could pretend that this was a blissful holiday rather than the first part of a life she hadn't planned for.

"Ferguson's manor is ahead," Malcolm said, loosely gripping the reins.

She shaded her eyes with her hand. "But it's so…"

"Small?" Malcolm suggested. "Not all clans have castles, darling."

"Its size is adequate, but it's so much plainer than I expected," Amelia said. The house, still half a mile away, had none of the ornate, imposing dominance of Ferguson's London townhouse.

"Don't let Ferguson hear you calling his estate plain," Malcolm said. "It may be small compared to his English holdings, but he's utterly besotted with it."

"I'm sure I won't insult the duke's house."

Malcolm glanced at her. "I still don't understand why you despise each other so thoroughly."

"I don't despise him," she said.

"Really?"

Ferguson had been perfectly civil at their wedding. And Amelia had to admit he and Madeleine were happy together.

She said as much to Malcolm. "Ferguson is my cousin by marriage and your closest friend. I will gladly steal his sheep, but I won't insult him in his own house."

Even over the breeze, his laugh rumbled in her ear. "Say the word, darling, and we will toss it all aside to become reivers. We could be the most feared partners in the Highlands within the year."

She laughed with him. But his words squeezed her heart. "Would you really stay here? Abandon London?"

She glanced at him. His profile hardened into a frown. "If I could, I would. But…"

He trailed off. If he finished the thought, it was stolen by the wind.

*   *   *

Madeleine served them luncheon as soon as they arrived. She'd been a duchess for five months, but it still felt odd to watch her preside over a gathering rather than hovering around the sides of it. An outdated, drafty dining room in the Highlands was as far removed from the theatres of Covent Garden as anywhere Amelia had seen her — and yet, somehow, Madeleine was in her element.

"Do you not care for the dessert, Mellie?" Madeleine asked.

It was some sort of pudding, delicious enough, but Amelia had spent more time staring at it than sampling it. "Just woolgathering, I'm afraid. Everything is lovely."

Malcolm dug his spoon into her dish, drawing a giggle from Ferguson's sister Maria. "You mustn't waste it," he said. "Ferguson is known for his frugality."

The room seemed to verify his claim, with the ancient, faded drapes and the threadbare carpet. But Ferguson's perfectly tailored jacket and gleaming Hessians told a different story. "If I seem frugal in the Highlands, it's only so I have less for my neighbors to purloin," he drawled.

Malcolm raised his glass to Madeleine. "If the pickings are better in London, Duchess, I do hope you will invite us to Rothwell House as soon as we arrive."

Madeleine laughed. "Be warned that we've enough footmen at Rothwell House to raise a battalion. And our butler can count spoons better than Ferguson's shepherds can count sheep."

Even though Amelia could barely remember the food she'd just eaten, the luncheon was one of the loveliest entertainments she'd had in ages. Madeleine had settled into her role, directing the servants discreetly, keeping the conversation flowing. It wasn't a hard task, with the familiar company assembled — only the two couples, with Ellie, Maria, and Kate scattered around them. But Amelia saw the hostess Madeleine might become. She had always held the seed of it, and her love for Ferguson gave it space to bloom.

Malcolm set aside his spoon as Ferguson rose. "Ladies, shall we leave you to your gossip?" he asked.

"I'm sure we will speak of more edifying topics than gossip," Madeleine said.

"Then you're better souls than I — I intend to demand every bit of gossip from MacCabe," Ferguson said.

Madeleine smiled at her husband. Amelia saw something flit across her face — just an instant of it, before it subsided beneath her grin. Persephone might have looked at Hades that way, over her dish of pomegranate seeds — like she was ruined for all other men and wouldn't choose any other fate.

She wondered what her own face said when she looked at Malcolm. His eyes held hers for a moment, a dark lover ready to consume. His grin said he wanted to taste all of her. And his voice, when he told her not to miss him, held a contradictory command. He wanted her to think of him while she was visiting her friends, to think of nothing but returning to him.

Amelia shook her head as he followed Ferguson and the promise of a drink. She usually only thought of characters like this. Somewhere, somehow, Malcolm had become part of her story — the story of her life, which she hadn't let herself contemplate until now. Three weeks ago, she would have called him the villain. He would cast himself as the hero.

Either way, she had to clear her head. She needed reason and pragmatism, not emotions and fantasy.

"The pudding may not have been to her liking, but I think her marriage is," Ellie commented to Madeleine.

"Strange, isn't it?" Madeleine responded. "I thought she'd be spitting nails at the man, and instead she looks ready to swoon at his feet."

"I'm still capable of hearing you," Amelia snapped. She didn't enjoy being talked about, but at least their jesting brought some of her old spirit back. "And I won't swoon at anyone's feet."

"Careful what you vow, Lady Carnach. You also said you'd never marry, and yet here you are."

Madeleine's French accent was most obvious when she was amused, and Amelia's marriage had amused her enough that one might guess she was a just-arrived émigré. "You made that vow yourself, Duchess."

Ellie stood, tossing her napkin aside. "Can we adjourn to the drawing room? I would much rather hash over Amelia's marriage with a cup of tea and a comfortable chair."

"The comfortable chair may be too much to expect," Madeleine warned Amelia, leading all the ladies through the dining room doors to the nearby drawing room. "I suspect Ferguson spent every spare coin he could find on a set of chairs for his study several years ago, but until he inherited the duchy, there wasn't enough money for the renovations this house needs."

She was right about the chairs. No dust sprung from them, but the seats sagged so badly that perhaps the dust was trapped within the fathomless pits where the cushions had once been firm. Amelia sat gingerly on an ancient settee that might have been in service when James I had united the English and Scottish crowns. "Do you intend to remain in Scotland very long?" she asked.

Madeleine adjusted her skirts as she sat in an armchair, ignoring the ominous creak of outraged wood. "Perhaps another week. Ellie and I are making a list of everything that must be replaced, refurbished, repainted, restored — we've spent a fortune just on parchment."

"I do enjoy spending my brother's money," Ellie said as she sat next to Amelia on the settee.

"Not as much as Maria and I enjoyed spending it on new wardrobes," Kate interjected. The twins sat on a pair of backless, armless stools, looking like perfectly matched ladies in waiting, their elegant white day dresses an odd match to the faded, regal brocade of the wall covering behind them.

"Your dresses must be wasted in the Highlands," Amelia commented.

"Oh, we don't mind at all," Maria said. "Anything is better than living with our father."

She was so matter of fact about it, and the previous duke's reputation was so well known, that all Amelia could do was laugh.

"Speaking of being wasted in the Highlands, when will you and Malcolm return to London?" Madeleine asked.

"If I had my preference, it would be later rather than sooner," Amelia said.

Ellie raised an eyebrow, but a footman entered and she saved her comment until he arranged the teacart beside Madeleine's chair. Madeleine thanked him with impeccable grace, spooning leaves into the teapot as though she had been raised with the duty.

Amelia rarely served tea. She could do it, of course, but her mother presided over the teacart at Salford House. And even if she was Lady Carnach now, her mother-in-law still ruled the servants. It wasn't a situation Amelia had thought she needed to change — it was easier to write during the day if she didn't have to plan menus and consult with the housekeeper.

But watching Madeleine, she wondered.

As soon as the footman left, Ellie pounced. "So does your desire to stay in the Highlands mean you've found the answers to my earlier questions? Or are you avoiding them?"

Amelia was lost for a moment. Madeleine grinned at Ellie. "I would put my money on avoidance. If you think Amelia has realized why she was attracted to Carnach, you've been dipping into the sherry without my knowledge."

"Amelia isn't stupid," Ellie mused. "She's surely understood the attraction by now."

Madeleine and Ellie had grown close during their journey, close enough that they shared private jokes just as Amelia and Madeleine had always done. Jealousy added an edge to Amelia's voice. "Could you please stop discussing me like I'm not here?" she demanded.

"Only if you can answer the questions I posed when we visited before your wedding," Ellie said, taking a teacup from Madeleine. "What do you want from Carnach? And what will become of your writing?"

"You asked me what drew me to him, not what I want," Amelia said mulishly.

Ellie waved a hand at that. "It's all from the same cloth. Why stay in the Highlands alone with him if you don't want something from him? You must have feelings for the man if you're willing to forsake all other company."

Amelia paused, reaching for a cup of tea to stall her words. When she spoke, she tasted the lie on her lips. "It's not that I want to spend time with him. I just don't want to return to London."

"If I were Ferguson, I would say 'bollocks' to that," Madeleine said.

"The theatre did not improve your language, did it?" Amelia asked. Madeleine had acted, in disguise, on a public stage for a few weeks the previous spring, which was how she had become attached to Ferguson. The milieu she had found there expanded her knowledge in ways she couldn't acknowledge in more proper company.

Madeleine grinned. "Ferguson is even worse for it. But you like London well enough — unless you've a reason to be afraid of it? Have you heard anything more about Lord Kessel?"

Amelia looked at the twins. She hadn't taken them into her confidence. Ellie saw the glance and gestured at her sisters. "Out, girls. The adults must discuss something."

"We are one and twenty," Maria said, cloaking herself in dignity.

"And I am nearly thirty, which is ancient, as you so kindly pointed out yesterday," Ellie said. "So leave the ancients to our tea, and go off to play spillikins or whatever it is you children do."

Kate stuck her tongue out at her sister, but their grins said they weren't offended. They left, closing the door behind them.

Amelia picked up the conversation again. "I haven't heard anything of Kessel. Still, as long as I am here, I can pretend that nothing will come of his investigations."

She could also pretend Prudence would forgive her — and that Malcolm would never find out about her writing. Ellie didn't let that point slip away unnoticed. "Have you told Carnach?"

Amelia shook her head.

Madeleine sighed. "You should tell him, Mellie. He seems to have a sense of humor, and enough honor that he probably wouldn't beat you more than once for it."

She was joking, but Amelia shivered. "I'd rather not be beaten at all, thank you."

"Carnach doesn't look like the type," Ellie said, in a voice that said she knew what she was talking about. "I agree with Madeleine. Tell Carnach, before he finds out your secret from someone else. It's always better that way."

Ellie still spoke like an oracle on a mountainside, one who had seen more human dramas unfold than either Amelia or Madeleine could comprehend. Amelia was too far gone to heed her. "He won't find out. There is no one who would tell him."

Madeleine stood abruptly. "Stay here a moment — I must retrieve something from my room."

She was gone just long enough for Amelia to regain her composure. That composure fled again when Madeleine returned with a letter in her hand.

"Am I discovered?" Amelia asked, not wanting to take the note.

Madeleine shoved it into her hand. "I haven't read it. It arrived yesterday from Prudence, but the inside cover is addressed to you."

Why had Prudence sent the letter to Madeleine instead of to Amelia directly? Madeleine answered the question before Amelia posed it. "Her note to me said she trusted I could pass this letter along without Carnach knowing you'd received it."

Amelia slid a nail under the sealing wax, opening the sheet of paper. Whenever she'd received letters from Prudence before, they'd been densely written, crosshatched with vertical and horizontal lines to save on paper and postage. This note was bold, legible, and only one line.

Forgive me. -P

Amelia's heart rose into her throat, carried by a crest of bile. She should have been the one to beg for forgiveness.

What had Prudence done?

Ellie looked over her shoulder, shamelessly curious. Her voice was gentle when she spoke. "You should tell Carnach, dear. I've no idea what Prudence wants forgiveness for, but your writing seems the likeliest source."

The award Kessel offered for information was only three hundred pounds, but that sum would be enough to keep Prudence and her mother for another year if they lived frugally in the country. And there was no denying that Prudence and Lady Harcastle had left Scotland as women bent on revenge.

Her heart sank, but the nausea remained. If Prudence had betrayed her, Amelia deserved it.

But it didn't make the thought of telling Malcolm any easier. The moment all the hunger in his eyes flared out and crumbled to ash, she would have to face the reality of being married — and if he knew about her writing, he would surely take away that comfort.

Could she use his attraction to her to win him over? Or was that the surest way to ruin what was good between them?

"Can you write to Prudence and learn why she is asking forgiveness?" Amelia asked Madeleine.

Madeleine sighed. "This is your fight, not mine. Shouldn't you ask her yourself?"

She felt small and childish, but in that moment, for the first time in over a decade, she wished someone could sweep her up and fix everything for her.

"I will deal with it," Amelia said. "But no more talk of it now."

They didn't let her off that easily, of course, but nothing they said could dissuade her. And when Malcolm came to the drawing room to retrieve her, she hoped her smile looked real.

CHAPTER TWENTY-ONE

They were less than two miles from home when a storm came down from the Grampian Mountains, so suddenly that there was no time to reach the castle safely. The curricle had been a stupid choice. Malcolm knew it even when he chose it; the weather could be unpredictable, and he should have taken his wife out in a closed carriage, with a driver left to the elements instead of her.

But he wanted her to see Scotland the way he did, with nothing between her and the wilds. He wanted her to feel something deeper, something that went beyond the vague dreaminess he sometimes caught in her eyes.

And so they were about to be drenched — not the ending he wanted.

"Will we make it home?" she asked, nearly shouting over the wind.

He shook his head, turning the curricle off the road and onto a smaller lane, half overgrown by weeds. "If the rain holds another five minutes, we can shelter in the old dower house."

The rain only gave them three. By the time they raced up to the dower house, under a sky suddenly dark with angry clouds, the rain was sheeting down, pelting them both with drops that were just this side of hail. He shrugged out of his coat and tossed it to Amelia. She huddled under it, but even through the wool, she was drenched.

He steered the horses around to the back, where the disused stables still stood. As soon as they stopped, he jumped down and ran around the side to lift Amelia out of the curricle. He didn't bother to set her down in the rapidly forming quagmire of mud — instead, he scooped her up and ran with her to the kitchen door of the dower house.

As soon as he pushed the door open, she struggled out of his arms and landed on her feet on the cold stone floor. "I can handle myself," she said, her voice breathless.

"I know," he said, smoothing back her hair and tossing her ruined hat to the floor. "But if you caught your death…"

Amelia laughed. "Go see to the horses, if you don't want them to drag the curricle away. I won't die in the next five minutes."

She was right. He ran out into the storm again. The wind sucked away his breath. It was like wading half-dressed into a pond. His clothes were plastered around him, streaming water behind him. The horses hadn't bolted yet, but a crack of lightning in the distance warned him that he needed to shelter them before the thunder drove them away.

The stables were up to the task. No one had lived in the old dower house in three decades, but the house and stables were maintained just enough to provide shelter for stranded shepherds. He unhitched the curricle and dragged the horses into the stable, fighting the wind and their fear with every step. He quickly removed their tack, rubbed them down with straw, draped a blanket over each of them, and tossed some aging oats into a trough.

A nest of mice squeaked in protest when he disturbed the grain, but he ignored them. His attention was focused on Amelia. He never should have brought her with him in an open carriage over such a long distance, not when something like this could so easily happen. It was reckless, stupid, irresponsible — all the things he'd tried to wean himself of when he inherited the estate. He would deserve her anger.

But when he raced back across the courtyard and flung himself through the kitchen door, she didn't look angry. She looked oddly thrilled, with a flush across her cheeks that made him think she'd caught a fever.

"Have you taken ill already?" he asked, stopping just short of running her over.

She laughed at him again. "Really, Malcolm, it's only rain. Unless some dread pestilence lives here, I'm sure we'll be quite safe."

She had found the tinderbox on the ancient wooden trestle table and lit a candle. The reek of cheap tallow wasn't enough to cover the damp, musty smell of disused rooms, but Amelia didn't seem to mind.

He stripped off his gloves and ran his hands across his scalp. He'd lost his hat somewhere, and the water he wrung from his hair trickled down his neck.

Amelia watched him, oddly sympathetic given the censure he expected. "Your shirt is soaked through, Malcolm. Is there anything here you might change into instead?"

He took the candle from her and caught her arm with his other hand. "I'm more concerned about you — we must remove your gown before it chills you completely."

"You usually don't need an excuse to undress me."

She had been oddly tense after leaving her friends, but her voice still held heat for him. The last two weeks had felt entirely like a honeymoon, even though they hadn't left the estate — a blessed few weeks before real life would begin again.

Would her comfort with him survive? Or would they subside into the bloodless political marriage he'd claimed to want?

He didn't allow those thoughts. He pulled her through the empty rooms instead, seeking something that would make her comfortable. After all, if she didn't survive his stupidity, any question of their future would be meaningless.

The dower house had been old before Malcolm was born, built on earlier plans in which each room connected to the rest. The furnishings had long since been removed, other than a few pieces that were too large to be transported easily or too out of fashion to be bothered with.

He didn't like seeing houses in this state of decay. Amelia, however, had no such aversion.

She stopped to run a finger over the intricately carved wooden doorframe connecting the old dining room and drawing room. He handed her the candle and left her to her examination. The drawing room held two chests of extra clothes and linens, as well as a heaping pile of firewood in the far corner. He threw one of the chests open and found several plaid blankets. Like the house, they were musty and cold, but dry enough.

He took the blankets back to where she still surveyed the door. It bore an intricate combination of snakes and knots, an old Gaelic motif that had survived the centuries.

She looked up at him. In the dim light, her eyes sparkled. "This is lovely, Malcolm. Think of what it must have been like to live here."

"Cold, damp, and depressing," he said, unfurling one of the blankets. "Or so my grandmother thought. It should have been hers when my grandfather died, but she refused to move into it. My father built her a more modern cottage, and this house was left to rot."

"It's far from rotting," Amelia said, sidestepping the covering he offered to walk into the drawing room. "All this stone — it's like the castle in miniature. With tapestries and carpets, it would be quite charming."

He finally caught her and began undoing the buttons down her back. "You can tell yourself all the stories you like about the charm. But when you are widowed someday, I hope you have enough sense to live somewhere warmer than this."

Her shoulders tensed under his hands. He softened his tone. "Don't worry, darling. I don't intend to leave you for at least a few decades."

She bowed her head. Her hair didn't glow in the candlelight — it was too wet for that — but the curls that had escaped from her chignon had a burnished edge. He needed to start a fire so her hair would dry, but clothes had to come first.

"You seem sure that I will outlive you," she said.

She was somber — a tone she rarely used. As the final button slipped free, he tried to reassure her. "It seems likely, after all. The men in my family live long enough, but I am older than you."

Amelia didn't respond. She stepped out of her gown, picking it up to drape it on one of the chests. The dress had once been white, but the hem had turned black from the dust she'd trailed through in the dower house.

"Are you upset about your dress?" he asked, trying to read her pensive look.

She snorted. "I'd rather have my writing desk than a thousand dresses."

"Who are you in such a rush to write to?" he asked.

"Oh, just my acquaintances in London."

She let him unlace her stays, but that bit of obedience wasn't enough to quiet the doubting voice in his head. Amelia wasn't the type to sound vague — which meant her letters might be the first clue to whatever it was she was hiding.

"You haven't asked me to frank anything yet," he said.

Her stays came away. She turned around to face him. "Alex franked the postage for my letters. Old habits die hard."

Something about her tone was off, even if her answer made sense — with another peer in residence, she didn't need Malcolm for free postage. But he forgot the question when she reached down and grasped the hem of her chemise. When she pulled it over her head, he sucked in a breath. Even after two weeks spent more in bed than outside of it, the moment when he saw her body made him want her again.

He draped her in one of the blankets, tucking it around her like a makeshift dress and cloak rolled into one. She raised an eyebrow at him. "Do you really intend to act as a nursemaid, Malcolm? I'm not even sick. And I've never seen you want to cover me up before."

Her voice wrapped around him, warming him more thoroughly than any blanket. The heat in his blood urged him to follow her lead.

Instead, he turned his back on her and gathered an armload of firewood. "You're not sick, but you won't get sick on my watch," he said, dumping the wood beside the fireplace.

He found another tinderbox and a small pile of kindling, sealed in a barrel against the damp. As he started the fire, Amelia came to kneel beside him. "You can't stop me from becoming ill, you know."

He struck the flint and steel together savagely, showering sparks onto the hearth. "I made a vow to protect you, Amelia."

"I know," she said, stroking his thigh. "But not every vow can be kept."

"I keep my vows, whether you do or not."

The kindling caught flame. Her hand stilled. "What do you mean to imply?"

"Nothing, darling." He moved away from her, grabbed a piece of wood and laid it in the kindling.

She sat back on her heels. "You don't think I intend to keep my vows?"

"You could barely say the word 'obey,' let alone mean it," he said.

He didn't know where the words had come from — he hadn't meant to bring it up, certainly not now. But even though he didn't look at her as he built the fire, it felt like his whole life hung on her answer.

The fire was roaring by the time she responded. "I never thought it was a vow I would have to make. Or one a stranger could hold me to."

His temper flared. "Am I still that much of a stranger?"

"No, of course not. And you should know, Malcolm, that I do intend to honor you. If I had to make these vows, marry someone, I am glad it is you."

The beast within was slightly mollified, just enough that he could pause to strip out of his shirt and breeches and wrap himself in the other blanket. When he turned back to her, she wasn't looking at him — she was staring into the fire as though she could see visions within the flames.

"If such things matter to you, I intend to honor you, too," he said.

She looked up at him. Wearing his plaid, smiling that sad smile, she could have been any Scottish bride from centuries past — anticipating the day she would lose him. "You may feel differently when we reach London. It's *de rigueur* for powerful men to have mistresses."

He sat down beside her and pulled her against his chest. The stone floor chilled him, but she was warm and alive in his arms — more alive than he could have hoped, when he was searching for the perfect hostess.

He kissed the top of her head. "Not this powerful man, darling."

"Do we have to go to London?" she asked. She sounded strangled as she said it, as though she hadn't meant to address the subject any more than he had planned to question her vows.

"I thought you would want to return to your friends," he said, trying to sound neutral.

"I'll miss them, but there aren't so many that I can't bear to be parted with. And Prudence…"

She stopped herself. He squeezed her shoulder. "You cannot make things right with her unless you see her again."

"That's what I am afraid of," she said. But she dropped the subject, tried to inject lightness into her voice, even though her attempt to seem nonchalant was unsuccessful. "The Highlands are compensation enough. Everything here is absolutely lovely. I could write about this place for decades and never tire of it."

"Your correspondents will tire of hearing about it long before then," he said.

She sighed. "How can you leave, though? I understand now why you never went to London before. Surely you don't want to go?"

"I don't," he said. "But I must. I've made my decision."

She toyed with the edge of her plaid blanket, matching the pattern's lines to the edge of his. "Politics isn't a nice game, you know. And there are very few men in Parliament who will give a farthing for the problems of the Highlanders. They can barely be bothered to care for the working classes right under their noses, let alone crofters hundreds of miles away."

"I'm aware of that. But if I don't try…"

He trailed off. The fire popped, sending sparks up the chimney. Behind him, rain still pounded against the shutters that protected the aging, fragile glass.

She waited for him to speak again. When he finally found the words, they didn't feel like the right ones, but they were the best he could deliver. "I want this place to exist for our children, and our children's children, and every generation beyond that. If that means I must spend all my time in London, creating policies that enable our clan to stay on this land, then so be it."

"All things come to an end," she said softly. "Even Rome fell."

"This isn't Rome," he said, suddenly snapping. His voice rang against the bleak stone walls. "This is my home — our home. And I will save it."

Some part of him wanted her to apologize, to soothe him, to tell him that he could save her.

Instead, she dropped the edge of his plaid. "I hope the ending of this story is the one you want, Malcolm. But you can't save everyone. No one can ever save everyone."

He kissed her then, if only to shut her up. The kiss turned into more, as most of their kisses did, and their lovemaking warmed even the stones around them.

But it wasn't enough to ease the fist around his heart. He would save them all, or lose everything trying.

CHAPTER TWENTY-TWO

Hours later, Amelia held a torch aloft so Malcolm could lead the horses into their traces. The storm had long since subsided, but he insisted on waiting until her dress was dry, unwilling to risk either her health in a damp dress or her modesty in a blanket. Prudence's note in her reticule tugged at her thoughts, and the knot in her belly hadn't subsided. But at least Malcolm's company could distract her, even if it wasn't enough to make everything right again.

As Malcolm hitched the horses, Amelia considered her latest manuscript. Her heroine, Veronique, had been captured and kept in an ancient stone manor by her evil uncle, and was quickly losing all hope of a rescue from her lost fiancé, Gaston D'Ambergris. The story sounded good on paper. But now that she had an actual image of a stone manor in her mind, there was so much she could add. Veronique needed to feel the cold cutting to her bones and the damp air sticking in her lungs. She also needed to feel the heat searing her skin when her fiancé rescued her, and the knowledge that he had scoured the earth to find her.

Amelia couldn't write everything she had felt at the dower house, and she certainly couldn't have the fiancé strip Veronique to the skin — even anonymously, she wouldn't publish such sentiments. But the feeling that someone would do anything to save her, would sacrifice himself for her comfort, was a notion Amelia had never really believed before.

Malcolm went back into the house and returned with their blankets. He wiped down the seats of the curricle with one, then spread the other over Amelia's seat. "Are you ready, darling?" he asked, extending an arm.

She nodded. He lifted her into the curricle, then tucked her cloak and the edges of the blanket around her. "We are less than two miles from the castle. Unless the road has washed out, we should be home within the half hour. I hope Graves had the sense to save our suppers."

"I really haven't minded," she said as he joined her on the seat. "Rain and hunger aside, I thought the dower house was lovely."

"Wouldn't you rather have a nice townhouse with wooden floors? Perhaps some wallpaper? Or the gaslights that I hear are the next advancement in London?"

She laughed. "Give me a castle any day, my lord. Townhouses may be comfortable, but they have none of the magic of your library."

He drove them down the lane toward the main road. "Perhaps I should have married Miss Etchingham after all. I had no idea you were so intrigued by history."

The reminder of Prudence, and the note she'd sent, sucked the humor out of Amelia's voice. "I don't care for history the way she does. The stories, though — much of the time I would rather live in a fairy tale than the horrid realities of London."

"Well, there are stories aplenty in the Highlands, although few of them are fairy tales." He turned onto the road. The horses slogged through the muddy rivulets running down toward the valley in front of them. The village lay between them and the castle, glowing orange.

But the glow was strange — the sun had set three hours earlier, and the moon was just a sliver in the sky. "What is that?" she asked.

Malcolm had already urged the horses into a canter, as fast as they could manage on the slick and treacherous road. "Fire," he said.

His voice was grim, intent on the village, not their previous conversation. Fire was always a risk, but she had seen many burned out crofts and dwellings when she and her family had traveled through the Highlands to reach Malcolm's home — more than she had ever seen between London and her family's estate in Lancashire.

"Is lightning particularly problematic here?" she asked.

"No more than anywhere, I should think. Why?"

"We passed many scorched ruins while driving here. Is it something about the thatched roofing?"

He pulled back on the reins, navigating the horses around a fallen branch in the road. After he flicked the whip above their heads to urge them on, he spoke in a voice she'd never heard from him before. "That wasn't lightning. That was improvement."

"Improvement? But there were no modern houses to replace them."

The words crackled between them like a storm about to break. "I wouldn't call it improvement either. But most landlords are clearing their tenants to make room for sheep. It is easier to keep the tenants off the land if there are no houses for them to return to."

"You can't be serious," she said, looking at his profile. There was little to see in the darkness, but his spine was a stiff line of rage. "I thought the clans were families?"

"That was true decades ago. And a few of us still hold to the old ideals. But if you're a distant landlord, living in London, and needing funds to fuel your gambling or drinking…"

He flicked the whip again. In the crack of sound, Amelia heard his judgment.

They covered the mile to the village much more quickly than was advisable on the sodden road. She wrapped the blanket around herself, but the wind cut through the wool. If someone's home or livelihood in the village wasn't being destroyed in front of them, it might have almost been funny. Malcolm had tried so hard to warm her up, to keep her safe, only to freeze her and risk dismemberment on the way home.

She didn't make the jest, though. When she glanced at him, she knew he focused solely on what lay ahead of them, not on the relatively new burden at his side. He'd cared for his clan long before he'd had a wife — and she understood the pull of old desires over the unexpected bond they found themselves in.

Her thoughts wandered, away from Malcolm and toward the stories whispering through the glens. There were tragedies lurking in the trees, stalking her in the mist. The modern MacCabes, who had been so exuberant at her wedding, seemed relatively happy. But over the centuries, the Highlanders had drunk to the very dregs of a cold, bitter cup. Tonight's fire was yet another stain on the fabric.

She hadn't lied when she told Malcolm that she could write about the Highlands for decades. She didn't know the individuals affected by tonight's fire, but she was already creating a story around them — perhaps a blacksmith with a beautiful daughter, whose forge was destroyed by arson so a nefarious stranger could force the father to sell the girl?

By the time they reached the village, she had constructed an entire plot in her head. They pulled to a halt near the burning cottage, separated from the flames by a brigade of men with buckets and shovels.

Half the village was watching the spectacle, but there wasn't a nefarious stranger in sight. As usual, the reality was almost disappointing in comparison to the story she had told herself.

One of the twins broke away from the crowd as Malcolm leapt

from the curricle. "It's a complete loss," Duncan said, dusting soot off his hands before clapping Malcolm on the back.

"And Sean and his family?" Malcolm asked, signaling for one of the children from the throng of bystanders.

"All safe. And they rescued their cow, even though it was the cow that caused the ordeal. A lightning strike frightened her and she knocked a lamp over. The fuel spread and reached her feed trough before Sean could put it out."

Malcolm handed the reins to the boy, along with a coin for minding them. Amelia threw off her blanket and slid down from the curricle. "How did the fire spread from the barn to the cottage?" she asked.

Duncan stared at her as Malcolm answered. "Most of the crofters keep their livestock with them in their cottages. A cow is too valuable to leave out, but none can afford a barn if they only have one animal to house."

The heat from the burning cottage prickled against her blush. "It must be different on Alex's estate."

Malcolm opened his mouth to say something, but a shout from someone near the cottage cut him off. "Stay here," he ordered, turning on his heel to cut through the crowd.

She didn't like to be left behind, but she knew there was little she could do in a fire brigade beyond getting in the way. So she remained with the rest of the observers, who were too occupied with watching the fire to notice her ruined dress and unkempt hair.

Malcolm didn't hang back, though. He charged into the very heart of the fight, picking up a pole when the men began pushing the smoldering thatched roof into the ruined interior. The building was mostly stone, and as soon as the roof was off, it would be less likely for a stray spark to spread to its neighbors. They were lucky it had rained earlier — while a fire started from within hadn't been contained by the rain, the nearby cottages were safer than they might have been.

There was an energy to Malcolm that Amelia hadn't seen with other peers — a driving need to satisfy and protect those around him. So far, she'd only seen that energy expended in their bed, with vastly pleasant results. But it was no wonder he dreamed of saving the Highlands. It was the type of battle he would feel honor-bound to take up.

She had wanted freedom and someone who wouldn't notice the hours she spent writing. But despite that desire, she hoped that when Malcolm did turn his attentions to politics, he would still have time to spare for her.

*　　*　　*

When the roof was off, Malcolm tossed aside his pole. The cottage was completely destroyed, as Duncan had said, but at least the village was safe.

He tramped around the side of the cottage and found Sean MacRae sitting on a stool, taking a rest after the worst of the fire had been fought. He stood when Malcolm clapped him on the back.

"Ye needn't've come, Laird," Sean said. "Nothing to be done yet."

"Your wife and children are all safe?" Malcolm asked.

Sean nodded. "Anne isn't happy I saved the cow, though. She thinks the beast is cursed, and this proves it."

"You can trade me for a different cow if that will make her feel better."

"Can I sell it to you instead? We will be wanting shillings more than milk, I think."

Malcolm frowned. "You don't want to give up your cow, Sean. I will find you a cottage for free for the next quarter, until you can get back on your feet."

Sean rubbed his forehead, smearing the soot that had settled on his skin. "I've a cousin — you remember Billy MacRae, don't you? He went to Nova Scotia last year and says if I join him, we can start a mill together."

"Canada? You can't be serious," Malcolm said.

"It's not that I want to go," Sean said hastily. "But wouldn't it be grand to see my boys be mill owners someday instead of shepherds?"

Malcolm tried his best to talk him out of it. He even said there was no use discussing it until morning anyway, and promised to visit again when the sun was out and Sean had calmed himself. But Malcolm knew, even though he wasn't ready to acknowledge it, that there was nothing he could say to change Sean's mind.

He cursed himself for it as he walked back to where Amelia and his curricle waited. Not that he wished his father had died sooner — he wished his father had lived many more years, of course. But maybe if Malcolm had inherited sooner, started this battle earlier, men like Sean would see opportunity here instead of thinking they had to sail across an ocean and start again.

Amelia was sitting on a stump a dozen feet away from the nearest villager, staring off into the middle distance between herself and the smoking ruins of the cottage. Even with the grime on her dress and the pensive, brooding look on her face, he wanted to see her. Maybe she could talk him out of his blue devils. Maybe in their bed, he could forget tonight's failure.

He froze. She hadn't seen him yet and didn't notice his hesitation. But why was he thinking in terms of forgetting? He should be working, not playing. These precious days after their wedding had been lovely.

But they were just a dream of what could have been, if neither of them had responsibilities to anyone else. Malcolm did have responsibilities, though — responsibilities he'd utterly neglected in favor of spending time between her thighs.

Amelia came out of her daze and looked around. When her eyes met his, he realized she was looking for him. She smiled slowly, wonderfully, radiantly, and even though the village was dark, she burned as bright as a torch for him.

Malcolm shook his head, hard. Her smile faltered just a bit. But she stood and walked toward him, extending a hand to take his arm.

"I hear the family is all unharmed?" she asked.

He nodded.

She patted his forearm, an instinctual gesture of comfort. "You must be relieved."

He wasn't. Their lives were saved, through no effort of his, but they would leave the Highlands. He couldn't save them from that. But he also couldn't keep delaying his plans, not if he wanted to save the rest of them.

"They'll live," he said shortly. "Let's return to the castle. I have work to do tonight."

Amelia frowned up at him. "You never work in the evenings."

He ignored the censure in her voice and escorted her to the curricle. He had always worked in the evenings before she came, at least in the year since his father's death. He wouldn't — couldn't — regret the last two weeks. But he couldn't keep ignoring his duties for the pleasure she offered.

If their honeymoon was a dream, it would end tonight. And he would take up the life he was supposed to live immediately, whether either of them were ready or not.

CHAPTER TWENTY-THREE

The rest of the evening passed in silence. The storm had ended hours earlier, but Amelia felt another wave about to break.

And it wasn't just her worry over Prudence. Malcolm had barely said anything after the fire — not as he drove her home, not as he escorted her into the castle, not as they had a makeshift supper of warmed over food at a corner of the dining table. His answers were clipped, lacking all of the brogue he usually charmed her with. And his hand as he helped her out of her seat at the end of the meal didn't linger on the curve of her back.

"I trust you can find your way to your room," he said.

"I know where it is, but I haven't slept in it yet," she said. It connected to Malcolm's chamber, but she only used it for dressing — all of her nights since their wedding had been spent tangled in his sheets.

He nodded, feigning oblivion at the undercurrents between them. "I have papers to see to tonight and wouldn't want to disturb you when I finish."

She looked over his shoulder to the footmen who waited to clear the table. "If you could escort me before you return to your study, I would be most grateful."

He saw the line of her gaze and looked over his shoulder. He offered his arm to her, but as soon as they reached the foot of the stairs, he stepped away. "You don't need me, Amelia. Go to bed."

She frowned. "What is the matter? You've never behaved like this before."

"Never?" He laughed. "You've known me less than a month. Perhaps this is who I truly am."

His voice was grim. His mouth was hard, as though she'd stolen every last kiss his lips could ever give her. His eyes weren't the ones that had enchanted her in the library — they were the slate grey of rain on stones. Standing this close to him, he smelled of soot and peat and damp wool, ancient and elemental.

She shivered. "Tonight was difficult and I am sorry for it. But perhaps a bath and a bit of rest is all you need."

Malcolm stared at her. "You think a bath will solve this?"

"It might. There's no harm in trying, is there? You can join me if you like."

He'd shown her the pleasures of bathing together earlier in the week. She would have sworn that he enjoyed it too — and they could both use the distraction. But he showed no sign of taking her invitation. "I must work. If you cannot sleep, I'm sure you have a correspondent to write to."

The comment slapped at her like a gauntlet, part taunt, part question. "My letters can wait for the morning."

"How gracious of you to put off your letters for me," he said.

"Is that what is bothering you? My writing?"

He didn't respond. Instead, his eyes met hers. His gaze was a battering ram attempting to break through her calm façade.

Amelia refused to blink. She might not be Amelia Staunton anymore, but even as Lady Carnach, she hadn't changed so much that she would give anything away. She held his gaze steadily, unflinching even as his eyes narrowed.

He pulled back abruptly, raking a hand through his hair. "You are a cold one, aren't you?"

He had finally found the words to make her flinch. "What are you going on about, Malcolm? Is this about my writing? The fire? Something else?"

"Nothing, darling." The endearment sounded like a curse. "Go to your bed. I've much to consider after tonight's fire."

She thought about reaching out to him. Her hand was already lifting, drawn to him.

But she dropped her hand. She couldn't face the questions in his eyes, not when she didn't know what the consequences would be — or whether she could confess her sins without losing him. Prudence's letter was still tucked in her reticule, and while she didn't know what Prudence had apologized for, the note felt like a dangerous scrap of treason that Amelia might hang for in the end.

She feigned a yawn. "Very well, Malcolm. I'm sure I appreciate a night without you."

He scowled. Amelia wanted him to argue. She wanted him to demand that she take back the words. It was crazy, that desire for a fight, but her whole body throbbed as anger rushed through her.

He didn't give her satisfaction. He walked away instead. If this was a battlefield, she had routed the enemy — but her victory was decidedly hollow.

* * *

Hours later, Amelia scowled as she punched her unfamiliar pillow.

She tried fluffing it again, flipping it to the cool side, but it wouldn't stay cool for long. The mattress was new, and she should have slept dreamlessly without the weight of a solid male tipping her toward him.

Could she really not sleep without him?

Amelia rolled out of bed. She told herself that the excitement of the storm and the fire kept her awake, not the yawning emptiness beside her. She threw open the drapes of one of the windows, grabbed her writing desk, and settled into the window seat. If she couldn't sleep, she could pour herself onto the page instead.

But she couldn't write, not when her muse wanted to consider Prudence's request for forgiveness instead of her current story. Amelia tried all her tricks — adjusting the light by adding candles all around the room, sharpening her pen until it could draw blood, scrawling on the edge of the page and waiting for the lines to become letters. But her usual geometric patterns all turned into castles instead of squares and diamonds. And her heroine, Veronique, may have wanted to be rescued — but as Amelia looked out the window, she suspected she would never want to leave the Highlands again.

"Blast it all," she swore under her breath.

She set her desk in front of her, leaned back against the paneled embrasure, and hugged her knees to her chest. She hadn't wanted to marry, but she would be lying if she tried to convince herself that her former life — her boring, predictable life, brightened only by a passion she couldn't divulge — was better than this. Malcolm was nothing she'd expected from marriage.

Something within her whispered that she could like spending her life with him very much indeed.

But she wanted the life of the last two weeks, not the role he would expect his countess to play in London. Perhaps she could convince him to stay in Scotland. Then she could write every day and sleep in his arms every night, which just might be perfect. And if they stayed in Scotland forever, it wouldn't matter what Kessel discovered or what Prudence had done.

Amelia was dreaming of that conversation when Malcolm flung open the door connecting their rooms. She'd made her chamber as bright as day with her candles, and the light reflected the hunger in his eyes. He was already stripped to the waist. If his eyes hadn't proclaimed why he was there, the bulge in his breeches did.

She grinned at him. "I thought you wished to sleep alone."

He shut the door behind him. "I overestimated my ability to stay away."

"Why did you want to stay away?" she asked, capping her ink and stowing it in its box.

He leaned against the doorjamb, his hands behind him like a child denying himself a treat — or a prisoner awaiting the gallows. "I told you I had to work."

"So you said." She set her desk aside, slipping her papers into their case. But she didn't go to him. "Does your presence mean your work is finished?"

"My work is never finished. And it seems your correspondence isn't either."

He jerked his head at her desk. His hair was wet, like he'd dunked it in a washbasin, and his jaw glistened as he ground his teeth.

She didn't want to lie to him. But he hadn't questioned her directly — just as he hadn't answered her question about his work, and why he had intended to avoid her bed.

And perhaps she was a coward, but she didn't want to tell him tonight. So she chose distraction over dishonesty. She yawned, stretching her arms above her head, feeling her nightrail tighten across her breasts. "Tell me what you want from me, my lord."

He closed the distance between them and crushed her against his chest. She laughed as he cupped her derriere. She felt the length of him against her belly. Perhaps he wasn't saying everything. Perhaps she couldn't tell him what she wrote. But there was no denying he wanted her.

She rubbed against him. "Surely you want to sleep, my lord? After such a long day…"

He nearly growled as he kissed her, nipping at the smile that curved her lips. She wrapped an arm around his back, twined her other arm around his neck, felt his wet hair glide through her ink-stained fingers. She hadn't been able to pour herself onto the page that night, but perhaps giving herself to this kiss would be enough.

Their kiss was slow, deep — devotion rather than demand. She let him sink into her, met his tongue with her own, burned under his clever hands. She felt like an altar and an offering all at once, unable to tell who was the worshipper and who was the sacrifice.

That question would have mattered to her once. She didn't worship any man, and she would never be a sacrifice. But by the time he pulled away and started blowing out the candles, she wanted him badly enough to play any role he asked of her.

He unbuttoned his breeches as he extinguished the light. His fingers were as steady and sure as his steps around the room, still utterly in control despite his obvious need. She turned to close the drapes, eager even though everything fluttered wildly at the intensity of his purpose.

"Leave them open," he ordered.

She stepped back, still looking out the window at the valley below, suddenly uncertain. Behind her, his breath hissed. The last light was snuffed out. The smoke from a dozen dying candles threaded through the room.

She would have turned, but his hands on her shoulders stopped her. He kissed the base of her neck, just under the heavy mass of braids pinned to her scalp. The gesture drew a moan from her lips.

"Amelia," he breathed into her hair.

His voice was rough, as rough as the hand he dropped to her breast — as rough as the slamming of her heart against her ribcage as his fingers bit into her sensitive flesh. She twisted her head back and tilted it as he kissed her again. The angle was awkward, and she would have turned if he'd let her...

But he didn't let her. There was an edge to him she hadn't felt before. As he slid down to kiss her throat, she felt that edge pressed against her vein. She shuddered as his caresses turned more demanding, as every flick of his thumb against her nipple turned into a taunting symphony of sensation. His other hand moved lower, tracing the flare of her hip, then slowly bunching up the fabric of her nightrail in his fist.

She was still conscious enough to notice the glass in front of them and the vast swathes of countryside beyond. She started to push away his hand, but his fist kept her skirt — and her — pinned.

"The window," she whispered, still enthralled enough that her modesty couldn't entirely overrule her desire.

"No one will see. Not without light behind us."

Then his hand slipped under her skirt and settled between her legs. She was already wet for him. She bit back another moan as he slowly stroked her.

"Still want me to stop?" he asked a few minutes later, when she was trembling on the precipice he'd driven her to.

"Never."

He kissed her earlobe, then tugged it with his teeth. His hand stayed buried in her wetness, enough to keep her on edge without letting her come. His other hand dropped away from her bosom, and she arched back toward him in protest.

"Greedy wench," he whispered.

"Only with you."

His fingers stopped, just for a moment. The world stopped too. In the dark, with the stars as their audience, she felt like she might be left hanging there forever, a swirling constellation of need.

Then he stroked her again. He freed himself from his breeches to press insistently at her back. He pulled her against him, then leaned over her, forcing her to lean too, until she was bent toward the windowseat.

"Brace yourself with your hands," he ordered.

The edge was back in his voice, and it had cut through his control. If she was a proper lady, she would run from such a beastly act. But she wasn't proper — and the emptiness between her legs wouldn't let her go until he'd filled it.

She put one shaking hand, then the other, on the windowseat. The cool brocade was textured enough to hold her steady. He nudged her legs apart, tapping at each calf with his foot until she'd taken the stance he demanded.

He was still wearing his boots. She almost came at the thought, at the touch of polished leather against her skin when she was nearly naked before him. He planted himself behind her and lifted her nightrail until cool air caressed her backside. He replaced the air a moment later, and his manhood grazed against her cleft as he moved to enter her.

"Amelia," he whispered again.

He plunged into her as he said her name. She screamed as he filled her, deeper than he'd ever gone before, deeper than she'd realized was possible. She tried to pull away, but his fingers dug into her hips and held her beneath him. He'd often let her set the pace over the previous two weeks, but not tonight. Tonight he made the rules. He pulled back, then slammed into her again, and again, and again. She shuddered, her legs trembling, her arms wanting to give out, to bend lower, until she was a mindless beast beneath him.

Her orgasm, when it finally crashed over her, was strong enough to break her. She sobbed his name as she came. He wrapped an arm around her waist, holding her up as he drove into her again. Then he went rigid against her, and his grip was unbreakable as he shot his seed into her womb.

She floated for a few minutes, trapped between him and the sky. But she fell back to earth when he pulled out. He swatted her nightrail back into place. She felt like a meal half finished and left abandoned, with tears on her face and his seed on her thighs.

When she turned to him, he was buttoning his breeches. "Aren't you coming to bed?" she asked.

She hated the quaver in her voice. But if it should have earned his sympathy, it failed. "I must be up early in the morning. You'll sleep better undisturbed."

She was already disturbed. But even though she'd let Malcolm take her like an animal — even though she'd let him take her at all, after he'd dismissed her like a servant for the night — she still had a few scraps of pride. She gathered them around her like armor, until she could look at him like the Virgin Queen dismissing a courtier.

"Do go on then, my lord. I hope you'll pick an earlier hour next time you choose to use me."

She could have sworn he almost grinned at that — but why? And why did he bite down on his smile? Why did he nod curtly, like he was accepting a business proposal?

Why did he leave her standing in the middle of her room, messy and aching for him?

She crawled into her bed, knowing she wouldn't sleep but unable to sit on the windowseat again after what he'd done to her there. She lay stiff and unyielding, staring up at the ceiling, hoping the darkness would smother the question she didn't want to hear, let alone answer...

Why was she falling in love with him?

CHAPTER TWENTY-FOUR

Malcolm awoke at dawn and was at the village an hour later. The cottage ruins still smoldered under the brilliant early sunlight. The neighbors took turns watching for errant sparks, but the danger to the village had passed.

The danger to him, though, was likely still asleep in the castle. And unlike a fire, she couldn't be quenched, not even with the roughness he'd displayed the night before. Did she dream of him, like he had dreamed of her?

Did she curse him for taking her like an animal?

The residents were stirring when he arrived. He progressed slowly, asking after sick relatives, livestock, crops — everything that might need his attention. He hadn't spent more than an hour in the village since his wedding. Not that his clan seemed to mind. If anything, they encouraged it.

"Better for ye to be clucking over her than us, is what I say," the baker proclaimed when Malcolm asked about his new oven.

"It's been a regular honeymoon for all of us," the blacksmith said as he dunked a red-hot horseshoe into a barrel of water.

"Shouldn't you be at the castle to wake up your bonny bride?" the pub owner asked, with a leer that Malcolm might have punched him for if the man wasn't so good-natured about it.

And Sean MacRae wouldn't hear any of Malcolm's offers of assistance. He and his wife agreed — they would go to Nova Scotia as soon as they could arrange passage.

Malcolm scowled as he accompanied Alastair back to the vicarage after he finished his rounds. "Our clan won't win any awards for gratitude."

"And you won't win any for humility," Alastair said, pushing open the gate to his yard.

"Your point?"

Alastair shrugged. "It may be my religious persuasion, but unlike you, I don't think you are the only one who can help them."

"I don't believe I'm the only one."

Alastair laughed.

"I don't," Malcolm repeated. "But it's my duty to do what I can for them."

"True," his brother said. He paused outside his house, turning to look down the lane toward the rest of the village. "Father would be proud, you know. Whether you keep everyone in the Highlands or not."

Malcolm ignored the compliment. "How can Sean want to go to Canada? It's a hard place, full of savages, without roads or schools. Who would want to live there?"

"Likely how we're thought of in London," Alastair pointed out. "Join me for breakfast?"

"No. Speaking of London, I shall leave for the capital within the week. There's too much to do before then to waste time talking about Canada over a plate of kippers."

Alastair sat on his steps, plucking a weed from a crack in the stone. "Is your countess eager to return to her circles?"

Malcolm tapped his riding crop against his boot, suddenly unable to look at his brother's face. "We haven't discussed it."

"You haven't discussed it." Alastair shaded his eyes against the sun and looked up at Malcolm. "Are you leaving her here?"

He should leave her here. She was a distraction — a glorious distraction, but still a distraction. Last night had proven it. In his study, sifting sightlessly through his ledgers, he couldn't last more than a minute without thinking of her. Trying to focus only increased his desire, to the point that he could think of nothing but having her.

She was a disease in his blood.

He suspected there would be no cure.

But the idea of leaving her behind was worse than the distraction of having her at his side. "She'll go with me. She's lived in London off and on for decades. I'm sure she'll be glad to return there."

"Good luck with that, brother," Alastair said, in a tone that said Malcolm was beyond salvation.

Malcolm laughed. "She's half in love with me already. Why wouldn't she want to go with me?"

"That means she's half out of love with you," Alastair observed. "You should at least discuss this with her, don't you think?"

Malcolm didn't acknowledge the point. Instead, he took his leave, ignoring Alastair's final muttered comments about duty and marital bliss. What did Alastair know of marriage? And it was all well and good to believe that God would provide when one wasn't the landlord responsible for half the county.

He was still religious enough to wince at the thought, but it didn't stop him from spurring his horse. His original intent the night before, when taking her in front of the window, was to remind himself that their marriage existed to save the land around the castle — that he needed obedience and heirs from her, not pleasure.

But he'd lost himself in her, as he always did. The fact that his distraction with her was already so profound...

He had to end it. He had to remind them both what their marriage was supposed to be. It had to be business, a proper, passionless union that wouldn't distract him from all the duties he needed to fulfill.

And if they were to be passionless, he had to make it happen now — before he was too addicted to her passion to leave her.

*   *   *

Amelia shoved her writing desk aside when her maid came in with a cup of chocolate. She'd awoken almost three hours earlier, when she'd heard Malcolm's footsteps pass by her room without a moment's hesitation.

It was the first time she'd awoken alone since their wedding day. She supposed she should be grateful that she wouldn't have to talk to Malcolm before she cleaned her teeth or brushed her hair. But she never felt the way one was supposed to feel.

The previous night was no exception. From the whispered conversations she'd overheard when matrons thought their charges were out of earshot, she knew many women of the ton found little pleasure in their marriage beds. Imagine how a woman like Lady Harcastle would feel about being bent over a windowseat?

"Are you feeling well, my lady? You look overwarm," Watkins observed, handing Amelia the steaming cup from her tray.

She didn't feel well — she felt a little ill thinking of Lady Harcastle, and by extension Prudence's note. But for the maid, she said, "Quite. Although perhaps a bath would be in order."

"I am glad we are returning to London, if you don't mind me saying so, my lady," Watkins said, ringing the bell to call a maid for water. "The kitchen is so far from the bedchambers here that it is difficult to keep the water hot until it arrives."

"What?" Amelia demanded.

Watkins looked at her blankly. "The castle is bigger than Salford House, and the kitchens..."

"I don't care about that," Amelia snapped. "What's this about going to London?"

Watkins's confusion grew. "I heard it from his lordship's valet, who said he was packing this morning. I'll start as soon as we have you dressed. Unless you're not going with Lord Carnach?"

Amelia gulped her chocolate to conceal her reaction, but only succeeded in burning the roof of her mouth. "Damn him," she muttered as she sucked in air over the burn.

"Did I speak out of turn, my lady? I am sorry for it."

Amelia waved her hand. "You're not the one who is out of turn, Watkins. Do you know if the earl is in the castle?"

"He was in the breakfast room when I brought your chocolate from the kitchen."

She rolled out of bed, setting aside the half-finished cup. "No bath. I need to dress. Something black."

Her maid didn't argue, even though she looked like she wanted to. Amelia went to the washbasin and poured water from the pitcher Watkins had brought with the chocolate. She stripped and washed herself ruthlessly, her fury increasing with every swipe of the washcloth across the skin Malcolm had used the night before. There were bruises the shape of his fingertips on her hips.

If she could kill him twice — once for making her think he cared, and again for proving her wrong — she would.

Watkins helped her into a fresh chemise, stays, a petticoat, and a black crepe gown better suited to mourning than a honeymoon. Amelia sat still as Watkins unbraided her hair, then repinned it in a strict twist. When they were done, she smoothed her skirts. She wore no jewelry but her wedding band. She didn't want to wear it — the reminder that, by law if not by right, he owned her. He could make her go to London with no notice at all. But there was still a chance this was a misunderstanding.

It had to be a misunderstanding.

The maid Watkins had rung for bathwater arrived. "Does my lady need something?" she asked.

"Not any longer," Watkins said, coming out of the dressing room with a pair of shoes. "But she will need a footman to bring up her trunks."

"Don't pack yet," Amelia said. "I do not go anywhere just because a valet said so."

She saw the look that passed between Watkins and the upstairs maid, but she ignored it as she slid her feet into her shoes and stalked from the room. How dare he embarrass her like that in front of the servants?

She walked down the stairs, trying to breathe, to calm herself. She reminded herself that she wanted a separate life from him, that being close to her publisher would make everything easier, that London was preferable to the Highlands.

And she tried to remember a time when the only thing that heated her blood was her writing, not the caresses of an autocratic boor. If he was so selfish that he would move them to London without any discussion at all, then she had no doubt he'd put an end to her writing the moment he discovered it.

"Stay true to yourself, Amelia," she ordered herself as she neared the breakfast room.

But when she walked into the sunny morning room, her resolve faltered. Malcolm sat at the table, the remnants of a large breakfast spread around him. He read a newspaper as though he was any country squire — one who'd slept perfectly by himself and was well satisfied with life.

He stood when she entered. At least he still had some courtesy. "Did you sleep well, darling?" he asked.

She felt the blood rising in her face. It was irrational to be angry without waiting for an explanation, but even if it was all a misunderstanding, she was still hurt that he seemed so unaffected by last night's lovemaking.

So when he pulled out a chair for her, she didn't take it. "Perfectly well, my lord. My bed is preferable to yours."

His hand clenched the back of the chair. "Then what are you mourning?"

"I'm not in mourning...yet."

"What in the devil do you mean?"

She glanced at Graves, who hovered with a footman near the sidebar. Then she tossed propriety to the devil Malcolm had referenced. "Black seemed expedient. It won't show blood, and when I've killed you, I won't have to waste time changing into mourning."

He crossed his arms. "You didn't want to kill me last night."

If she hadn't wanted to kill him before, his smug tone undid her. "That was before I recognized you for the man you are," she hissed. "How can you decide our lives without even a by-your-leave? I'm your wife, Carnach, as much as we both regret it. Not some strumpet who must do what you tell her."

"Wrong," he said flatly. "A whore could leave, if she had the funds. You're bound to me forever."

"As if I could forget," she snapped. In her rage, even her ears were burning. "And you wonder why I would want to end you."

"Graves, count the knives tonight," he said to the butler.

"I always do, my lord."

She glared at the servants. "Out. Now."

The footman jumped at her tone. Graves, oddly, had the temerity to smile before he refused. "If I might be so bold, my lady, may I suggest you murder his lordship elsewhere? His mother has not yet come down to breakfast, and you wouldn't want her stumbling upon your crime."

She wanted to scream. But she would save her breath for Malcolm. "Then you. Out. You don't want to hear this in front of anyone else."

"You aren't the one who decides when we talk," he said.

"I don't want you to talk. I want you to listen. But I'll let you express a preference after I'm done, which is more courtesy than you've shown me."

He shifted, oddly uncomfortable. "I thought you…appreciated what I decided."

She snorted. "If you don't want Graves to hear what I think of you, we should adjourn to another room."

He scanned her face, and whatever he saw there convinced him that she would make good on her threat. He took her arm, but not as a polite escort — he grabbed her as though she was a prisoner bent on escape.

She shook him off. "Handling me so roughly isn't advisable in my current mood."

He bowed deeply, somehow turning the subservient gesture into an insult. "Then if the lady would be so kind as to follow me, I will find an appropriate place for this discussion."

He stalked away. She missed the feel of his hand on her arm, and as soon as she realized it, she fisted her hands until her nails dug into her palms. Where was the resolve she'd promised herself?

She'd make do without it. She followed him silently as he strode out of the main wing, across the great hall, up a short flight of stairs to the dais, and through the long portrait gallery that connected the hall to the ancient tower. She'd seen the portraits when Lady Carnach had shown her and Prudence around the castle a lifetime ago, but they hadn't bothered with the tower itself.

Amelia shivered. Her blasted imagination was already thinking of dungeons. Centuries of MacCabes watched their progress, and Amelia wondered how many Carnach earls had dragged their wives through the gallery to the tower beyond.

Malcolm moved fast, their pace set by his anger. She had wanted to insult him, to draw blood, to upset him as much as he'd upset her. But now that his anger was unleashed, she worried she may have pushed him too far.

They reached the end of the gallery. Malcolm pulled open the thick oak door. It groaned on its hinges, revealing a circular room large enough to hold the remnants of the MacCabes's earlier armory and several decades of abandoned furnishings. A stone staircase started to the right of the door, spiraling along the wall and disappearing through an open trapdoor to the second floor some fifteen feet above their heads.

She walked in and Malcolm slammed the door behind them before gesturing her into the only intact chair. She sat as though she wanted to, but the effect was ruined when she sneezed as a cloud of dust flew up around her. He ignored the dirt. He watched her with those unfathomable grey eyes, like a predatory hawk waiting for the mouse to leave its hole.

She shifted under his gaze. The chair creaked ominously. He towered over her, a brooding inquisitor prepared to force a confession. When she tried to stand, he pushed her back, leaning over her and planting his hands on the arms of her chair. "You got what you asked for — no servants can hear us. Will you explain to me why we're here?"

His voice was quiet and deadly, warning her to take care. Amelia was too angry to back down. She leaned up toward him, inches from his face. "You do take pleasure in lording your authority over me, don't you?"

"If you don't want me to, say the word."

"As simple as that?" she asked, arching an eyebrow.

"As simple as that," he agreed. But then he leaned in and kissed her. Their fury melted them together, until she sighed against his lips. When he pulled away, that smug smile was back. "Deny me all you want in the morning, though. I vow you enjoyed what I gave you last night."

She fell back against the chair. "What does that have to do with anything?"

He straightened. "I should have been gentler, perhaps. If you came downstairs seeking an apology, though, I'll only give it if you genuinely dislike our lovemaking."

She snorted. "Wherever did you get the idea that I wanted to discuss last night?"

"Few women of your class would allow themselves to be used like that, at least not without a token protest. If this is your token protest, I'm all ears."

She blushed. The only part of last night she hadn't enjoyed was when he left — everything before that was quite enjoyable indeed. "You think I'm too...passionate to be a proper wife?"

His grin was wolfish. "You're the proper wife for me, darling. If you're to give me an heir, we may as well enjoy our duty."

His voice teased, but the words scorched her like a brand. "That's all you see me as, isn't it? A vessel to carry your heir? And a bit of sport in the meantime?"

She came to her feet and drove her fist into his chest before he realized her intent. The air whooshed from his lungs and his arms wrapped around her, drawing her too close to allow another punch. She kicked him instead, and he winced as she hit his shin. But he didn't relax his grip. "What the devil is the matter with you?" he yelled, his cool composure finally destroyed. "Are you breeding already?"

She kicked him again for that. "Why didn't you ask me whether I wanted to go to London? Why did I have to hear it from your blasted valet instead of you?"

He let her go abruptly and stepped back, out of range of her foot. "Is that what you're carrying on about? Not last night?"

"I hardly call a legitimate grievance 'carrying on,'" she muttered. "But yes, I'm upset about this, not your...forwardness in my bedchamber."

"I meant to tell you about London when you awoke, you know. Word traveled faster than I expected."

"Is that supposed to be an apology?"

"You forget, wife," he said, his eyes narrowing. "I don't need to consult you. We've indulged ourselves since the wedding, and it has been pleasant, but I have duties I've neglected for too long. Apology or no, we will be leaving for London by week's end."

"You are so mad for duty that you care for nothing else," Amelia spat out. "What of your duty to me?"

He seemed truly puzzled by that. "I haven't mistreated you, have

I? You'll have the finest of everything in London, once we've settled there. Ferguson said yesterday that he has a townhouse he'll sell us, and you can decorate it however you like."

The Duke of Rothwell knew they were going to London before Amelia did? "You should have your precious Ferguson choose the colors. I'm sure he's more *au courant* than I am."

Malcolm's lips quirked. "If we're stealthy, we could steal the furnishings from him."

She grinned, then bit her lip. Malcolm's humor was too appealing, too distracting. She found her anger again and held onto it.

"You can't treat me like a piece of baggage, Malcolm. I had a life before you, and I don't want to lay it aside at your say-so."

"And what, pray, was that life?" he asked, crossing his arms. "Your correspondence?"

She lifted her chin. "Among other things."

"I haven't asked who you write to. But know that I could burn every scrap of paper and open every letter you receive if I have a mind to."

"I know," she replied. Beneath her anger, she felt panic — and somewhere beneath that, unacknowledged tears. It turned her into a trapped animal, frenzied and violent. "At least I know duty is all you care for. When I've given you a son, you'll surely let me seek my own pleasure like any other dutiful wife."

She had no desire to sleep with anyone but him — she just wanted to turn his attention away from her writing. But his sudden scowl was gratifying.

"You're not writing to other men," he said. It almost sounded like an effort to convince himself, not a question. "You were innocent when we married. You can't have tired of me yet."

"I tire of this conversation already."

He barked a laugh. "It's your conversation, not mine."

"Are you really set on going to London? On doing your duty rather than indulging for another few months? I thought we wouldn't go to town until the start of the Season next spring."

He sighed. "It must be done, darling. And if you're so determined to be rid of me, I'd best take you with me so I can keep an eye on your traitorous body."

His tone was a jest, but as he dropped his gaze to her breasts, his longing was real. She flushed. He may have thought her body would betray him — but from the heat she felt as he inspected her bosom, she knew it was dangerously close to betraying her as well.

She reached up and poked him in the chest. He brought his attention back to her face. "So that's all you want?" she asked. "Duty and fidelity? Nothing else?"

He didn't answer. She held her breath without realizing it as his hand came up to caress her face. His thumb traced across her cheekbone, remarkably gentle, and she leaned into his touch. She thought he would kiss her, would apologize, would relent...

But he pulled away. "Duty and fidelity," he repeated. "Anything else for our class is a distraction."

A distraction. Of all the villains she'd ever written, none had been as cruel as this. She gasped, sucking in the air her lungs suddenly screamed for. Her rage flared up and flamed out, a bonfire smothered by endless cold.

"A distraction," she whispered. The word etched itself in the ice on her heart, like a pattern traced on frost-covered glass, one that would return again and again at every touch of cold.

"A pleasant distraction," he amended, looking at her oddly. "A wonderful distraction. A better distraction than I ever thought to find."

There was a compliment buried there, but if she reached to grasp it, she only felt the thorns. "I think we understand each other, my lord."

He eyed her warily. "Do we?"

"Yes." She nodded, trying to be as coldly cruel as he was. "I distract you. And I've let you distract me for far too long."

He hadn't reacted yet. She smiled sweetly and aimed for his heart. "Don't fear, though. We can set up separate households as soon as we return to London. Now that you've got the wife you wanted and I'm not ruined, I see no reason at all why I should stay at your side."

CHAPTER TWENTY-FIVE

Malcolm should have been elated. He should have ushered her back to the breakfast room, fed her, and arranged separate housing within the hour.

He should not have felt like throttling her.

And he most certainly should not have turned on his heel, walked through the door, and locked it behind him.

He didn't plan to leave her there — he just needed a few minutes to think. And it was easier to think when he wasn't confronting those expressive blue eyes, or considering how her breasts looked better cupped in his hands than they did covered up by yards of black crepe.

Admittedly, the vibrations from Amelia pounding on the door as he leaned against it weren't conducive to rational thought. But now that she had admitted exactly what he already realized and acknowledged that they shouldn't be ruled by their passion, why did he feel like he was making the worst mistake of his life?

Malcolm banged his head against the door.

"Let me out before I make you regret this!" Amelia shouted. The words were muffled by the wood, but her annoyance rang through.

He grinned. He already regretted it, but whatever revenge Amelia planned would likely amuse him.

That amusement wasn't what he wanted in a marriage. He'd always thought his wife would be a paragon, one who could preside over his dinner table and perform credibly in the ton.

Amelia was better suited to preside over a battlefield than a teapot.

Malcolm knew what kind of wife he should have looked for. But faced with a choice between Amelia in all her glory and prim, dull Miss Etchingham, his body had made the choice for him. It wasn't just his body that wanted her, though. He could lose hours talking to her, let days pass without wanting the sound of a fresh voice.

He would have to control himself if he wanted to leave her long enough to accomplish anything for his clan. But while he would force himself to find some distance, he only needed it during the day. He hadn't even survived one night without her. Surely they could find a compromise rather than parting ways entirely?

His wife cursed on the other side of the door. Something metallic scraped across the stones. He turned the key and pulled the door open. Amelia stood inches away from the threshold, dragging an ancient broadsword.

"Not very sporting of you to try to kill me," he said.

Amelia grunted as she lifted the sword. "I came downstairs planning to kill you — no sense wasting this dress."

But a laugh lurked in her eyes, and she didn't struggle when Malcolm took the sword from her. It was meant to be wielded with two hands, and he swung it in an easy arc before replacing it on the wall. "Darling, violence will not solve our problems."

"Neither will locking me away when the mood strikes you," she said. "If we cannot even finish a conversation without wanting to kill each other, how can we live together?"

"Not all of our conversations end like this. We haven't fought at all since the wedding."

"We haven't spent our time talking, you dolt." He snickered at that, but she didn't rise to the bait. "If we were accustomed to talking, you would have consulted me about London."

He held up his hands. "I'm sorry."

She glared at him.

"Truly," he said.

"Do you know what you are apologizing for?"

He didn't — he just wanted her to calm down. But he knew better than to admit it. "I apologize for not asking your opinion."

She crossed her arms. "And if I said I wanted to stay here? What would you do?"

"Do you want to stay here?"

"I find I love the Highlands more than I expected."

That had nothing to do with him, but he still felt a boost of satisfaction at knowing she was settling into their home. "We'll return for Christmas. But I must go to London for the start of Parliament in November if I'm to meet potential allies."

"So you've decided about Christmas too?" she asked. "Really, are you such an autocrat that you cannot even feign interest in my opinion?"

He winced. "Marriage requires adjustments. I'll admit I'm not accustomed to asking anyone's preferences."

She didn't seem mollified by that, so he went on the attack. "You know, darling," he said, watching her face. "You're not so good at this marriage business either. Have you met with Graves or the housekeeper a single time since becoming my countess?"

She deflated. He hadn't seen her shoulders drop like that before. He almost felt guilty — almost.

"Your mother has things well in hand," she said.

"But it's not her house anymore. It's ours. She'll remove to the dower house when she's finished redecorating it, and then the castle, our house in Edinburgh, and the house we'll open in London will all be yours to manage."

Amelia scowled. "You sound like that's a reward."

He spread his arms to encompass the room around them. "You said you loved the Highlands. If you want this to be your home, then make it so."

Her eyes were stark. He knew she still had secrets — knew it even more now that they'd spent several weeks together. A woman of her passionate leanings wouldn't have spurned the attentions of all men for a decade unless she was hiding something.

Malcolm doubted that he wanted to know what she was hiding, even though the question ate at him. He wanted her to tell him freely, not because she'd been caught. Still, he wasn't above prodding a bit, if that would encourage her to compromise and keep living with him.

He strolled around her, like a wolf circling a deer, and sat in the chair he'd previously placed her in. She turned, watching him, sensing his shifting mood.

He leaned back. "If you don't want to share my house, of course, there are other alternatives."

"What are those?" she asked, her eyes narrowing suspiciously.

"I've a house on the western isles, utterly remote, that would give you as much solitude as you desire. Although I must warn you that your bed there will be quite chilled without me in it."

She grinned before she caught herself. "You are remarkably self-assured."

"You make it easy to be," he said.

"Would that I could be so confident."

Her voice was soft, suddenly uncertain. Doubt should have no place in her heart — she was too strong for that.

He held out a hand for her. When she took it, he pulled her into his lap. "Come to London with me, Amelia. I want you there, distraction or no."

She toyed with a button on his waistcoat. "What if I can't be what you need? I don't want to be a mere distraction, but I never aspired to be a hostess, or a mother, or a wife."

"What did you aspire to be?"

She didn't answer. Was this her secret? Some hidden longing? A secret passion she couldn't name?"

He tried to guess. "You aren't... I mean to say..."

He cut himself off. She looked up at him, her eyes wide. He finished his question before he choked on it. "You and Miss Etchingham aren't of the, er, Sapphic persuasion, are you?"

She paused, just for a moment, just long enough for his heart to stop. Then she burst into laughter, and the peals of it bounced off the bare stone walls.

"You thought Prue and I were lovers?" she asked when she could speak again. "Really?"

"Not really — not after everything you and I have done. But few women dream of something other than children. What's your dream?"

She closed her eyes. When she opened them again, there were tears there, but he didn't know if they were from laughter or mourning. "It was just a dream, my lord."

"Tell me," he urged, shamelessly going back on his plan to give her time.

She searched his face, looking for something. Then she said, "What if I told you I wanted to write?"

"Is that all?" he asked.

"All?" she echoed. "You really think it's nothing?"

She looked affronted. He had just broken through — he couldn't let her shut him off again. "I didn't mean it as an insult," he assured her. "But compared to being in love with someone else or committing high treason with your letters, writing seems preferable."

"No treason," she promised. Then she sobered. "It's just not something I had planned to give up, and yet marriage to you…"

He kissed the side of her neck, reveling in the way she opened for him. "As long as it doesn't cause a scandal or keep you from your duties as my countess, what's the harm? I'm sure it's fashionable in some circles for you to write bits of poetry or what not."

"So if I don't cause a scandal, I can write?" she asked.

Her voice was breathy from his kiss, but the look in her eyes said that the fate of their marriage rested on his answer.

"Yes," he said. "I'll even go you one better and say that as long as your nights are mine, you can use your days however you wish."

Her eyes lit up. He almost felt guilty — it wasn't much of a compromise, not when he knew he would need to stay away from her during the day if he was to accomplish anything meaningful in Parliament.

His guilt buried itself when she kissed him, hot and hungry. He let her take the lead this time — and she nearly broke him on the stone floor. When they finished, her black skirts were covered in dust and his trousers were hopelessly creased.

But she would go to London with him. And her secret, now that she had divulged it, was benign enough.

It was a victory. He had won their battle. But he may have lost the war.

Because looking up at her, as they both came undone, with the sunlight streaming through her hair and the light in her eyes, he realized he had fallen in love with his wife.

Bloody hell.

CHAPTER TWENTY-SIX

London - 26 November 1812

Amelia pushed her loathsome eggs around her plate. She should have hired a new cook, but she didn't want to admit that they would stay long enough to need one. Malcolm sat at the head of their new breakfast table, thumbing through the morning papers and making notes in a ledger that had rarely left his side since arriving in London a month earlier. His fingers, when he came to their bed at night, were almost as blackened by ink as hers.

Every night, he was ravenous for her. It was astonishing, the speed with which he could transform from the proper, duty-bound Earl of Carnach to the passionate, playful man she'd married. When they were in their chamber, he shed his reserve like he shed his clothes, claiming her like he had to take everything he could before the sun rose.

If this were a fairy tale, he had fallen victim to some dark enchantment — a magical lover at night, destined to turn back to stone in the morning.

He was always out of bed when the sun rose. In Scotland, they had lain in bed for hours some mornings, making love and laughing and getting crumbs from their breakfast in the sheets. In London, he was already cloaked in his mental armor before her sleep-fogged brain could register the change. He would eat breakfast with his papers and leave the house shortly thereafter, obsessed with meeting peers and keeping abreast of the issues of the day. And he wouldn't return until it was time to dress for that night's parties — parties where he made all the right noises and said the right things to the right people.

Parties where he never laughed.

It was maddening. Amelia had thought she wanted her days to herself. But when they stretched endlessly in front of her, broken by dull duties to her household rather than passionate demands from her new husband, she wanted the old Malcolm back. She wanted the seductive sorcerer from their library, not the sober politician from their breakfast room. She wanted him to see what the life he'd chosen would cost them — and to understand that there were possibilities other than hardening his soul into a graveyard effigy before his body was even dead.

Amelia sipped her tea. It had grown cold while she brooded. She found she hated it almost as much as her eggs. As she set the cup onto the saucer, she let it slip from her hand. The tea rushed over the lip, flooding the tablecloth and cascading onto Malcolm's untouched copy of the *Gazette*.

He jumped, pulling his ledger out of the way before picking up the dripping paper between his thumb and forefinger. She felt a swift stab of satisfaction as the ink ran and the paper reverted to pulp.

Malcolm looked up at her, but there was no heat in his gaze — just concern. "Are you feeling well, dear?"

Dear. Not darling. It shouldn't have bothered her. But her voice couldn't hide the chill. "Quite. I am sorry my clumsiness has ruined your morning."

He dropped the paper back into the puddle. "Warwick, send a

footman out for another paper."

The butler bowed. He shouldn't have had to be told — but then, Amelia suspected the hiring agency had not had many appropriate butlers to send on such short notice, and she'd done little to train him.

"Do you care to go upstairs while you wait for the paper?" she asked her husband. "I'm sure we can entertain ourselves."

She didn't even want to — she was too annoyed to fall into his bed so easily. But her request was a test.

For a moment he looked like he might pass. His eyes lit up, turning to that warm silver she now only saw at night, and his hand reached out to caress her cheek. His touch melted some of the ice around her heart, once again erasing the memory of his decision that she was just a distraction...

But when she melted, he hardened. He dropped his hand. "Would that I could. But Parliament just opened two days ago. I cannot miss a session already."

"Does it matter?" she asked before she could stop herself. "Does anyone care whether you're there?"

His silver eyes turned to steel. "I must start as I mean to go on. Someday they'll care. But they won't unless I'm there enough that they know me."

"How lovely that you're giving them a chance to know you," she murmured.

Malcolm raked a hand through his hair. He looked like he wanted to argue. She hoped that he would. Their fight in the tower before leaving for London had cleared the air for a moment — but as she suffocated in the ton and he did his damnedest to conquer it, she knew their marriage was far from sorted.

They might not be ruined by her secret writing career after all —

while Prudence refused to see her, there wasn't a single whisper about *The Unconquered Heiress* with Amelia's name attached to it. But after four weeks in London, Amelia knew the biggest danger to their marriage likely wasn't her writing — it was all the words they weren't saying to each other, welling up between them. Soon those words would be an ocean, unbridgeable, with dangerous riptides that could suck them both away.

She wanted him to say how he felt. Instead, his voice cooled. "You're overset. I trust your tongue will be more civil at the parties we're attending tonight."

She sucked in a breath. When he grasped her hand to kiss it, she kept it in a fist. He kissed her knuckles anyway.

"If all you want is civility, you should have married someone else," she said through gritted teeth.

"Can we not talk about our marriage yet again?" he asked, gripping the arms of his chair. "What's done is done. We'll have all the time in the world once I'm settled in Parliament. But I trust you can amuse yourself for now."

They had talked about their marriage — just enough for her to feel nauseated and depressed, and vaguely homicidal.

She lifted her chin as she rose from her chair, tossing her napkin into the pool of tea between them. "Very well, my lord. I will amuse myself. And tonight I will be exactly the type of wife you need."

He stood, still pretending to be a gentleman despite the glare in his eyes. "If you aren't, you'll get that conversation you seem to want — but I promise you will not enjoy it."

She swept out of the room, ignoring his threat and the servants who gaped at them. He seemed to forget that these people were newly hired and not at all as loyal as his family retainers in Scotland.

But she didn't care about her reputation. She needed to be away from him, to think about which of them was the guilty party in the mess that their marriage was quickly becoming. She wasn't innocent either, not with her secrets, not when she was too scared to tell him how she felt or what she'd done until she was certain of his reaction.

And eventually she needed to decide whether to fight for him — or whether her writing, which is all that had mattered for so long, was still enough.

*   *   *

That night, Malcolm leaned back into the cushions of their new town coach. Amelia had greeted him quietly when he'd knocked on her door to escort her downstairs — not with annoyance, as he expected, or pleasure, as he wanted, but with calm resignation. Even now she refused to look at him. She looked down at her hands instead, where they were primly folded in her lap.

"What ails you, dear?" he asked. "You haven't seemed yourself today."

Her temper sparked. But if it melted the ice, it only melted it enough to drown her emotion. By the time she spoke, she had frozen again.

"Isn't this what you want, *dear*?" she retorted. "Propriety?"

She'd promised that morning to be the type of wife he needed. Now he knew she was doing it to provoke him — and she had succeeded. But the carriage was rolling to a halt at the first rout party of the evening. He couldn't afford to discuss their marriage now, not if he wanted to stay cool in the face of the ton.

So he let her statement pass. She glared at him before she

remembered the show she was putting on for him. She returned to staring at her gloves and didn't look at him again.

The first event passed in a blur of faces and a procession of inane conversation. Malcolm had never liked rout parties, so called for the route taken through the house — he and Amelia made a circuit of the drawing rooms, greeted the hostess, touched fingers and exchanged civilities with the other people they passed, and were out the door a quarter of an hour later.

When their carriage finally came back to them through the crush of vehicles outside the house, Malcolm handed Amelia up into it. She settled her skirts around her, remaking herself into a statue. He saw now why she'd been dubbed the Unconquered. Everything about her was icy perfection, contained, constrained, unattainable.

He wanted to smash through her façade. He wanted to bury his fingers in her hair, rip out the pins, and free her curls to let them flow over his hands. He wanted to hear her laugh, low and throaty and only for him.

The harsh blast of desire startled him. He clenched his fists against his thighs, vowing to stay in control.

"Wasn't that lovely?" she said, after a few minutes of silence. "I do so love a good rout party."

Her voice was drenched in sarcasm. He would have laughed, but his mood was too foul. "Then I'm sure the next one will make you even happier, dear."

She looked out the window of their carriage, watching their slow progress through Mayfair. And she didn't speak to him again, not at the second rout party, not when they returned to their carriage, and not when he escorted her up the stairs to Lady Delamar's ball.

It was their final party of the evening. Malcolm didn't even want to go in. He wanted to take her home, take her to bed, seduce her out of her pique, make her beg, make her scream for him — make her feel everything he felt. Make her accept their life together.

Make himself happy instead of miserable.

But he handed their cloaks to a maid, escorted Amelia into the ballroom, and greeted the hostess instead. He had turned thirty-five two weeks earlier — more than half the age his father was when he had died. Malcolm would run out of time to save the Highlands — he couldn't waste the opportunities these social events offered.

"How long do you wish to stay, my lord?" Amelia asked when they left the receiving line.

He shrugged. "It depends upon the guests. If there are men worth meeting, we shall stay longer."

There was a flash of something on her face — sadness? It surely wasn't pity, but for a moment he saw her as he had in the old dower house, mourning for him even though he was alive at her side.

"May we dance first?" she asked. "I know it's not proper for me to ask, but they are starting a waltz."

He'd denied her that morning when she tried to lure him back into bed. But he wasn't strong enough to deny her again.

"One dance," he said.

"Of course. And then you can go be Lord Carnach."

There was no accusation in her voice, just resignation.

He pulled her onto the floor. She'd taught him the waltz while they were in Scotland — it was still unacceptable in some circles and hadn't been danced in London at all when he'd last visited the capital. In their castle, he could get as close as he liked, molding himself to her, teasing her until most of their lessons ended in lovemaking.

Here he held himself at the proper distance. But as they moved together across the floor, the music lured Amelia out from behind the wall she'd created. Perhaps it lured him out from behind his own wall, too. Somewhere, somehow, their marriage had devolved into a siege.

But when they were in each other's arms, all of that faded into the background. As long as the music played, he could believe that the last few weeks were just a bump in the road, that their marriage would right itself again once they settled into their roles.

"I would ask your thoughts, but I think mine mirror them," she said.

"I doubt that."

She raised a brow. "So you're not experiencing the same confusing mush of wanting to do murder or run off to the nearest bedchamber?"

He laughed. "You win the point, darling. That is what I was thinking."

"Did you just laugh?" she asked with a quizzical frown.

"Is there something wrong with that?"

She paused while they negotiated around a slower couple. Then she looked at his face again, trying to read what else might be lurking in his eyes. "You never laugh at these events. I've missed it."

"I didn't think you'd noticed," he said.

It was her turn to laugh, but hers was pained. "Romeo and Juliet had it easy, didn't they?"

His hand tightened on her waist. "What do you mean by that?"

"It's easy enough to have a wedding. But everything that comes after…do you think they really would have been happy together? Or would their passion have flared out?"

"If you plan to drink poison, I'll murder you myself," he warned, suddenly worried.

"You know I'm too violent for poisons," she said. This time her laugh was genuine. The light in her eyes was back, the light he now saw only in their bed.

He caressed her hand. Her other one dug into his shoulder. "Our passion shows no sign of slowing," he said.

She didn't answer. They finished the dance. Every time their bodies touched, the friction wore away at his resolve. Neither of them were happy — it was as plain on her face as it was in his gut.

But what would it take to be happy? And how could he put their happiness above the livelihoods of an entire clan?

Just as the music ended, Amelia sighed. "Thank you for the dance, my lord."

She was wistful. He realized that she expected him to walk away. His last bit of resistance snapped. He could spare them a night, even if he couldn't promise her tomorrow.

"Shall we go home?" he asked. "Only if you want to, of course."

She smiled, slow and sultry. "Do you promise to laugh at least twice?"

"You're making a bad bargain, wife."

"I'm happy with the terms," she said.

"You shouldn't be." He lifted her hand and kissed her knuckles, each one on its own, far less discreet than he should have been. "There are many things I want to do at least twice tonight — things you'll find much more pleasure from."

Amelia laughed. For a moment, it was like they were in Scotland again — just the two of them, with nothing hanging between them. He wanted to bottle that feeling, cork it and keep it someplace safe, so he could pull it out and quench himself with it during their next silent battle.

In the next minute she froze.

"What?" he asked, turning to look over his shoulder in the direction of her stare. Prudence Etchingham sat ten feet away, alone, at the periphery of a circle of spinsters and chaperones. It was the first time they'd encountered her at an event — either Lady Harcastle was economizing, or they weren't usually invited to the caliber of parties that Malcolm and Amelia attended.

He turned to stand at Amelia's side. She took a single step forward, then stopped. The movement drew Prudence's attention.

Her face suffused with color. It wasn't a pretty blush. Splotches of red spread down Prudence's throat and across her chest. She straightened her cap and smoothed her hair unconsciously, as though she needed to do something with her hands.

"Shall I escort you to her?" he asked Amelia, his voice low.

"No," she said. "I must talk to her without you."

But even though her voice sounded sure, almost strident, her hand still clutched his arm. So when Prudence stood and walked toward them at a pace more appropriate for a cemetery than a ballroom, he didn't leave Amelia's side.

Prudence finally reached them. He bowed over her hand. "Miss Etchingham, it is a pleasure to see you again," he said.

"Lord Carnach," she murmured. But her eyes were locked on Amelia's. "Lady Carnach, I trust you are well?"

Amelia's fingers tensed on his arm. "Perfectly, Miss Etchingham. And you?"

Their proper titles, after years of friendship, sounded like insults. Prudence briefly closed her eyes. "Tolerably well, I suppose."

The silence immediately grew awkward. Malcolm tried to step away. "If you want to converse, ladies, I'll seek out other circles."

"That would be wonderful," Amelia said, flashing him the first grateful look he'd seen outside their bed in weeks. "Perhaps you could fetch us some lemonade while we talk?"

Prudence hesitated. "I'm not sure talking is advisable, Lady Carnach."

"I'm sure we have much to discuss," Amelia said. He heard a question in her voice, almost an accusation — odd, when the only sentiment he'd heard her express about Prudence was guilt.

"Yes, we do. But not here."

"When, then?" Amelia asked. "I left my card ages ago, nearly the moment we arrived in London. And you've avoided meeting me at Ellie's house."

"Tomorrow?" Prudence said. "I will come to Ellie's for our usual gathering."

She didn't sound like she wanted to, though.

"Please do," Amelia said, low and urgent. "I must know..."

She broke off as Lady Harcastle bustled up to them. "Prudence, we must go home," the woman barked.

Prudence shifted, but she didn't look at her mother. "It's early yet, Mother. Surely you don't want to leave?"

"I find the company dreadful tonight," Lady Harcastle said.

She still hadn't looked at Malcolm or Amelia. The insult was clear. Malcolm didn't care what Lady Harcastle thought of him, but for Amelia's sake, he wanted to put her in her place.

"I trust you approved of the company in the post chaise I hired to take you to London?" he asked.

Her frown turned even uglier. "It was rude of you to invite us under false pretenses, and even ruder to fling your hospitality in our face. Prudence, we're leaving now."

"Mother, he wasn't..." Prudence said.

"Don't say you're defending him!" Lady Harcastle exclaimed. "After what he did?"

People were looking at them curiously. Prudence's flush spread higher, lower, until every bit of exposed skin was red.

"Lady Harcastle," Malcolm said, his voice low, "consider your words carefully before anyone misinterprets."

She finally looked around her. Perhaps she realized that her statements were vague enough to ruin Prudence. She lowered her voice, but the venom was still there. "Prudence should be on your arm, not her," she said, gesturing at Amelia without looking at her. "You'll regret what you've done."

Prudence grabbed her mother's arm. "Come, Mother, you're right — we should leave."

Lady Harcastle looked at Malcolm for a long moment. He stared her down. "If you were a man, I would call you out," he warned, his temper snapping. "But as you're not, I suggest you stay away from Lady Carnach. She should not have to hear your slander."

Amelia placed a quelling hand on his arm. Lady Harcastle closed her eyes at the gesture. When she opened them, the venom was gone — but there was a resolve there that Malcolm didn't understand.

"I wish you both happy," she said, in a dark voice that sounded like a curse. "I hadn't before, but now I see how very much you deserve each other."

Malcolm raised an eyebrow, but she turned without saying goodbye. Prudence mouthed an apology to Amelia, but she hurried after her mother even though the woman shook off Prudence's attempt to touch her shoulder. Prudence slowed then, but she still trailed in her mother's wake — she had nowhere else to go.

Amelia's hand slid from his arm. He reached out and clasped it with his own. "I'm sorry we encountered them," he said.

"I had hoped Prudence would forgive me someday," she said.

"I think she will," Malcolm predicted. "But her mother is another matter."

Amelia squeezed his fingers. "Can we still go home? Or do you want to make use of our audience?"

The other spinsters and chaperones had watched their conversation with Lady Harcastle with wide eyes. It would be smart to stay another hour and show they were entirely unaffected by her accusations — but Malcolm again found that he couldn't deny the need in Amelia's voice.

They returned to their house. By the time they reached his chamber, they were mindless for each other. And as he'd promised, he did everything twice. The first was hard and fast, with his hands buried in her hair and her name on his lips. Her limbs wrapped around him, clinging, stroking, like the woman he needed rather than the statue she'd become.

The second was deep and slow. Devastatingly slow. He didn't let either of them come until her voice was hoarse from begging — until his heart burst from everything he couldn't find the voice to say.

After, he cradled her in his arms. Her finger traced patterns across his chest, teasing him as he caught his breath.

"I don't think our passion is in any danger of flaring out," he said when he could speak again.

Her hand stopped. She pushed her hair back off her face. There were tears in her eyes, but she didn't brush them away. "Don't tempt Fate, Malcolm," she whispered. "Our lives are far from finished."

He kissed the top of her head. "You make me want to live forever."

She didn't answer. Her finger resumed its tracing. Maybe she was a witch, binding him with her touch — because his words hadn't been a lie, even if they sounded like an empty compliment.

He wanted forever with her.

But the only way to claim forever was to accept how she felt in his arms — and acknowledge that her love was more important than any of the duties on his shoulders.

CHAPTER TWENTY-SEVEN

The next afternoon, Amelia took a cup of tea from Ellie's outstretched hand. The conversation between Ellie, Madeleine, and Amelia had been desultory while they waited for Prudence, but Amelia needed their advice. And she finally seized the moment before she lost her nerve.

"Do you mind if we discuss Carnach before turning our attention to art?" she asked.

"Am I hearing you correctly? You are volunteering to discuss Carnach?" Madeleine asked, raising a brow.

"Yes," Amelia scowled. "And I may never do so again, so you should take the offer if you're curious." She doubted she wanted to hear their opinions — they would never parrot back only what Amelia wanted to hear. But if anyone could help her untangle her feelings, it was her fellow Muses.

Ellie dropped a lump of sugar into her own cup. "You know I haven't painted in an age. I'd much rather hear your latest tales."

Madeleine settled back into her chair, sprawling like she did when she wore breeches on the stage. "I haven't memorized any new roles lately, so I've nothing to discuss. Ferguson is too inventive for us to play the same characters twice."

She blushed as she spoke, but her smile was supremely self-satisfied. Amelia laughed. "As much as I dislike the man, he is good for you, isn't he?"

"He has his uses," Madeleine said with a secretive grin over her teacup.

"If I have to hear yet another time that you and my brother are so perfect, I may scream," Ellie said, rolling her eyes. "Should we wait for Prudence? Or do you want to start, Amelia?"

Amelia looked at the clock on Ellie's mantel. It was ten minutes past their appointed time. They were ensconced in the marchioness's private sitting room in Folkestone House, an opulent, comfortable room that Ellie had turned into an Oriental fantasy. Ellie perched regally on her chaise-longue, her red hair and pale skin lit up by the gold velvet cushions. Amelia and Madeleine sat in matching armchairs, backed by an ornate chinoiserie screen, but the settee waited for Prudence.

"Prue said she would come when I saw her last night, but she didn't sound like she meant it," Amelia said.

"Where did you see Prudence?" Madeleine asked. "I thought you hadn't spoken yet."

"At Lady Delamar's ball. And we still haven't truly spoken. We just exchanged a few words. Then her mother dragged her away before I could ask about her note. But Prudence didn't seem to want to talk anyway."

Ellie scooped up another lump of sugar. "She'll come when she's ready. But if she didn't cut you last night, you still have a chance."

Amelia sighed. "It will be a shame if I can never repair the breach with her and am saddled with Malcolm forever in the bargain."

"Is he really so bad?" Madeleine asked. "Even if he cannot rival Ferguson, he still seems friendly enough."

"You've been married for five months. Surely your honeymoon is over?"

"Not yet," Madeleine said. "Or if it is, I still like him anyway."

"Is yours over, Amelia?" Ellie asked. "You seemed happy enough when we saw you together in Scotland, even if you still couldn't answer my questions."

Amelia stayed still, fighting the urge to stand and pace the room. "In some ways Malcolm's better every day. I would wager that he is as...inventive...as your precious duke, Madeleine."

Ellie snorted as Madeleine choked on her tea. "So the Earl of Carnach is good in bed," Ellie said. "Unsurprisingly, I must admit. He has a sense of humor and a strong body. He'd have to be an utter dolt to make a mess of things."

Ellie was the most brutally frank woman Amelia had ever met — it was little wonder they hadn't socialized when Amelia and Madeleine were still confined to the spinsters' set and Ellie was blazing a path through the most scandalous reaches of the ton. Amelia grinned at her. "Carnach is good. Quite a bit better than good."

"Now who is going on too much about her husband?" Madeleine teased.

"Fine," Amelia said, holding up her hands in surrender. "I won't go on about Carnach's prowess."

"A pity," Ellie murmured. She dabbed at her mouth with her handkerchief, dusting away a crumb from her biscuit. "I don't suppose you'd let me paint him?"

"His portrait?" Amelia asked.

"I could paint him as Caesar Augustus. With those arms and calves, he would be a sensation in Roman garb."

The flare of jealousy was so sudden that Amelia gasped from it

— and so bright that Ellie and Madeleine couldn't help but notice it. "No painting," Amelia bit out.

Ellie raised an eyebrow. "Perhaps you have answered why you kissed him. Have you admitted yet that you're in love with him?"

Amelia broke a biscuit in half, then slowly pulverized it between her fingers. When she looked up, Ellie's eyebrow was still raised. Madeleine leaned forward with her arms on her knees, eager for the tale.

She set aside the saucer with its pile of crumbs. "I may be in love with him," she said slowly.

Then she smashed her reserve like it was yet another biscuit. "Damn him, I *am* in love with him. I never prevaricate — you know I hate prevaricating."

"Indeed," Madeleine murmured, giggling.

"Yes. I'm in love with him. And yet I'm telling you, not him, because the bloody man won't stay in the house long enough for me to say three words to him. And bedding is *not* the same as a real conversation."

Every night she traced her feelings on his chest, but she hadn't been able to say them aloud — not when she had no idea whether he would embrace them or fling them in her face. She gave in to her desire to pace, leaping up with the force of her speech. Ellie's private salon was too small to pace back and forth, so she circled around their chairs like a caged beast.

"She's in a bad state, isn't she?" Ellie observed.

Madeleine sipped her tea. "She'll come through in the end. She always has a plan. What do you plan this time, Mellie?"

Amelia came to a dead stop between Ellie's chaise and Madeleine's chair. She braced a hand against the back of Madeleine's chair to steady herself.

Madeleine knew her better than anyone else — better than her husband ever would, if he kept avoiding her during the day. And Madeleine had seen all of Amelia's schemes. So it was little wonder that she snorted when Amelia whispered, "No plan. I have no plan."

"You must have a plan," Madeleine insisted. "What is it? Flirting with someone at a party? Withholding sex like the Grecian women in *Lysistrata?*"

"Perhaps a slow-acting poison like the Florentine women used?" Ellie supplied.

Amelia and Madeleine both stared at her. "You've never thought of poison?" Ellie asked. "I declare, if Nick ever returns, he should bring an official food taster."

Amelia laughed. "I would almost pity the man if I didn't believe he deserved it."

"If I do kill Nick, I won't have the patience for poison." Ellie drawled the words as though only humor lay underneath them, but her blue eyes were stark. Amelia leaned over and squeezed her shoulder in silent sympathy. Ellie's former lover was her dead husband's cousin and heir — and Amelia suspected that if he ever returned to claim the title, their battle would be a story for the ages.

Ellie shrugged away from Amelia's hand. "No poison for Carnach, then. What will you do instead?"

Amelia slumped back into her chair. "I don't know. I hate not knowing, but there you have it. The great Amelia Staunton, plotter extraordinaire, brought low by a mere man."

"At least her pride hasn't been utterly destroyed," Madeleine observed.

"Careful, Amelia," Ellie said, taking Amelia's cup and refreshing it from the teapot. "Sentiments like those will have every would-be women's suffrage supporter in London beating a path to your door."

"Malcolm would hate that. He will only let me write if I don't cause a scandal — imagine what he would do if I led a radical uprising in my sitting room."

She snickered at the thought, but her words caused a stir among her companions. "Did you tell him you're writing?" Madeleine demanded.

Amelia took her teacup back from Ellie. "Yes. Before we left Scotland."

"And he approves?"

"He said writing a bit of poetry seemed like a proper pastime," Amelia said, mimicking his dismissive tone.

Ellie stifled a laugh. "You must have wanted to stab the poor man."

"I may have tried to do him violence," Amelia allowed, thinking back to the broadsword she'd hauled off the wall of the tower. Then she thought of their lovemaking on the stone floor…

She somehow mastered her blush before either of her friends caught her. "He said I could write as long as I don't cause a scandal. And I intend to take him at his word."

Madeleine's eyes narrowed. "Did you tell him you *want* to write? Or did you tell him that you *have written*? And that what you have written was the sensation of London this spring?"

Amelia waved a hand, then blew on her tea to cool it. "He didn't ask. If he wants to assume that I write poetry for myself with all the hours he leaves me to rot in that house, then he's welcome to that assumption."

"He'll catch you eventually," Madeleine warned.

"No. He won't. There hasn't been a hint of rumor about me."

"So your plan is to keep him from finding out that you write the most in-demand Gothic romances of the day, whilst ignoring that you're in love with him?" Ellie asked.

Amelia scowled.

Ellie clapped her hands. "Oh, this shall be fun. If he hasn't caught you by Christmas, promise you'll invite me to Scotland with you. I don't want to miss it."

Amelia threw a cushion at her. "You're no help at all. Why we asked you to join our club is beyond me."

"You'll be outvoted if you try to oust Ellie now," Madeleine said. "Ferguson and I will come to Scotland too. It sounds like the best house party I've ever attended."

"It's so unfair — you are so assured that Ferguson will go where you want to go," Amelia said, retrieving her cushion from Ellie and stuffing it behind her back. "That's the problem with Malcolm. Ever since he decided it was time to take his seat up in the Lords, he's mostly avoided me. He even told me that I'm too much of a distraction."

"He may be good in your bed, but he is a dolt after all, isn't he?" Madeleine asked. "I'm sure Ferguson thinks that at least half the time, but he's too smart to say the words to me."

"But Ferguson isn't so obsessed with his duties that he ignores everything else," Amelia said. "All I want is to believe that if the choice came down to me or the estate, Malcolm wouldn't sacrifice me for his damned castle."

"I could paint him as Agamemnon," Ellie mused, her eyes focused a thousand feet beyond the room. "And you as Iphigenia, awaiting sacrifice."

Amelia threw her cushion again. "No painting. And no death, particularly not with Malcolm playing the role of a father sacrificing his daughter. I'm overwrought, I know. I should be happy that he leaves me alone during the day. But once in awhile…"

She trailed off. Ellie tossed the cushion out of her reach, no doubt wanting to preserve the china. They lapsed into silence as Amelia stared into her teacup.

Once in awhile she wanted to feel important to him.

But she wanted to feel like it was real, not something she had tricked him into with yet another scheme.

There were footsteps in the hall. Ellie's butler, a sinfully handsome young man who could never be a butler in a proper house, tapped on the door. "My lady, Miss Etchingham has arrived."

He bowed as he stepped aside to let Prudence through to door. "Thank you, Ashby," Ellie said. He bowed again, flashing a smile far more brilliant than a butler should display before leaving and closing the door behind him.

"You do turn up the best looking staff," Madeleine said with a sigh. "Ferguson probably would have forced me to fire the butler you found for us if he wasn't so good at his job."

Ellie laughed as she stood to embrace Prudence. "Welcome, my dear. Would you care for tea?"

Prudence nodded. Her cheeks were flushed, like she'd just come in from the hunt. "I am sorry for my tardiness. Mother was rather beastly about letting me go."

Amelia rose to her feet, hovering as Prudence turned to hug Madeleine. They exchanged small compliments about their dresses, even though Amelia was sure Madeleine had seen Prue's dress before — but Amelia's nerves overruled her impatience.

When Prudence turned to her, Amelia braced herself. Prudence's dark eyes were serious — but oddly, there was little judgment in them. Instead, her eyes looked dead. If her usual spirit was there, it was buried so deep that even Prudence's talent for unearthing the past might never find it.

They stood awkwardly for a moment. Amelia rushed to fill the silence. "I trust the rest of your evening was pleasant?"

She winced. It was a stupid thing to say, but the banal pleasantry was the first sentence that popped into her head. Prudence nodded, though. "And yours?"

"Yes, quite," Amelia said.

They paused again. Ellie busied herself with the teapot. The tang of fresh lemons in the air made Amelia ache with memory. Prudence was the only one of their circle who took her tea with lemon. How many hundreds of afternoons had they spent like this?

And would it ever be comfortable again? Or would she always rush to say the wrong thing just to break the silence?

Prudence took her cup from Ellie and sat on the settee. The rest of them sat as well, the easy comfort of moments before mostly gone. Ellie tried her best, though. "Are you and your mother staying in London for the holidays?"

Prudence stripped off her gloves and reached for a biscuit. "The lease is paid through the end of the year, so yes. After that…"

She trailed off. She didn't look at Amelia. Instead, she examined her biscuit like it was the most fascinating confection she'd ever had the pleasure of seeing.

Amelia couldn't contain herself any longer. "Prudence…Miss Etchingham…I am sorry. Really, truly sorry for what happened in Scotland. I only meant to help."

Prudence sighed. She took a tiny bite of her biscuit, savoring it, before she finally looked at Amelia. "I know, Mellie."

She took another bite of her biscuit. Amelia waited. The whole room waited. Perhaps the whole world waited — or at least that's how it felt to Amelia, balanced there between damnation and forgiveness, between wanting to apologize and demanding to know what Prudence had done.

"And I don't hate you for it," Prudence finally continued. "I felt nothing for Carnach. We had nothing in common, other than our mutual need for a spouse. So when it comes to your marriage, you're forgiven."

Amelia exhaled. Prudence regarded her gravely, leveling a stare at her that would have cut her heart out if she hadn't heard Prudence's last words.

But Prudence wasn't finished. "I know what you were trying to accomplish. And I might have even thanked you for it eventually, had you succeeded. But you can't carry on with your meddling, Mellie. It's already cost you more than you know."

Amelia felt her face crumple. Tears burned at the corners of her eyes. But she was so accustomed to controlling herself that she ignored the imminent flood. She took a breath, steadying her voice so it wouldn't betray her. "I couldn't forgive myself if it cost me your friendship. I vow I will never meddle in your affairs again."

"The damage is done," Prudence said. Then she shifted in her chair. The afternoon sun through the window lit a stray wisp of guilt in her eyes. "And, truth be told, I should make the same promise to you."

Amelia thought back to the letter she'd received in Scotland and Prudence's cryptic request for forgiveness. "What happened? Why did you apologize to me?"

Prudence took another biscuit. She nearly inhaled this one, as though it could go straight to her backbone.

Ellie nudged the plate of biscuits closer toward her. "Take all the time you need, dear," she said gently. "Amelia won't bite."

"Do you know what she's talking about?" Madeleine asked Ellie.

"I have my suspicions," Ellie said, shrugging. "And even if they're correct, we'll muddle through together."

Prudence threw Ellie a grateful look and lunged for another biscuit. "I shouldn't eat so many of these — I can't afford to let out my gowns. But Mother and her marriage schemes can go hang."

Amelia laughed despite her apprehension. "What's her latest scheme?"

Prudence sobered. "Nothing to do with marriage. Do you know, I almost wish she'd kept her focus on the marriage mart? But with my latest failure, she's seeking other incomes."

"She should write a gossip column," Madeleine suggested. "Her tongue would cause quite the stir."

"It's already caused enough trouble," Prudence said.

Then she looked at Amelia. "I'm sorry. Very sorry. And I am apologizing now, because you may not be able to hear my apology when I divulge what I am sorry for."

Amelia sucked in a breath and held it, using the extra air to push down her rising nausea. "What happened?"

Prudence screwed her eyes shut, grimacing before letting the words go. "Understand that I was still angry with you. But in my annoyance, I slipped in front of Mother. And she knows that you wrote *The Unconquered Heiress*."

CHAPTER TWENTY-EIGHT

If Amelia was one of her heroines, this would be the moment when the vague feeling of doom coalesced into a living, breathing threat. She loved writing those moments — but when confronted with a threat of her own making, one that could destroy the pretty palace of lies she and Malcolm had built, her heart stopped.

"What is she doing with that information?" she asked.

Prudence swirled her tea in her cup, perhaps looking for leaves that might tell their fate. "She had promised not to do anything with it. I didn't want to ruin you, even if she did, and I swore her to secrecy. And she is still friends with your mother, even if they aren't speaking at the moment."

Prudence drained her teacup, then continued. "But when she saw the two of you last night, dancing together like you were a love match, all her anger came back. She was apoplectic — I haven't seen her like that since she found out my brothers were going to fight on the Peninsula. She was raging all night about Carnach being a liar and seducer of women. It's possible she hates him more than she hates you, Amelia. And that's saying something — she's convinced you set a trap for him."

"I could buy her off," Amelia said, already trying to think of alternatives. Coming up with a plan was better than giving in to her panic. "It would be hard to get three hundred pounds without telling Malcolm, but I think it could be done."

"I don't think it's about the money, much as we need it," Prudence said.

Her empty cup clattered in her saucer. Ellie removed it gently from her shaking hands. Prudence looked up, and Amelia saw her doom written on Prudence's face. "I talked to our driver on the way here — we've let go of our footmen. He said Mother sent him to White's this morning with a note for Kessel."

Panic overwhelmed her then, leaving no room for plans. Amelia suddenly felt lightheaded. She collapsed against the back of her chair, hitting her head on the frame since her cushion wasn't there to stop her. The starburst of pain was nothing compared to the sudden knot in her stomach, a clenched fist demanding penance.

Amelia dropped her head into her hands. "Malcolm will murder me. And I deserve it. In fact, I hope he does it quickly, just so I'm not left wondering when it will happen."

"Carnach isn't the killing type. I've seen murderers and he isn't one," Ellie said.

Madeleine knelt at Amelia's feet and started chafing her hands. "He won't kill you, Mellie. If he tries, I'll kill him myself."

They were all silent as Madeleine rubbed Amelia's hands. Amelia fought to breathe, forced herself to take in deep lungfuls of air instead of the shallow, tortured breaths her panic had induced. When she finally had enough air to think again, Madeleine looked her in the eyes. "He won't kill you," she said again, clear and solid. "But you should tell him about this immediately."

Amelia stood, swaying just a moment as she gained her balance. "You're right. If I can tell him before he hears it from someone else…"

She trailed off. Her friends nodded.

For once, they all let her believe what she wanted to believe.

"It will come off all right, Amelia," Ellie said. "And there are worse scandals than being a writer."

Amelia didn't care about the scandal anymore. She cared about how Malcolm would look at her, and whether those eyes would ever light up for her again — or whether their whole lives would become their daytime distance, rather than their nighttime passion.

But she smiled at Ellie like she agreed. "I'm sure it will. Thank you for the tea, and for the advice."

Then she turned to Prudence, who watched her carefully. "Prue — can I call you Prue, or are you still Miss Etchingham to me?"

Prudence grinned, just a bit. "I suppose you can call me Prudence if I can still call you Amelia."

Amelia smiled. Everything else was crashing around her ears, but this first step at reclaiming their friendship gave her heart. "Prudence — thank you for the warning. If your mother hasn't said anything irrevocable, tell her I'll pay her. Anything she demands, so long as she stays quiet."

"I will tell her," Prudence said. But there was too much doubt in her voice to give Amelia any comfort. "She is so angry, though — has been ever since Carnach threw me over for you. I'm not sure she'll accept."

Amelia pulled on her gloves. "No matter. I've made my bed. I won't complain when I must lie in it."

Madeleine hugged her before Amelia could escape. "You will feel better when you tell Malcolm," she said. "And no matter what happens, you'll always have us."

They let her go then. There was nothing they could do to cheer her, not when her marriage had suddenly veered onto the thinnest of ice.

And where once she would have lit a bonfire on the edge and watched happily as their marriage drowned, she knew that she and Malcolm were worth saving.

She just had to pray that she was not too late to pull them back from the abyss.

*   *   *

Malcolm swirled his drink in his glass, letting it lap right up to the edge. His hands had stopped shaking an hour earlier — a good sign, if he was to emerge from the upcoming confrontation without committing violence.

But his mind still raced. It was only four o'clock, hours earlier than he had told Amelia he would be home. He had come straight to his study when he returned at three. It didn't feel like his study, not with the empty desk and the books rented to fill the shelves until he could order according to his preferences. It was better than waiting for Amelia in his bedchamber, though.

With a bed, it would be all too easy to pretend, one last time, that they were perfect.

He felt like he was suffocating. He yanked at the knot in his cravat, tossing it on his desk when it finally came free. The cloth covered the book he'd flung there an hour earlier. Ferguson had warned him, a lifetime ago, to ask Amelia about it. And he had asked — but he hadn't pressed, even when her request to write should have roused his suspicions. At the time, he told himself it was because he had already ruined her, and nothing could get him out of it.

But now he knew — he hadn't asked because Amelia was the only bright spot in the life he'd given over to his duties. He hadn't wanted to lose that. And his selfish desire to keep a bit of pleasure for himself, to keep his faith in her intact, may have cost them everything.

Malcolm drummed his fingers against the desk, letting some of his anger leach away so he wouldn't resort to draining the entire decanter before Amelia came home. The rhythmic tapping reverberated in the room. There were no carpets yet, and the wood floor did nothing to dampen the aggressive sound. It sounded like his heart pounding in his ears — the way it had earlier, trying to drown out Kessel's voice.

Malcolm and Ferguson had adjourned to White's for luncheon. Ferguson didn't enjoy Parliament, even though he could one day dominate the government if he wished to. With his scheming tendencies and the dozen seats his duchy controlled in the Commons, the new Duke of Rothwell was an undeniable force.

But Ferguson didn't want that type of power. "Do you finally believe me that governance is a vastly boring endeavor?" Ferguson had asked as they cut into their racks of lamb in White's main room.

Malcolm had looked around the club. The men who were most interested in politics seemed to directly overlap with the men he liked the least. "I won't argue that point. But if you leave the act of governing to this lot...it's little wonder there's so much that needs changing."

"Are you the one to do it, though?" Ferguson asked. "It's rather like Sisyphus pushing his boulder up the mountain."

"Someone must be Sisyphus," Malcolm said. "And if I'm cursed to push this boulder up the hill, so be it."

"Wouldn't you rather be Zeus? King of your mountain castle, lovely bride at your side, making babies and ruling your world? Make someone else be Sisyphus."

Malcolm laughed. "Zeus's wife was a jealous bitch and most of his children hated him."

Ferguson grinned. "I know. I hoped you'd take the metaphor without remembering the rest of the story."

"I've only been here a month. Once I've made some allies, there is progress to be made."

"I'm sure you'll go to the devil in your own way, MacCabe — you always do," Ferguson said with a shrug.

They'd lapsed into companionable silence, punctuating their chewing with the occasional jest. If London was full of women like Amelia and men like Ferguson, Malcolm might have tolerated it quite well.

But instead, there were men like Kessel, who stopped by their table with a slap on the back that seemed friendly and dark eyes that were full of malice. "Carnach!" he exclaimed. "I haven't seen you in years."

Kessel was several years older than Malcolm and Ferguson, and Malcolm had barely known him at Eton or during his brief trips to London in his youth. But Malcolm's voice was smooth as he invited Kessel to join them. "It has been an age. Rothwell, I trust you still remember Lord Kessel?"

Ferguson gave a cursory nod as Kessel took a seat. "Kessel."

"I am still so very sorry about your brother, your grace," Kessel said, his oily voice finding the crack in Ferguson's armor. "Carriage accidents are so tragic."

Ferguson's smile was all teeth. "I'm sure he would be glad to know someone mourns him."

Ferguson's brother died in a poorly hushed-up suicide, not a carriage accident — a fact Kessel, like the rest of the ton, was all too aware of. Malcolm tensed. Kessel was after something. And even if he wasn't after something, Malcolm disliked the man for what had happened between him and Amelia the previous year. But Kessel was also a powerful figure in the Lords, one who spoke often about the superiority of England over all the other British isles. He would never be an ally — but Malcolm hadn't wanted him as an out-and-out enemy.

Of course, hours later, in his study, Malcolm knew that Kessel was his enemy — perhaps was always destined to be his enemy, no matter what Malcolm could have said. Still, as he hashed over the conversation again, he grimaced. He shouldn't have offered the man a chair. He shouldn't have let him speak. He shouldn't have listened.

He shouldn't have let his words burrow into his soul, where they would fester and bleed, just as Kessel wanted them to.

But it was too late for "should." The conversation had happened, and there was no taking back the words.

Malcolm had tried to claim Kessel's attention, to distract him from his odd attack on Ferguson's brother, not knowing it was just Kessel's opening salvo before turning the battle to Malcolm. "What can we assist you with, Kessel? I'm sure you'd rather take your luncheon than sit about reminiscing."

"Oh, but reminiscing is such fun, isn't it? And I couldn't let another day elapse without offering you felicitations on your marriage."

It was Malcolm's turn to bare his teeth. "How kind of you to remember."

"How could I forget? Lady Amelia — forgive me, Lady Carnach — is hard to forget. I hope you don't regret the circumstances of your marriage."

His voice was quiet, but it carried. Heads were beginning to turn. Malcolm leaned in, maintaining the slightest veneer of civility. "I offered for her hand, and the lady was kind enough to accept. Any other story you've heard is a lie."

"I did not mean to impugn her honor," Kessel said, holding up his hands in mock surrender. "Of course, why a woman called 'the Unconquered' would marry so quickly does raise eyebrows. I'm sure she's pleased with her bargain, though."

Ferguson had been examining his fingernails while Kessel spoke, but he finally interjected. "I find you quite tiresome today, Kessel. If you have something to say, say it."

Kessel's cheeks flushed a dull red, matching the nose that was already showing the longterm effects of drink. His gaze shifted from Ferguson to Malcolm, but neither of them apologized. Malcolm may not have approved of Ferguson's attack, but it was the slightest bit gratifying to see Kessel squirm. Ferguson was a duke, after all, and Malcolm's earldom outranked a mere barony — there was little Kessel could say.

It should have ended there. Malcolm and Ferguson both turned back to their plates, expecting Kessel to leave. But then his voice turned from oil to fire, igniting the air between them.

"I hope you can control your wife's pen better than you can control your friend's tongue," he said to Malcolm.

Malcolm kept cutting at his lamb. He knew how this game was played. "My wife's pen is none of your concern."

"Is it not? When she would make fools of everyone in the ton?"

Malcolm made the mistake of looking up. Whatever Kessel saw on his face made him smile. He continued without an invitation. "Don't say she didn't tell you. How shameful that I discovered her secret before you did."

"Careful, Kessel," Malcolm said through his teeth. "You would regret dishonoring her."

"Does she regret dishonoring me? If she were a man, I'd call her out for what she's done."

Everyone around them had grown silent. The silence fell across the dining room, doing nothing at all to distract Malcolm from the heartbeat in his ears. "What, precisely, has she done?"

Kessel reached into his coat and pulled out a slim volume, bound in calfskin. He threw it on the table like a gauntlet. "She wrote that nasty bit of filth. I'd wager she's sitting at home even now, penning more stories under your very nose. Perhaps this time you'll be the villain instead of me."

Then he stood. "Again, I wish you very happy, Mr. Rosefield."

The name on the book was A.S. Rosefield — a pseudonym, as everyone knew, although he hadn't known who the name protected until that moment. The murmurs broke out around them, sounding like hundreds of scuttling beetles coming to pick over his bones. Malcolm ignored the crowd. He ignored the book. He even ignored the voice that told him to stay calm, to smooth the waters.

Instead, he had lunged up and punched Kessel in the face.

CHAPTER TWENTY-NINE

Amelia arrived home at four-fifteen. The carriage ride from Ellie's house on Portman Square to her new house on Curzon Street was not overly long, but her dread made it feel like a lifetime. She wondered if Madeleine's mother, the Marquise de Loubressac, had felt this way as she was driven to the guillotine.

Then she winced and told herself not to be dramatic. Her aunt had lost her head in the French Revolution, which was why Madeleine had grown up with Amelia instead. No matter what happened, Amelia wasn't at risk of being executed. Losing Malcolm wouldn't be as bad as that, would it?

She couldn't answer that question.

She had offered to drop Prudence at her house in Bloomsbury, even though it was a substantial detour from the more exclusive streets around Hyde Park, but Prudence had declined. If talking to Lady Harcastle could prevent the impending scandal, she would have gone, but Prudence thought Amelia's pleas would fall on deaf ears.

So when the carriage rolled to a halt outside her front door, there was nothing she could do but wait for Malcolm to return — and hope she could tell him everything before he heard it elsewhere.

When she walked up the steps to the house that still didn't feel like a home, her butler greeted her. "His lordship has returned, my lady. He requests your presence in his study."

She handed the butler her cloak, her reticule, her gloves — everything she could think to give him, but it only delayed the inevitable by a few moments. She walked down the hall alone, her half-boots echoing on the bare floor. She heard herself slowing down, until the cadence of her steps sounded like a funeral cortege.

When she reached Malcolm's study, the door was closed. She paused outside it. Her hand, when she raised it to knock on the door, trembled in front of her like a dying leaf as she exhaled.

"You did this to yourself," she whispered. "Now see it through."

She rapped her fist on the wood.

"Enter," his voice rumbled.

She pushed open the door. He sat at the other end of the room, between his desk and the French door behind him. In the twilight of encroaching winter, she couldn't read his face. He hadn't lit any candles, or lamps, or even fires. The room was cold — but he blazed with heat. Sprawled in his chair, with his jacket and waistcoat missing and his cravat lying in a heap on his desk, he looked like the king of hell awaiting a concubine.

She shivered as she closed the door behind her. Her imagination was wild even in the best moments — in this, perhaps the worst since her father's death, it threatened to undo her.

When she turned back to him, he was still seated, watching her with hooded eyes as he sipped from the glass in his hand. "Come here," he ordered.

He rarely stayed seated in her presence. She swallowed hard. She had a sudden urge to run, to hide, to crawl into the deepest cellar and hope the storm would break over her.

But she walked toward him. She owed him that. Whatever happened, he deserved better than a coward.

And she wasn't ready to give up just yet.

It was still the longest walk of her life. He didn't smile. He didn't rise to greet her. He didn't show the slightest hint of encouragement. Over his glass, his eyes dropped to her breasts, then to her hips. He watched her like she was a dark goddess. And he was a pagan hunter, torn between his lust and his need to destroy her.

She reached the chair opposite his desk. She gripped the back, waiting for him to speak, knowing that if she spoke first her words would disintegrate into a babbled plea. When he finally broke the silence, his voice was full of gravel.

"Light the candle."

She looked down at the table beside her. Her hands shook as she picked up the tinderbox. She'd never had trouble before, but it was a futile effort. She couldn't get the sparks to light.

Malcolm cursed. He set down his glass with nearly enough force to break it, then strode around the side of the desk and took the flint from her hands. He lit the candle on the first attempt. The flare of light threw demonic shadows on his face. There were questions in his eyes she couldn't face — and judgment in his jaw she didn't want to see.

He returned to his chair and leaned back. She started to sit, but he stopped her with a gesture. "You don't have permission to sit, wife."

His mouth twisted on her title. She sucked in a breath. "Will you let me speak? Or have you already decided to end us?"

"Wherever did you get the idea that I would end us?"

She exhaled, letting out just a bit of fear. As long as he didn't leave, they had a chance...

But he wasn't finished. "You know divorce is unacceptable. And

I still want my heirs from you, even if I must tie you to my bed until you provide them."

She sat down, permission or no. She couldn't stay standing when her knees buckled — and his voice was so cold she doubted she could anger him further. "You don't have to be cruel, Malcolm. I was coming here to beg your forgiveness."

"Beg my forgiveness?" he asked. His laughter was bleak, cutting through the last scraps of her defenses. "You'd best start on your knees. And use that pretty mouth for something other than your lies."

Something snapped at his crude language. "How dare you. Banish me if you will, but I won't be spoken to like that."

If his eyes softened, it must have been a trick of the flickering light. His voice was still brutal, uncompromising. "I'll speak however I wish. You wanted a conversation about our marriage yesterday. Now you have it."

"What changed?" she asked.

It was beyond obvious that he'd learned the extent of her secrets, but she tried to delay, tried to give the lover she knew a chance to emerge from behind the warrior who faced her.

The fury that rode him made him too ruthless to be rescued. He reached forward, unearthing a book from beneath his discarded cravat. She recognized it as soon as he grasped it, holding it between a thumb and forefinger as though it might poison him.

"Now, wife," he said, deadly calm, "tell the truth, for once in your life. Did you write this?"

She met his eyes. He'd already made up his mind. But there was just a bit of hope there — that, against all odds, she would redeem herself, that she hadn't hidden this from him.

She didn't want to lose that look.

But it was inevitable. She confessed the way a good hunter killed her prey — mercifully swift, but implacable.

"Yes. I wrote it."

He dropped the book on the desk. It landed badly, falling open and creasing the pages. He picked up his drink again, leaned back in his chair, and closed his eyes.

"I didn't intend to cause a scandal."

"I'm sure you didn't."

Amelia drew a breath. "No one who knew would have betrayed me. If you'd married Prudence…"

His eyes snapped open. "Don't you dare say this is my fault."

"I know where the fault lies. But I wrote that book long before I met you. If I had known…"

She stopped herself.

"Why didn't you tell me?" he asked. The words were dragged over the gravel of his voice, then flung bleeding at her feet.

She spread out her hands. "When? When should I have told you? When we were first married? Why ruin the best weeks of my life? Or in London, where you've barely said two words to me outside our bed?"

Her anger sparked, burning dangerously alongside her guilt. "It was wrong not to tell you," she continued. "But don't pretend that my secret is the only wedge driving us apart."

"It's not your secret I care about," Malcolm said. "It's that you didn't trust me enough to tell me everything. Instead, I find out from Kessel, in front of an entire room of men at White's."

"Oh, my God," she whispered. "Truly?"

"I'm not the liar in the room," he snapped. "All I required from you, all I requested, was that you not cause a scandal. Was that so much to ask?"

It was little wonder he'd gone so cold. To have her writing made so public, in such a humiliating way…

"I'm sorry, Malcolm. I am truly, truly sorry. If I'd known when I wrote it that it would lead to this, that it would cost you so much…"

"It's too late for apologies," he said. "If you'd told me, if you had trusted me, perhaps there would have been a different outcome. But you didn't."

"Fine. I didn't do enough. At least I am honest about what I failed to do for us."

He didn't acknowledge the blow. "What am I going to do with you?"

It was almost a whisper, more of a question for himself than anything she could answer. "Do I get a say in the matter?" she asked.

"No."

She stood. No matter how angry he was, no matter how badly she'd behaved, she wouldn't be a martyr. "Fine. Send me a note when you've decided what to do. I'll be at my mother's house."

That threat was finally enough to draw him from his chair. "You aren't leaving," he said, coming around his desk to grasp her arms. "You may be a liar, but you're still my wife."

She stayed still within his grip, as though his touch didn't affect her at all. It was another little lie, she supposed, but it was better than giving ground. He would just take the gesture, like he took everything else — and keep taking, until she was nothing but a porcelain doll, doing his bidding. "And you may be my husband, but that doesn't mean we have to live together. If you don't want me, let me go."

Malcolm fixed his steely grey eyes on her. "You will stay here until you give me an heir. You will take up your responsibilities as my countess — all of them, starting with this house you've neglected since arriving here. But if I catch you publishing anything ever again, I will rid myself of you."

Like she was vermin. She narrowed her eyes. "You can't sue for divorce unless you prove I'm an adulteress," she scoffed. "And you will find that an impossible challenge."

"Divorce is only one option. I could have you deemed insane and committed to an asylum. Or I could confine you to that house in the western isles — your writing would never reach the mainland if I didn't allow you letters."

"You wouldn't," she said.

His eyes were as cold as the sea and just as relentless. "You do not want to see how far I will go if you push me."

She wanted to apologize. She wanted to make him see how she felt — to tell him that she loved him, that they could overcome this. But if he didn't love her, did it matter? She would always come second to his estate.

And as much as she loved him, she knew she would hate herself if she made her life a footnote to his.

She stiffened her spine, straightened her shoulders, and stubbornly met his gaze. "If you trust nothing else I say, trust this. I would rather be sent to your island than stay here and serve your whims. If you intend to treat me like a prisoner, we might as well make it official."

Malcolm held her still, scanning her face, looking for the truth in the shadows cast by the candlelight. He flinched at whatever he saw there. She burned under his touch, but she would rather flame out than melt back into him. If he could see what he had, admit what she meant to him…

He couldn't. She saw the moment when he hardened himself again. "You'll stay here for now. But I have as little wish to see you as you have to see me. I have business to attend to and no need for your distractions."

She felt another hot flare of anger at that word. "Good. Leave me. I've enough to do without you."

"You'll never publish again," he reminded her. "I'll burn every scrap of paper in this house if I have to."

"It will be hard for you to stop me if you're not here," she said.

She was baiting him, wanting to snap him out of his frozen judgment. He just smiled thinly. "The servants won't deliver your letters. I pay their salaries, not you. And if you want to leave the house while I'm gone, you're welcome to. But will anyone receive you?"

"You think I care about that?" she asked. "Writing was all I cared about. And you. And now you're taking both away, for something I did before I ever knew you."

He ignored the statement. He caressed her cheek, just once, before stepping away. "Goodbye, Amelia. I'll ask Ferguson to check on you. Send word through him if you're breeding so I know whether my presence is required next month."

Amelia sucked in a breath. She would have kicked him for that, but he was already out of reach. She heard him stride away, heard him open the door and shut it behind him. She stayed still, as impassive as he had been, until she heard the answering slam of the front door.

She picked up the book he'd tossed on the desk, smoothing the pages with her fingers. She couldn't mend the creases. And when her tears started to fall, she couldn't save the ink.

She sank to the floor and buried her face in her skirts. How could she have fallen in love with him? And how would she go on now that everything was gone?

CHAPTER THIRTY

A week later, Amelia sat silently in one of the main drawing rooms of the house she hated, watching the afternoon rain pour down against the windows. It was easy to stare at the rain — she still hadn't ordered drapes. The room had all the cheer of a tomb. She supposed it was fitting.

She never thought she would be reduced to the languid, fainting air of all those stupid society misses. But since Malcolm had walked out of their house and their marriage, she could barely summon the energy to get out of bed, let alone charge through her days like she usually did. What was there to charge toward? How could she fight a battle in which the enemy never showed his face?

Ferguson, drat the man, sat in the armchair opposite her, reading a copy of her book. He came every day, without fail. She'd asked him to leave her alone, but he took his loyalties to Malcolm seriously. Luckily he hadn't asked her if she was expecting — she might have killed him for that, no matter how much her cousin loved him.

The duke had tried conversation every other time he'd visited, but he hadn't bothered today. He had taken a seat, pulled a flask from his pocket since she wouldn't offer him a drink, and started reading the book he'd brought with him. When she realized he held *The Unconquered Heiress*, the book that had ruined everything, she knew he was baiting her.

He snorted at something on the page. He looked up, and his blue eyes twinkled as he examined her. Then he looked down at the book and chuckled again.

She felt the first stirring of curiosity over anything since the afternoon Malcolm had left. "What?" she asked.

He held up a finger. "You've waited days to say something. At least let me finish the chapter."

She sighed, but was startled when she realized she was more amused than angry. "You don't have to guard me."

He made a show of marking his page before setting aside his book. "This is quite good, you know."

She was flattered — hugely flattered. It was the first time someone outside the Muses had acknowledged her as a writer, and it still mattered, despite the circumstances. But she didn't let the compliment distract her. "Really, your grace. You don't have to be here. I'm not a traitor in need of guarding."

"I know you won't run away. But you look morose enough to jump off a cliff if you could gather up the energy to find one."

There was sympathy in his voice, even after their spotted history. Did she really look so forlorn? Even in the awful months after her father's death, she'd still found the will to write, and talk to Madeleine, and try to comfort her mother. What had happened to her?

"Suicide was never my idea of a solution."

He shrugged. "I doubt my brother wanted to end himself either. I wasn't here to stop him, but I wouldn't have MacCabe feel that guilt over you. Even if he likely deserves it."

She hadn't given Ferguson enough credit. He was probably a better man than she realized.

Then he grinned. "I do love seeing MacCabe brought low by marriage, though. I wish you both very happy."

Her little flicker of appreciation died. "Little chance of that, is there?" she snapped.

"Well, you aren't Mad, and he's certainly not me," Ferguson mused.

She rolled her eyes. "You are so astute."

He nodded. Then he stood, picking up her book. "I must be off. Same time tomorrow, though. Perhaps I'll win a laugh from you yet."

"Why hasn't Madeleine visited?" she asked abruptly. "Is the gossip so bad she can't come?"

In her prison, she'd heard nothing about the ton's reaction to her writing. The butler brought no papers or letters; no cards were left at the door. Only Ferguson breached the walls — and his eyes turned wary. "She was told you wouldn't receive her."

"What?" Amelia demanded. "Who told her that?"

"Your butler. MacCabe's orders, of course."

"And did he order you to come every day?"

"He asked me to come once. After seeing your sorry state, I took it upon myself to come back. But don't mistake me for your ally, Amelia," he said, displaying a sudden flash of the ducal hardness that lurked under his rakish façade. "If you'd seen Kessel accost him at White's, you wouldn't forgive yourself lightly either."

She shifted in her chair, her cheeks flaming with embarrassment. But his voice softened back into its usual drawl. "But as I said, I would hate for you to do yourself violence before MacCabe comes to his senses."

She had felt dead inside before, thinking her scandal had touched her friends so badly they couldn't visit. But knowing she'd been left to rot under Malcolm's orders, with only his friend and watchdog for an occasional companion, made her seethe.

"I am going to do violence to him before I ever hurt myself," she declared.

Ferguson toasted her with his flask. "Don't tell Mad I said this, but just this once, I'm relieved to see your spirit."

She came to her feet. "Did my blasted husband say I can't leave the house?"

"Why? Do you wish to kill him in front of an audience?"

"No. But if I'm to rot, I can do it somewhere more comfortable than an empty house."

"He did ask me not to take you back to your mother," Ferguson said, serious again. The duke may have wanted to see her in better humor, but he would still honor the letter of Malcolm's requests.

But there was just enough of a devilish gleam in his eyes that Amelia wondered if he could be convinced to ignore the spirit of those demands.

"Not to my mother's, then," she said. "I have a better idea, if you'll consider it."

She left Ferguson cooling his heels in the drawing room while she stuffed a few dresses and her pin money in a satchel. If Malcolm wouldn't come home, she would draw him out.

And either they would hash things out properly and forgive each other, or she would force him to let her go.

She loved him. Even now, even after everything he'd said. But if he was still as unreasonable after she explained herself as he was before he left, she would leave him and not look back. She was no longer convinced that her writing was enough to keep her happy. The idea of growing old alone with her books no longer held quite so much appeal now that she had the memory of Malcolm's caresses.

But she would rather be moderately unhappy alone than thoroughly miserable with her husband. If she had to see that cold, awful look in his eyes every day for the rest of her life, she did not think she could bear it.

Amelia MacCabe would scheme one last time. If she succeeded, she would win him. If she failed...

She refused to consider what would happen if she failed. She walked out of her room, out of their house, and didn't look back. Either she would return as his wife in all ways — or she would never return again.

*   *   *

The next morning, at dawn, Malcolm stood at the far end of Gray's Inn Fields. He picked up a pistol from the case Ferguson held and tested the weight in his hand. Extending his arm in front of him, he squinted down the barrel. He'd never wanted to murder someone — but he had to admit that Kessel tempted him to reconsider.

"Don't say you'll actually shoot the man," Ferguson said, hunched under his greatcoat against the chill. "Half the ton still thinks I'm insane. I'd rather not prove them right before I've had my breakfast."

Malcolm dropped his hand, careful not to let the pistol discharge between them. "I must say I'm tempted to wound him."

"You aren't half the shot I am. If you pierce his heart, you will have to flee for the Continent."

"I'd wager fifty pounds that I'm a better shot than you."

Ferguson snorted. "Done. But we'll test it on targets the next time we're in Scotland, not on Kessel's sorry hide. His second said he won't aim for you — if you murder him, you'll hang for it."

"Fine," Malcolm said ungraciously. "I won't kill him. Taking your money might make up for it."

He should be spending the morning preparing for Parliament. But in a cruel irony, he had discovered that the task he'd set for himself — getting into politics, saving the Highlands — was possibly the last thing on earth he really wanted to do.

He wanted to be in Amelia's bed. He wanted to watch the sun filter through her hair. He wanted to let his hands tell her everything he couldn't say.

But he wasn't where he should be, or where he wanted to be. He was standing in one of the most notorious fields in England, in dying late autumn grass, ruining his second best pair of boots on ground still sopping wet from last night's rains, waiting to fight an illegal duel that could cost him everything with a stray shot. He was supposed to be calm, sober, dutiful. He should be more like Amelia's brother, and nothing like Ferguson.

Of course, Ferguson had agreed to be his second. The Earl of Salford was probably still abed, or, equally likely, holed up in his study reading about rocks. Perhaps there was something to be said for being a bit disreputable.

Malcolm exhaled, watching his breath float away on the chilled air. "Where is the bastard? I want to end this."

Kessel had called Malcolm out after Malcolm punched him at White's. To be fair, it wasn't the punch that caused the duel, although Malcolm could understand the man being put out after his nose was broken for a second time in a year over his dealings with Amelia. It was when Malcolm had called him Lord Grandison — the thinly veiled name Amelia gave him in the book.

Ferguson pulled out his watch. "They still have five minutes. His second, Lord Beale, agreed to bring a doctor along, so perhaps they are later than expected."

Malcolm put his pistol back in the case. "We're too old for this, Ferguson."

"Too old for what? Tardiness?"

"You know what I mean." Malcolm gestured at the field. "An illegal duel, with our titles?"

Ferguson opened his mouth. Then he clamped it shut.

"What?" Malcolm asked.

His friend shook his head. "After the duel. No sense making your blood boil until you're safe."

Malcolm sighed, but he didn't argue. The sound of a carriage in the distance announced Kessel's arrival. Ferguson was right — going into a duel angry was a sure way to accidentally kill one's opponent.

It was all more petty than Malcolm expected. Kessel stepped down from the carriage, accompanied by Lord Beale. A sleepy man riding above the coach with the driver watched the proceedings with an utter lack of interest. If either of the combatants did need the services of the doctor, Malcolm hoped he would wake up before attempting to treat them.

Ferguson and Beale had already settled the particulars of the duel. All that was left for Kessel and Malcolm was to finish it.

"Lord Kessel," Malcolm said, nodding curtly.

"Lord Carnach," he replied. "Ready to apologize for your wife's behavior?"

"No. Will you apologize for speaking badly of her?"

Kessel sneered. "Never."

Malcolm sighed. "Very well. Rothwell, if you would be so good, give us our paces."

Ferguson nodded. Kessel chose his weapon from the case. Malcolm picked up his pistol. They strode out the appointed number of steps.

Malcolm breathed deep. The cold air seared his lungs. If everything went according to plan, this would be over in another minute. But his heart still raced. If it didn't go according to plan, the last memory Amelia would have of him was their fight.

And his last act on earth would be dying for a woman who didn't know he fought for her.

He steeled himself. No Carnach laird had died at the hands of an Englishman, and he wouldn't be the first. When he heard Ferguson's shout, he turned, took aim, and fired.

CHAPTER THIRTY-ONE

"I cannot believe you shot my hat," Ferguson said for the fifth time as they drove back to White's.

Malcolm sprawled on the seat opposite him. "You wouldn't let me shoot Kessel. I didn't want to waste the morning entirely."

Kessel had deloped, shooting his gun into the ground rather than aiming at Malcolm. The duel was enough to salvage his pride — he wouldn't risk killing an earl with a stray shot. Malcolm should have deloped as well, but he gave in to the last-second impulse. Hearing Ferguson shriek like a girl had been worth it — although he would save that tidbit for a day when he needed a favor.

"I suppose I should be grateful," Ferguson mused. "I'm no longer the maddest Scots laird in London."

The story would spread. When Ferguson's hat flew off, Kessel's eyes had bulged out, looking particularly gruesome over the bruises from his still-healing nose. And the shot awoke the doctor — just before he fainted, no doubt at the thought of losing the Duke of Rothwell on his watch. The man almost fell off the carriage box, but Lord Beale's driver hauled him upright before he tipped over the side.

"At least Kessel will have a different story to tell at White's today than how my wife is a reckless hoyden."

"What were you saying before the duel? Your claim that we were too old for this?"

Malcolm shrugged. "We're peers of the realm, not schoolboys. We should be working, not dueling."

Ferguson snorted. "I forget, you never come to London. Look around the next time you attend White's. If they're not addicted to gambling, drinking, or wenching, they're so obsessed with Beau Brummell that they don't have time for anything more strenuous than tying their cravats."

"Just because other men neglect their duties does not make it right for me to do so."

"True." Ferguson worked his finger through the hole in his hat, then twirled it around his hand. "But why force yourself to be only the one, or only the other?"

Malcolm thought back to the moment before he turned around on the dueling field. He had thought there were two paths in front of him — either give up Amelia and be the laird he should be, or keep her and give up his ambitions. Each path had its own rewards, just as each path required its own sacrifice.

On the path he had chosen, there were defined waymarkers: marry someone, take up his seat in the Lords, make allies, make heirs, craft speeches, gather power, use power, win, die. It was a path — but it didn't leave any room for joy.

But what if life wasn't a path? What if it was an ocean, with endless tides and currents — and endless opportunities to change course?

"Drop me off at my house instead of White's, will you?" he asked abruptly. He'd stayed at the club since leaving his house, although he'd kept to his room most nights rather than endure the sidelong glances and whispered gossip about Amelia's writing.

"Of course." Ferguson rapped on the roof and shouted up the new direction, then leaned back into the corner, still toying with his hat.

In the silence, with the clarity that had gradually replaced his rage over the past few days, Malcolm forced himself to acknowledge what his heart had known for weeks.

He was in love with Amelia. He loved the way she stood up to him when he was at his most insufferable. He loved that she had opinions of her own. He loved that she thrived in Scotland where other ladies would have faltered.

He loved her secret desire for adventure. He loved how often she blushed, and especially loved how she could say and do the most outrageous things despite her own inherent modesty. He even loved her writing, not that he had confessed it to her.

The same woman he had plotted to drive away had captured his heart. And until he'd been so awful to her, she had looked more than willing to give him hers in return.

He groaned. He wanted to go home and tell her all of this, but he did not know what reception she would give him. She would either rage at him and throw things — or coolly, efficiently cut him from her life just as he had threatened to do with her. To keep her from leaving, he would need to apologize. Even worse, he would have to confess his feelings and hope he was right about her, that her affection for him was strong enough to withstand the fight they'd just had.

Malcolm never thought he would be in this position, but at that moment, he had to admit he was a coward.

"Maybe I should go to the club first," Malcolm said. "Freshen up, have breakfast."

"Perhaps you should," Ferguson said agreeably, even though the carriage was rolling to a stop in front of Malcolm's door. "Without

Amelia in residence, your cook has probably given himself a holiday."

Malcolm leaned forward, all his clarity swept away again by Ferguson's nonchalant pronouncement. "Where in the bloody hell is she? I thought you visited her yesterday."

Ferguson put his hat back on his head, the entry hole prominently displayed right in the center. "She was there yesterday. She hadn't said anything to me, other than to tell me to leave, every day I visited before that. But by yesterday, she was done waiting for you."

"When did you intend to tell me?" Malcolm asked, keeping his voice calm even as his eyes narrowed.

"When I dropped you at your door — and here we are. I thought about telling you before the duel, but I'm glad I didn't. You might have shot me in the face instead."

"I told you not to take her back to her mother."

"I didn't. She's with my sister. Anytime you want to thank me for watching over your wife when you couldn't be bothered with her, I'll accept your appreciation."

Ferguson's voice suddenly turned cold. Malcolm glimpsed the steel he usually hid under his rakish, devil-may-care attitude. "You know I appreciate it," Malcolm said.

He wanted to beat down the path to Ellie's townhouse, pound on the door, and demand to see Amelia. But his temper had already done enough damage. It wouldn't help him now, no matter how easy or gratifying it felt in the moment to give in to it. A week of remorse was enough to keep it in check as he pondered Ferguson's news.

Ferguson eyed his friend's unusual forbearance with surprise. "Are you feeling well, MacCabe? I'm prepared to defend myself if you want to go to Gentleman Jackson's and take out your aggression with some boxing."

"Boxing won't help," Malcolm said, pretending to relax against the seat, ignoring the panic clawing at his throat. "If Amelia's gone, it may be for the best. She was none too happy with me when we last saw each other."

"She seemed happy enough before you came to London."

Malcolm couldn't listen to Ferguson any longer. He needed to walk, to think, to decide his own path — or decide whether to abandon the paths entirely and fight the current to get back into her arms. He grabbed his hat and flung open the door. "I'll find my own way from here."

Ferguson nodded. "I wish you luck, MacCabe. Wherever it is you decide to go."

Malcolm stepped down onto the pavement in front of his house. Ferguson's carriage rumbled away, melting into the noise of London coming awake. His windows, uncovered and unlit, held the ghosts of what the house could be — if anyone lived there, or loved it enough to make it a home. But it wasn't a home, and it wasn't what he needed right now.

Instead, he started to walk.

*   *   *

Amelia's day did not proceed precisely according to plan. But then, Ellie was not a woman who could be managed.

The marchioness was ever ready to help someone in need, even if her definition of "help" was sometimes at odds with that of her beneficiaries. When Ferguson had deposited Amelia at her doorstep the day before, Ellie had sprung into action. Twenty-four hours later, Amelia dazedly suspected that if Ellie had helmed the command in the

Peninsula, Britain would have destroyed the French armies years ago.

"I really don't think a dinner party is a good idea," Amelia protested again as Ellie nearly dragged her to the drawing room.

"Nonsense," Ellie said briskly. "If you ask me, you should have gone out the night Kessel told everyone about your writing. You do have sympathizers, but it would have been easier to tip them in your favor if you'd stood up instead of hiding like you knew you'd done something wrong."

Ellie probably had a point. Still, Amelia tried to stand her ground. "I only want to talk to Malcolm. I moved to your house to shake him into action, not host half of London."

"It isn't half of London. I haven't invited more than thirty to dinner. Compared to the party I gave last week, this is the smallest, most intimate affair imaginable."

Amelia sighed. Ellie was uncompromising when she took the bit between her teeth. But Amelia no longer wanted to scheme. She wanted a quiet moment with Malcolm and a chance to tell him what was in her heart.

But she couldn't talk to him when the note she'd sent to his club earlier in the day went unanswered. And Ellie said she hadn't invited him to dinner. Would he ever give her the chance to speak? Or was he really as done with her as he had seemed the day he walked out of their house?

Sir Percival Pickett was the first to arrive. "Fair Lady Carnach!" he cried, ever dramatic as he bowed over Amelia's hand. "If you had only told me you were an authoress, I would have redoubled my efforts to conquer your golden citadel!"

Amelia choked back a laugh as she heard Ellie snicker beside him. "I do hope you aren't too scandalized by my efforts, Sir Percival."

"Scandalized? I am enchanted! I knew there was a spark of the divine in you. I must write another poem for you now that you are no longer the Unconquered."

"I'm sure that won't be necessary," she said. In her second London Season, Sir Percival had written a horrid poem, "On the Unconquer'd's Cornflower Orbs," that had given her her nickname and caused Alex and Sebastian to rib her mercilessly for months. She didn't need another of his dubious poetic efforts.

Sir Percival could not be quelled. "You dubbed me Sir Galahad in your book. I am honored. Nay, I am humbled. Nay, I am rendered speechless. I can only hope to repay the favor. I shall consider a name immediately."

He wandered off in search of brandy to fuel his art. Ellie snickered again. "Sir Percival does not seem inclined to call your husband out for your book, does he?"

Amelia scowled. One of Ellie's callers earlier in the day had delighted in telling them all about Malcolm's duel with Kessel. "Of all the stupid things men do, that must be by far the worst," Amelia said.

A footman ushered Ferguson and Madeleine into the drawing room. "I hope you aren't casting aspersions on all men just because you're plagued with poor Percy," Ferguson drawled as he kissed her hand.

"Sir Percy is harmless. It's duelists I cannot abide by," Amelia said.

Madeleine kissed her cheek. "No need to lecture Ferguson on the matter. If I had known why he left the house before dawn today, I would have shot him myself. But I agree with him — it is nice to know that another Scottish peer is more scandalous than he is."

"You have my felicitations," Amelia said drily. "And how did my dear husband acquit himself?"

"Tolerably, although he owes me a hat," Ferguson said. "Your honor is defended for another day, my lady."

His younger sisters, Kate and Maria, greeted her next. "How could you not tell us you wrote *The Unconquered Heiress*?" Kate squealed.

"It is grossly unfair of all of you," Maria complained. "First Madeleine, now you!"

Ellie pinned her with a glare. "If you are so indiscreet, it's little wonder the grown-ups don't tell you their secrets, is it?"

Maria flushed. The twins knew of Madeleine's acting, but no one else in the ton did — and Amelia didn't think any of them wanted to risk that scandal being unearthed. "I am sorry, Ellie," Maria said. "It won't happen again."

Kate and Maria linked arms and walked to the far side of the room, escaping the muttering Sir Percival, who was entranced by a painting of a mostly nude woman near the fireplace. Ellie's drawing room was perfectly arranged for both large parties and surreptitious encounters. Her reputation for scandalous gatherings was borne out by the lavish oil paintings, the little alcoves lined with velvet drapes to keep sound from carrying, and the lush undercurrent of perfume from the hothouse flowers rioting in enormous urns throughout the room. It had the feel of an expensive boudoir, not a prim, prudish widow's hermitage.

Amelia kept a smile pasted on her face as more guests streamed in. It really was a select gathering of the cream of the aristocracy. Ellie's influence, at least in some circles, was enough that she could fill her table with only a day's notice.

But then, in November, the company was thin and there weren't as many entertainments as there would be at the height of the spring Season. Between Amelia's writing, Malcolm's dueling, and their mutual feuding, she was the *on dit* of the week. No one invited to such an event as this dinner would decline the invitation, unless they meant to blackball her.

Ellie's Aunt Sophronia, the Dowager Duchess of Harwich, strode imperiously into the room. "Is the Duchess of Bodlington supposed to be me?" she demanded, ignoring the pleasantries.

Amelia blinked. "Yes, your grace."

"Good. The Duchess of Devonshire tried to claim her, but I said the author had more sense than to honor such a scandalous woman."

The duchess was a force in the ton and always spoke her opinion bluntly. The fictional Duchess of Bodlington was one of the more comical aspects of Amelia's satire. Amelia tried to read the woman's face, but saw the same inscrutable, vaguely displeased look in Sophronia's eyes that she always saw. "I am sorry if the book caused you offense, your grace."

Sophronia laughed. "Nonsense. It was the best flattery I've had in an age. You may not receive vouchers to Almack's after this, but you'll be invited to every party I have influence over."

She turned away. Amelia exhaled, thinking she was safe.

But then Sophronia turned back. "I am offended about the cane. Must you have given me a cane like I am yet another gouty old woman?"

"If anyone could make a cane seem appealing, I'm sure it's you," Amelia offered.

Sophronia nodded. "That is true. You are forgiven, Lady Carnach."

The duchess proceeded into the room. Ellie smiled smugly. "I told you this party was a good idea."

Amelia sighed. "I vow, if I ever write another satire, you will not be spared."

Amelia's brothers turned up next. She hadn't talked to either of them since her Malcolm-imposed isolation, but their greetings were warm even though the look in Alex's eyes promised an imminent rehashing of everything that had happened. Sebastian, though, had just arrived from his plantation in Bermuda two weeks earlier, and cared more for regaling the lovely Maria and Kate with stories of his exploits than he did for Amelia's scandal.

Augusta came with them, accompanied by Lord Tarrier, her usual companion at these sorts of events. She was slightly cooler than her sons when she embraced Amelia. "I was surprised you wouldn't let me call on you this past week," she said.

"Malcolm takes the blame for that. I didn't know it, but he told the butler I wasn't receiving."

If Augusta had been annoyed with Amelia, all her anger suddenly switched sides. "That man is a beast. I do hope you have a plan to teach him a lesson."

"Why do you all think I have a plan?" Amelia asked.

"You always do," Augusta said. "Even if you don't share it, as you neglected to share your writing these past years."

Amelia winced, even though there was no anger in her mother's voice. "I won't scheme again. And I'm sorry..."

Augusta cut her off. "I only wish you'd told me. I feel like a first rate fool for having discussed *The Unconquered Heiress* with you without realizing you'd written it. You must have laughed when I was blathering on about who I thought each character was."

"It was hard to keep from telling you then," Amelia admitted.

"Well, what's done is done." Then Augusta frowned. "Though I must say, you have more of a talent for attracting scandal than I ever expected. I hope your friend Prudence isn't similarly inclined."

"Why do you say that?" Amelia asked, stepping back with her mother from the open doors so that Ellie could greet the next arrivals.

"I can't abide by what Lady Harcastle did. No matter how angry she was about your marriage, you would think her friendship with me would have held her tongue. But I'm fond of Prudence, and the daughter shouldn't hang for her mother's mistakes. And I may be lonely without you and Madeleine. I've asked her to move in with me and be my companion, if she would like."

Amelia's mouth twitched. "You have less need of a companion than any woman I know."

"That obvious, am I?"

"It's a lovely gesture," Amelia said. "Really. And it would be wonderful to know that Prudence has somewhere to stay in London, especially someplace without her mother. But you don't need a companion."

"True. But with you and Madeleine both moving on, perhaps I would like another young lady in the house. And you're not the only woman in the Staunton family who can scheme."

Her gaze flickered to Alex. Amelia laughed. "I wish you luck with that. Alex won't look up from his books long enough to see Prudence."

Her mother smiled mysteriously. "We shall see, dear."

Lord Tarrier returned then with a glass of champagne for Augusta, and they went off together to examine the paintings.

Within another fifteen minutes, the full company was assembled. Ellie was conversing in low tones with Ashby, her butler, about how to move everyone to the dining room when loud voices in the entry interrupted them.

"Who could that be?" Ellie said.

She didn't sound particularly concerned. Ashby bowed. "I will attend to the matter, my lady."

The matter came to them instead. They heard booted feet moving quickly down the hallway toward them. Amelia took a step back from the door. Ashby moved into the gap, ready to defend his mistress.

"Step back, Ashby," Ellie murmured.

The butler stayed where he was. Ellie sighed. "At least have a care for your face — you can't be my butler if he breaks your nose."

Ashby did step back then, just as Malcolm turned the corner. He stood framed in the open doorway, alone, and yet somehow as dangerous as if he had an entire army behind him.

Behind her, Amelia heard women gasp. She couldn't look away from him, though. He wasn't dressed for dinner — in fact, if she had to guess, he was still wearing his clothes from the morning's duel. His buff breeches were more suited to a morning ride than a social call, and his boots were covered in dried mud that flaked off onto Ellie's pristine carpets.

He looked like William the Conqueror, come to claim the woman who had tried to spurn him. At least William and Queen Matilda had ended as a love match, even if the legends said he'd whipped her for refusing him.

Amelia drew a breath and told herself to focus on them — on what she saw on Malcolm's face, not the stories she could make up about them. His face was more compelling than any fiction — fierce, rugged, a little wild, with sleepless, bloodshot eyes and dark stubble on his chin. His eyes were locked on her, had been since the moment he stepped into the doorway, like he knew unerringly where she was and could always find her, no matter the obstacles.

Her heart leapt. Everything else in the drawing room fell away. Even the air disappeared — she couldn't breathe anymore, not with him looking like he wanted to devour her.

"Amelia," he growled. "Let's go home."

CHAPTER THIRTY-TWO

Home. That word meant something with him, something more than it had ever meant to her before. She used to think she could be happy anywhere, as long as she had her writing. But with him, she wanted roots. She wanted a place that was theirs. Above all, she wanted him.

She almost ran to him. The instinct was there — to go home with him, drag him up to her chamber, and let their lovemaking stand in for all the apologies they owed each other.

But she had to know whether there was more behind his eyes than lust.

She sucked in a breath. Then she gestured to the butler. "Ashby, escort Lord Carnach to Lady Folkestone's salon? We can talk after dinner, if you're inclined to wait."

Malcolm's eyebrows slammed together. She heard Sebastian's laughter, Sophronia's clucking, even Sir Percival's murmured exclamation of adoration. But she kept her eyes on Malcolm's face.

He was angry, yes.

But he wasn't defeated.

"I'm not inclined to wait," he said.

She lifted her chin. "You've waited a week — surely another three hours won't be the death of you."

"I only need three minutes."

From his vantage point a few feet away, Ferguson snickered. "I would have wagered less than that."

Some of the women tittered. Malcolm's scowl deepened. "Three minutes, without this helpful audience you've assembled."

"Do take your time, Lady Carnach," Ellie said, gesturing at the door. "You can use the salon across the hall. Dinner can wait three minutes."

From the expectant air in the room, Amelia suspected they would wait even longer if they got the show this dinner suddenly promised them. She scowled. "Very well. Three minutes. If I don't return by then, send a rescue party."

She walked forward. The five feet separating them had seemed unbridgeable, but suddenly his hand was on her shoulder as he turned to walk with her. It wasn't heavy, or angry, or even demanding, though.

For the crowd, he was a lord asserting his rightful authority. But his touch on her shoulder was tentative, as though he worried he could break her.

The first cracks split across her armor. If he had lashed out at her, she would have hardened. But the soft graze of his fingers across her arm was a greater threat to her composure than any accusations.

The salon was smaller than the drawing room, but not as intimate as the room upstairs that Ellie used for their private Muses of Mayfair meetings. The room was empty, but lit candles abounded and a fire burned merrily in the hearth. Ellie spared no expense when entertaining, making sure all the public rooms were open even when the party didn't intend to use them.

Amelia wanted to pace, but she forced herself to stand still. She needed to keep her composure — and keep from begging — long enough to hear what she needed Malcolm to say.

"Will you sit?" he asked.

"No. What do you wish to say?"

He ran his hands through his hair. If he'd worn a hat earlier, it was missing, and the dark tendrils were damp from the day's rains. He clasped his hands behind his head, as though to keep from touching her. The gesture, and the taut lines of his arms and chest as he looked at her, only emphasized his air of barbaric suffering.

"I'm sorry, Amelia. For everything."

He ground the words out through his teeth.

She waited.

He waited.

She sighed. "Is that your apology?"

He dropped his arms and crossed them on his chest. "That's what you want, isn't it? An apology?"

"Is that why you said it? Because you think that's what I want?"

"I have no bloody idea what you want," he said. "I thought I knew when we were in Scotland. But you've changed."

She laughed, but it sounded just as ragged as his words. "I haven't changed. You just saw what you wanted to see."

"Isn't that what you did?" he countered. "Saw me as the amusing lapdog you would have preferred?"

Her laugh had been pained, but her snort was genuine. "You're no one's lapdog. Where did you get that idea?"

"You'd prefer it, though. If I waited at your feet, accepting whatever scraps you give me when you're not too busy with your 'correspondence.'"

He said the word contemptuously. Her anger flared. "That's your dream, not mine. For me to be at your feet, waiting for you to have a free moment after Parliament, letting you have a quick fuck before you go back again."

Her vulgarity shocked him, drove the dark look off his face and replaced it with something closer than pain. "God, Amelia," he sighed. "Where did we go so wrong?"

She was tired, suddenly — achingly weary, and wanting nothing more than to lean into his arms and let him cradle her as she wept. "I don't know, Malcolm. I'd take it back if I could."

She paused. In the flickering candlelight, she saw the same desolation on his face that had swept away everything else in her soul.

"But I can't take it back," she whispered. "Perhaps we should accept that this wasn't meant to be."

"I don't believe that."

His voice was firm. No matter what he thought of her, no matter how angry he was, he wouldn't concede that point.

"How can you be so sure?" she asked.

"Call it intuition."

The same intuition that had ruined her in his library so many months ago — the same fate he'd seemed to want then was still glimmering in their future.

But she couldn't see how to grasp it. Maybe it was a fairy light, always dancing just out of reach, leading them on to destruction.

"There's no such thing as intuition."

"I've read your books, Amelia. You believe in fate. You believe in destiny. And your destiny is here, with me."

He stepped forward, pulled her into his embrace. "Tell me what you need. Tell me what I can do to win you."

His voice rumbled in his chest, against her cheek. His lips brushed her hair. That soft touch was back, the one that would undo her.

No schemes, she reminded herself.

But even though she would tell the truth, it was too hard to look at him while she did it. So she buried her face in his chest. "I want to believe that you see me when you look at me. That you see *me*, not your countess, not your hostess, not your broodmare. That you'll love me even when I fail you."

She wanted to stop. But she owed him the rest, even if she could do no more than whisper it. "I want to believe that someday you'll love me as much as I love you."

*   *   *

Malcolm tightened his arms. She felt so right within them. Even if she had lied. Even if she'd made him a laughingstock.

Even if he didn't deserve her.

He didn't know how to confess his feelings, but he knew how to seduce her. One of his hands moved down her back, a prelude to the delicious battle he would wage. He could show her how he felt, even if he couldn't find the words to tell her.

She pulled away. In her eyes, he saw her heart transform from a bleeding offering to a hardened wall. "You cannot kiss me into submission, Malcolm."

"I wasn't," he protested.

The lie was too obvious. She took another step back. "Either say how you feel — how you really feel, not what you think I want to hear. Or set me free."

He panicked. He never panicked. But his life hung on a string. She held the scissors, as effective and as merciless as the fate that had driven him there. He couldn't get this wrong. He couldn't lose her for want of the right phrase.

"You belong to me, Amelia. Always. I meant it when I made those vows. Let me take you home and prove it."

He knew the words weren't right, but she must have heard the feeling behind them. Her eyes flickered. He thought, if he had another moment, he might be able to convince her...

But someone knocked on the door. "Are you alive, Amelia?" Alex called through the door.

"I'm sorry," she whispered.

He reached out to grab her, but she evaded him. "When you went looking for a wife, you wanted something bloodless. You wanted something that would save your clan, not yourself. I'll be married to you regardless — it's too late for anything else."

Then she leveled a glare at him that should have destroyed him. "But you must decide what you want. I'll be your cold society wife. Or I'll be your lover. But you can't ask me to switch between the two — neither of us can live like that."

She stalked over to the door and threw it open. Alex waited, glaring daggers at him as he offered Amelia his arm.

Amelia's words were combative — but her eyes had said she still wanted him.

Which was good, because Malcolm was damned sure he wanted her.

CHAPTER THIRTY-THREE

When Amelia opened the door, Alex offered her his arm. "Shall I escort you in to dinner?" he asked.

The other guests milled as close to the doors of the drawing room as possible, casting blatantly speculative glances at them. She held her head up high, as though she spent every party closeted in a room discussing the fate of her marriage with her stupid husband.

"How lovely of you to offer," she said.

She felt Malcolm come up behind her, even before she saw the hostility flare in Alex's eyes. She wouldn't turn to face him. She wouldn't let him affect her this badly, so badly that she was having trouble remembering what she needed to hear from him.

It was a coward's decision to leave before they were finished, but she was glad Alex had knocked on the door. If he hadn't knocked, she might have accepted Malcolm's apology — and only later realized that saying she belonged to him wasn't an apology at all.

Malcolm wouldn't let her off so easily, though. His hands settled on her shoulders. "Three more minutes, Amelia," he demanded, his voice a low growl in her ear.

She started to shake her head.

He leaned in. "Please," he said.

It was funny, how one word could undo her.

She dropped her hand from Alex's arm. "Go on to dinner without me," she said.

Her brother crossed his arms. Behind him, Sebastian stepped up to lend support. "Do you need me to show this blackguard out?"

Sebastian was wild enough to do it. Amelia scowled at him, warning him away.

Then she turned to Malcolm. He pulled her back into the salon, slamming the door against their audience and turning the key in the lock.

"Well?" she asked, crossing her arms.

He looked like he wanted to seduce her. And she might have let him, if she thought it would help. But they'd solved all their previous arguments with lovemaking, and it had turned out that their arguments weren't solved at all.

Perhaps he finally recognized that fact. He moved away from her, slowly, deliberately, just far enough that they couldn't touch even if they both stretched their arms toward each other.

She kept hers crossed, denying the temptation. He ran a hand through his hair, gripping the back of his head, and she felt the tension rolling off him in waves before he finally spoke.

"Listen to me, Amelia. You want to believe that I see you for who you are. And I want you to know that I do. I see a lovely woman at the height of her beauty, who could have any man in Britain with a single gesture. I see a headstrong, stubborn schemer who will do anything to get what she wants. I see someone whose intellect and sense of humor are so delightful that she could only be bored with the ton — there's no challenge here for you."

His words were an odd mix of compliments and near-insults. She opened her mouth, not sure whether to accept his praise or deny his condemnations.

But he held up a hand. "I see a woman who will always help her friends, even when her plans don't come off perfectly. I see a woman whose passions are so boundless that she can only contain them by putting them onto the page. I see a writer whose talent grows with every book, whose artistic pursuits will get her shunned in some circles even as others adore her even more for it."

She leaned against the doorframe behind her to keep from falling. Her husband still wasn't done. "I see the only woman I ever could have married, the only woman I will ever love. The only woman I would happily lose everything for. The only woman who could destroy me if she walked away."

He finally stepped forward, like a penitent and a conqueror rolled into one, a king in the unfamiliar act of penance. With his disheveled appearance, he looked like he had crawled through hell to get back into her arms.

When he was inches from her, he gently took her hands. She held her breath.

Then he sank to his knees. "I didn't ask you to marry me, Amelia. But I can beg you to stay with me. And I can vow to you that no matter what happens, no matter how many books you write or how many duels I have to fight because of them, I will only love you more."

Those last words were the end of her. It wasn't just that he'd found the right sentiment to share — it was that he meant it, so honestly and so scorchingly that it was written across his face as though etched there by a divine hand. There was nothing but love in his eyes, nothing but need on his lips.

Despite all the odds, and all her denials, she'd found what she needed. And it wasn't in the pages of a book. It was in his heart, bleeding on the ground in front of her, waiting for her to pick it up.

She pulled him to his feet. "You're the maddest, most demanding man I've ever met. But I've never laughed as much as I have with you — never *felt* as much, never realized how much I had missed until I found you. And I've never been as desolate as I was when I thought my past had driven you away."

She knotted her fingers with his. "I love you, Malcolm MacCabe. No matter who you are and no matter what you want to do."

His eyes lit up, fiercely ecstatic. He kissed her then, claiming her lips with tender hunger. That moment, when they finally recognized each other's hearts, was worth any scandal that could come from it. And her memory of it, carried in her heart like a little fire, could rekindle her love on the days when she needed a reminder. That flame would outlast anything that might come between them.

When Alex knocked on the door again, she groaned. "Let's pretend we're dead so they leave us be," she murmured against Malcolm's lips.

He ran his thumb across her cheek, then pulled her in to kiss her again.

Alex's knocking grew more insistent.

"Damned persistent beggar, isn't he?" Malcolm said.

Amelia laughed. "It's a Staunton trait, I believe."

"If that's what gave me another chance with you, then I suppose I am thankful for it."

She slid her hands off his shoulders, down his muscled chest, until they came to rest on his backside. "We should go, shouldn't we?"

"No." His hands trailed down to settle on the curve of her hips. "You're right. We'll pretend we're dead. Then we can go back to Scotland and be free of the lot of them."

Alex tried the handle.

"Go away, Alex!" she shouted through the door.

She heard Ellie laugh, but at least Alex stopped pounding on the door.

Amelia rested her head against Malcolm's chest. She was right where she wanted to be. Scotland, London, the smallest house party, the grandest ball — it didn't matter, as long as she was in his arms.

He brushed a kiss across her hair. "I mean it, darling. Let's return to Scotland."

She tilted up to meet his eyes. "But I thought you needed to be here for Parliament? I don't mind staying."

"We'll come back. There is still work I can do in Parliament, even if it's just voting against every measure Kessel supports."

His grin made her laugh. "Better that than breaking his nose again, I think."

"Say the word, and I'll break it every week."

This was the man she'd married — the sorcerer from the library was back.

And the light in his eyes said he would never hide from her again.

"We don't have to return to Scotland for my sake," she said.

He kissed her, slow and deep. When he pulled away, his breath was heavy. "I'd rather spend my life saving you than the Highlands."

"You don't need to save me," she said.

"I know," he replied. "If anything, you're the one who saved me."

By the time they emerged from the next kiss, neither of them could breathe — and Amelia's only thought was to find the nearest bed.

Malcolm must have felt the same way. "Shall we go home, Lady Carnach?"

She smiled as he reached around her to unlock the door. When they walked through it, the assembled crowd took one look at the smile on her face and started clapping.

But she didn't blush, not even when Malcolm said they would leave immediately. The rumors would spread through the ton. They would say that the mad Scottish laird had won the Unconquered. Or they would guess that she had conquered him.

It didn't matter what stories anyone told about them. All that mattered was that she and Malcolm would write the rest of their story together.

And that was the best ending of all.

EPILOGUE

MacCabe Castle, the Scottish Highlands - 23 December 1812

Amelia laughed as Malcolm entered her bedroom an hour before dinner with a dark silk muffler and a look of mischief in his eyes. "Must you really? Your infernal brothers are still teasing me for the last time we missed dinner."

"I think you'll be happy for the diversion," he said.

She laughed as he stepped behind her and kissed the side of her neck. He wound the silk around her eyes. Neither his inventiveness nor his tenderness surprised her.

But she was surprised when he scooped her up into his arms and strode forward. And even more surprised when he opened the door to the hallway. "Malcolm, you devil," she said. "Are you really taking me out in front of our families like this?"

Amelia's mother and brothers had joined them for Christmas, as had Prudence. Ferguson and Madeleine were supposed to join them the following day if the snows allowed them to visit. With Malcolm's family in residence as well, their holiday had been merry despite the weather.

"I suspect most of them already know what I have in store for you."

"I suspect most of England knows, after that display in London," she muttered.

He laughed. "I don't care if most of the world knows. But I'm not carrying you off to ravish you — or rather, that may be a hoped-for addition, but not the main event."

Amelia relaxed against his chest. He wouldn't let her down until they'd reached their destination. But really, there was no place she would rather be than in his arms. She'd finished her latest manuscript before leaving London, and so there was no need to return anytime soon. And that meant she could spend the winter months focused on a more exciting project.

Malcolm whistled as he stepped carefully down the stairs. He kept walking, and she felt the unmistakable chill of the great hall as they passed through the ancient room. At some point there were more steps, and he reached forward and opened another door, but she was too disoriented to know where he was taking her.

Finally, he set her on her feet and unwrapped the blindfold from her head. As her eyes adjusted to the dim light, she saw that they were in the portrait gallery. The door to the tower was mere inches from her nose.

He nodded at the door. "Open it, darling. Your surprise is inside."

"You don't intend to lock me in again, do you?" she asked over her shoulder.

"You won't know until you open it."

She laughed as she gripped the handle. The iron was cold against her bare skin, but the heat of Malcolm close behind her pressed her onward. She opened the door. Inside, the room looked like something out of a fable — a happy story, not one of her Gothic tragedies. The daylight had died hours earlier, but the room was bathed in the glow of dozens of white candles perched on the staircase that spiraled around the room. A fire roared in the large fireplace, banishing the chill of the stones. Large tapestries and thick carpets replaced the ancient weaponry, although the broadsword she'd once threatened him with still hung on the wall, now in a place of honor. The lone, decrepit chair was gone, and an elegant sofa and armchairs were grouped near the fire.

The tower had been transformed into retreat fit for a medieval princess. She looked back at Malcolm, a question forming on her lips. He placed his hands on her shoulders and gently pushed her into the room, turning her toward the section she had not seen from the door.

Amelia shrieked. A mahogany desk sat to one side of the room, as large and imposing as the one in Malcolm's study. She nearly ran to it, dimly registering his laugh as she examined the desk. There were several quills and bottles of ink on top, along with a sander and a blotter. She opened the drawers and found heaping stacks of creamy writing paper, all waiting for her next stories.

Amelia looked up. Malcolm leaned against the doorframe, his eyes silver with love instead of mischief. "How did you know I wanted a study?" she asked.

"As much as you write, it seemed silly that you spend your time in a converted sitting room with a traveling writing desk. And this room is far enough away from the family wing that no one will disturb you."

She sank into the chair and ran her fingers across the polished desk. "So you did not bring me here to lock me up?"

Malcolm laughed and pulled the door closed. "Only if I am locked in with you. The door locks from the inside now," he said as he slammed the iron bolt home.

He strode toward her desk. In the candlelight, with a smile playing on his lips, he looked just as magical as he had the first night they met.

"This would be the perfect place for an illicit assignation," she teased.

He reached out and tweaked her nose. "You're not going to use that paper to invite a lover here, are you?"

"Only if you will frank a letter to yourself, my lord."

Malcolm pulled her up into his arms. "Then you like your present?"

"I love it," she said. "This is the best present I've ever received."

He kissed her then. She kissed him back, matching his hunger. It didn't have the same forbidden edge as their first kiss, the one in the library that had bound them to each other all those months ago.

But if the thrill wasn't quite the same, the devotion and love more than made up for it.

Finally, she broke away. "I haven't given you your present yet," she said.

"You are the only present I need," he replied, leaning in to kiss her again.

She laughed. "No, I think you will like this one. I want you to choose the title for my next project."

Malcolm raised his eyebrows. "Can the title be *Amelia Spends the Year in Bed with Malcolm*?"

She swatted him. "Beastly man. I've come up with three for you to choose from."

He crossed his arms and waited.

"The first," she said, "is *The Evil Earl*."

"Absolutely not. It sounds like you're setting me up as the villain," he said.

"Then what do you think about *The Mad Highland Laird and the Innocent English Lady*?"

He shook his head decisively. "Based on my experience with Highland lairds and English ladies, that is entirely inaccurate."

She paused and pretended to think, anticipating his reaction to her next words. "And how do you feel about *The Expected Heir of Carnach*?"

His smile widened. "Now that shows definite promise. How long do you think it will be until you release this gem?"

She ran a hand over her belly, still flat beneath her gown. "Perhaps seven months."

Malcolm's eyes lit up. He wrapped his arms around her again. "This may be the best story I've heard you tell yet."

"Then are you happy?" she asked. "Even though I won't be able to go with you to London for the Season?"

He kissed the top of her head. "Only if you're happy to let me stay here with you."

She pulled back and pretended to scowl at him. "Unfair, my lord. You will be an absolute tyrant by the end of my pregnancy, I'm sure."

"You do know me so well."

"There is still one problem, Malcolm."

"And what is that?" he asked, catching her wrist to pull her back into his embrace.

Amelia tilted her head up and looked into his eyes. Intuition or not, she saw their future in his eyes — and it was brighter than any story she could write.

She grinned at him, embracing her fate. "What can we possibly tell our families when we miss dinner again tonight?"

THE END

Books by Sara Ramsey

<u>Muses of Mayfair</u>

Heiress Without a Cause
Scotsmen Prefer Blondes
The Marquess Who Loved Me
The Earl Who Played With Fire - coming 2013

A Note From The Author:

As I continue to write the Muses of Mayfair series, I've realized these books are my love letter to the power of female friendships. I couldn't have written this book, or anything else, without my own muses, and I'm so grateful that they're in my life. While all of my friends and family have been wonderfully supportive throughout my writing journey, I especially want to thank Katie, Heather, and Terry for reading early drafts and being invaluable friends and sounding boards. I also must thank Vidya, Claudia, Lauren, Katrina, Ritu, Tammy, and all my other friends for their support and love -- and for dragging me out of the house and plying me with Champagne when I'm getting too hermity.

On the business side, I must thank my indomitable agent, Jennifer Schober, and everyone else at Spencerhill Associates (especially Carol Guerin, who keeps me from going mad if Jenn is out of the office). Thanks also go to Krista Stroever, who did an amazing job editing this book — her insights amazed me, and any mistakes remaining in the book are entirely mine. I also want to thank all the book bloggers and reviewers who've picked up my books, and Joan Schulhafer and Deb Tobias for their help in marketing this series.

And finally, I want to thank you for spending your time with Amelia and Malcolm. I'm so thrilled that this book found its way into your hands, and I hope you enjoyed it! If you want to be notified when future books come out, participate in my online contests, or get special sneak peeks of upcoming works, please join my mailing list at http://www.sararamsey.com/wordpress/newsletter/.

Thanks again! Ellie's book, *The Marquess Who Loved Me*, is coming in Summer 2012, and I can't wait to share it with you.

Sara Ramsey
San Francisco, California
March 2012

Stay in Touch

Do you want to be the first to hear about new releases, special content, and giveaways? Sign up for Sara's newsletter at: http://www.sararamsey.com/wordpress/newsletter

Sara loves to hear from readers and usually responds quickly, barring deadlines. Please send questions, criticisms, or compliments to dearsara@sararamsey.com

If you want to share this book with your book club, Sara is happy to talk to groups in person or via Google Hangouts/ Skype. Please send Sara an email to discuss possible options.

You can also find Sara on Twitter (@sara_ramsey), Facebook, or Goodreads.

Photo by Misti Layne

Sara Ramsey writes fun, feisty Regency historical romances. She won the prestigious 2009 Romance Writers of America® Golden Heart® award with her second book, *Scotsmen Prefer Blondes*. Her first book, *Heiress Without a Cause*, was a 2011 Golden Heart finalist.

Sara grew up in a small town in Iowa, and her obsession with fashion, shoes, and all things British is clearly a rebellion against her hopelessly uncool youth. She graduated from Stanford University in 2003 with a degree in Symbolic Systems (also known as cognitive science) and a minor in history. She is currently living the hip romance writer life in San Francisco, California. Read all about her Regency obsessions and upcoming works at www.SaraRamsey.com.

,